614
Scarlet Ct.

By
Dr. Bon Blossman

First Paperback Edition: April 2011
First published in hardcover in April 2011 by Zakkem
Publishing, a division of Zakkem Productions.

ISBN-13: 978-1460978580
ISBN-10: 1460978587
BISAC: Fiction / Suspense

Acknowledgements:

First, I wish to thank Jason Myer for his efforts with feedback, graphics and never-ending love & support. You believe in me, you are my soul mate, my best friend, and I love you.

Thanks to Whitney and Zakk for continuing to be wonderful– I couldn't have asked for better, more loving kids even if I designed you both myself. Whitney you are a true diva and Zakkem, there's nobody more talented than you are.

Thank you to my awesome friends & family who have supported my writing career over the years. Scot & P and Dao, thank you for the first purchases of Take Heed to your Nightmares. Thank you to Brandi and Susan for your feedback on Take Heed. Thank you to Melody & Ryan for the first purchase of Chronicles of Zombie Town. Your support means more than words can say.

For my parents, Dr. Robert & Diana Blossman: You have always supported me and my endeavors – no matter how bizarre or out of reach that they seemed. Thank you, I appreciate you and I love you!

I love you Lauren, Madison and Ella – you are very special to me. My next novel series will be for you and I think your parents should get you the iPhones that you deserve as long as you continue to get good citizenship awards!

Last, I dedicate this book to my lovely Doberman, Ozzy. He gave me inspiration for the character Omen, even if most of the inspiration came from his neurotic barking at golfers.

CONTENTS

Fear is only a state of mind until it lives.

1 – Blazing Blackness

Drake failed in an attempt at a 50-50 grind on his skateboard, plummeting to the ground, rolling along the grass as Dominick's laughter filled the air.

"Give me my five dollars, Dom!"

"You didn't land it! No deal!"

Drake groaned, stumbling to his feet, catching something peculiar in his peripheral vision. He shot his caramel eyes into the sunny Texas sky, focusing on rising plumes of smoke from the middle of the adjacent neighborhood, Winding Heights Estates.

"Dominick, check it!" he shouted, grabbing his skateboard from the ground, taking off toward the source of the smoke.

"Wait up!" Dominick followed suit, jumping on his skateboard, pushing off furiously from the sidewalk.

The teens skated as fast as they could through the neighborhood toward the plumes. Both boys lived in the neighborhood as well as other friends and family members. Drake grabbed his iPhone from his pocket and feverishly thumbed the numbers 911.

"Emergency! Fire! My name is Drake Henry! Something's on fire in Winding Heights Estates!" Drake screamed into the phone, rounding the corner of Rosamond Street to confront the blazing house.

"Oh, no way," Dominick hollered, rolling up in front of the house, stopping himself by grabbing onto the mailbox. "Isn't that your—

Drake continued screaming into his phone, "It's my Uncle Basil's house!" Drake glanced down at the curb to read the address, "It's 5150 Rosemond Drive in Winding Heights Estates. Hurry!"

Drake chunked the phone into the grass, tossed his skateboard, and dashed toward the home in a panic. He swung around to face Dominick, eyes bulging and face turning pallid green underneath his tanned skin.

"Dominick, he might be in there! I have to go in!" Drake demanded, his face wearing a mask of panic.

Dominick shook his head back and forth rapidly.

"Drake, wait for the fire department. You made the call and that's all you can do."

A muffled bark from within the burning abode echoed into the street. Drake shot a glance at Dominick with horror stricken across his face. Blood pulsed fast and hot through his veins, his heart picking up the pace.

"It's Omen! His dog! He's in there! Maybe Uncle Basil's trapped in there too?"

Drake yanked Dominick's sweat infused beanie from his head, exposing his blackened dreadlocks in disarray.

"Don't know why you wear this crap when it's hot outside but it'll keep my hair from catching on fire," Drake rasped abruptly, covering his tousled bronze hair with the knitted cap, tucking the straggled pieces under the fabric of the cap along the edges.

"Don't go in there, Drake! It's a death wish!" Dominick objected harshly, eyebrows pulling upward into a plea.

Drake shuddered, gritting his teeth and tightening his muscles. Ignoring Dominick's protests, he raced up to the front door to discover it was slightly ajar, smoke trickling onto the front porch. The charred smell of burning wood hung thickly. He widened the door, releasing a gush of smoke into the front yard as he turned his head, taking a step backward, allowing it to filter through the air. He paused for a moment, wincing as he crossed the threshold into the front hallway, the intense heat from the fire saturating his exposed skin. The smoke, thick as darkened clouds, only allowed him to see a few inches in front of him.

Grabbing his t-shirt and covering his face to his eyes, he took shallow breaths through the cotton fibers. Sweat started streaming down his face as he felt his way along the wall, relying upon his memory of Uncle Basil's home. He had only been there two times before in the past. As if someone turned up the volume, the barking grew more distinct, louder. Upon reaching the doorknob of the master bedroom door, he was relieved to find it was still cool.

No fire inside, it must have started in the back, his mind comforted him as he continued to hold his t-shirt tightly around his face. The shallow breathing led to dizziness, his heart raced even faster. Blinking wildly to soften the sting of the smoke, Drake opened the door. Omen, a very frightened black and rust Doberman pincher, burst out of the bedroom to greet him, the fervent smoke pouring into the bedroom behind him.

"Hey, boy! Where's your daddy? Where's Basil?" His voice was gruff as the smoke stifled him, causing him to cough violently.

Omen scurried through the smoke toward the front door and Drake, still coughing, struggled to fight the reflex for a deep inhalation. He had to see if Uncle Basil was inside the bedroom. He would never forgive himself if he allowed his uncle to die in this fire.

He entered the bedroom, shutting the door behind him. The smoke dissipated, leaving a thin haze. The fire was closing in and he knew he would not be able to go back into the house the way he had come. Drake searched the master bedroom frantically for Uncle Basil. He was not in there. He continued into the bathroom. Each breath of air tingled his lungs, urging him to cough. Catching a glimpse of his horrific reflection in the mirror, he grimaced as he gazed at the swollen capillaries in his eyes, his handsome veneer covered with soot, his bright teeth glistening in brilliant contrast with his smudged russet skin.

After thoroughly searching the master bedroom suite, Drake felt assured Uncle Basil was not there. He rushed to the bedroom's front window and felt around for the lock on the sill. A wave of nausea seared his body as he discovered it was a permanently sealed window with double paned glass. The smoke billowed into the bedroom from underneath the door. Drake needed more time. Wheezing, he fought to breathe normally, needing to concentrate to find a way out of this nightmare. He sprinted into the bathroom and snatched a bath towel from the wall hanger. He hurled it into the bathtub, soaked it in water, and crammed it underneath the bedroom door.

"That should buy me a minute or two," he mumbled, scanning the room for a plan.

He rushed back into the bathroom to search for an alternate escape route. A round window taunted him from above the bathtub. It was also double paned, permanently sealed. The back of the house crumbled down with a vehemence, boards crashing, and fire roaring with an unbridled fury. The walls of the bedroom rumbled around him. He was sweating profusely and knew it wasn't long before he was in grave danger. The temperature abruptly climbed, feeling like the hottest, most smothering day in August, his sweating amplified. He frantically searched the room for something to hit the windows with as he heard the sirens blaring in front of the house.

"Thank God!"

Drake darted to the front bedroom window. He yanked the drapes and the steel drapery pole from above the window plummeted to the ground, missing his forehead by a mere centimeter. Bracing himself with one foot on the window ledge, he pounded on the window with a clenched fist, sweat bounding off the glass with each strike. The inner window absorbed most of the sound as his fist bounced back with every hit. Another wave of nausea took over his senses as he realized it was shatterproof glass. His lungs tightened as the murky air filled them.

"HELP! HELP ME!" Drake shouted over the roar of the fire, hands spread flat on the glass, the window absorbing the sound waves of his voice, sweat beading up and streaming down the window from around his hands.

He watched two fire trucks park haphazardly in the street in front of the house. The geared up firefighters darted out of the trucks, readying the fire hoses. Omen the Doberman ran circles in the front yard but it wasn't in playfulness, it was to communicate with the firefighters about Drake. Drake experienced a rush of self-gratification as he realized he had saved the dog's life. He hoped it wasn't in exchange for his own although it was quickly becoming a reality.

Catching a glimpse of Drake in the window, Omen tore at full speed toward him, his black fur sparkling in the sun with every motion. With his elongated snout pointing at the window, he relentlessly barked with vigor but the focused firefighters, as drones following a program, continued to unwind and hook up the hoses.

Dominick hysterically screamed at a firefighter, pointing his lanky arm toward the front door of house. Omen scurried to another firefighter by the fire hydrant, nudged him with his snout, and sprinted back to the bedroom's window like a Greyhound at the races, grass flicking into the air behind him.

"C'mon boy! Keep it going! C'mon Omen!" Drake gasped, pounding on the glass to no avail.

Dominick, noticing Omen's erratic behavior, drew his eyes to Drake through the window. Dominick spun around and grabbed the firefighter by the elbow, jerking his body around to face the window. He pointed at Drake, Omen still barking at the window.

"Domin—

Drake lost the fight to a cough, a forced dramatic inhalation of smoke tinged air following. The shift was up for the wet towel holding the smoke at bay underneath the bedroom door. It had served its purpose well and now allowed the smoke plumes to infiltrate the bedroom with elegant, artistic swirls. The temperature abruptly rose again as the thick gray cloud surrounded Drake like a fluffy blanket. Drake's lungs began to seize followed by a bout of intense disorientation. Uncle Basil's bedroom was no longer a bedroom. It was a cloud, a dark gray, sweltering cloud. The only way for Drake to keep his sense of direction was to focus on the image through the window. He clenched his fist and pressed them against his temples, clutching the t-shirt covering his face. He closed his eyes tightly while fighting to remain conscious as his heart raced wildly. He moved closer to the window, bodylines flat with the glass, sweat streaming downward as a liquid frame. He opened his bloodshot eyes to lock into a narrow gaze with the firefighter in the front yard. Dominick was standing by the fireman's side donning a panic-stricken expression.

"Dominick!" Drake's voice was breathless with exertion, choking on the invading miasma.

With another compulsory inhalation, Drake Henry's world turned black as his body crumbled to the floor.

2 – Farewell Austin

"You're finally back, man! Can't believe you spent two of your last three days at Winding Heights High School in the hospital! How are ya feelin'?" Dominick chortled, pushing back the shoulder length dreadlocks from his face, repositioning his beanie.

Dominick and Drake skulked down the corridor of Winding Heights High. They were best friends, polar opposites on the exterior. Dominick towered over most of the students in the hallway at 6'3 whereas Drake was a few inches shorter but well built, not as awkward and gangly as Dominick. Drake, with year round russet colored skin, had prominent masculine features. When he stood still, he appeared perfect as a mannequin. Dominick, pale, had a more cherub like face, less distinguished but with a raw appeal.

"I'm fine. I'm still coughin' but I'll be a'ight. I never had a chance say thanks. I know you're the reason they rescued me in time. The doc said I made a ridiculously fast recovery. He's amazed I didn't croak from smoke inhalation, said it was because I'm so athletic," Drake said, narrowing his eyes in a mock sarcasm, smiling.

"No big deal, man. However, that dog is the real hero, he's hella smart. Your uncle should let you have him since you rescued him. If it were up to your uncle, he'd have been a char-grilled Dobe. Now that's a stellar hot dog, ya know!"

"That's gross, Dom."

Dominick calmed his laughter, preventing a near stumble as they trekked down the hallway.

"But yeah, Omen's gonna live with us," Drake reported, tousling his chin length hair, smooth jagged points resembling flaccid golden dagger blades.

"That's cool. So, I heard old Basil was at Maggie May's Pub on 6th Street when it all went down."

"Yeah, that's right. Wow, insignificant news travels fast. We're relieved he wasn't home."

Dominick took a few breaths before continuing, searching for the right words.

"It was all on the news, dude. Everything about your uncle is on the news. If he uses too much toilet paper, it's on the news," Dominick said, searching for a topic to change the subject, "What's that's dog's name, again?"

"Omen. You know, from that old scary movie. My Aunt Kerstin was a freak about scary movies and she named 'em."

"Omen, oh yeah, forgot. That dog looks like he walked straight out of hell. He is a demon dog but he's so cool."

"Hollywood directors live to demonize Dobermans and give them evil roles in movies when they are actually one of the smartest and nicest dogs you could own as a pet," Drake defended, avoiding eye contact with a pair of known hallway gossips, obviously trying to get his attention.

"I guess I agree with ya, Drake. My cousin had a Doberman a long time ago and he was way cool too. Never even heard that dog growl."

Drake paused with an uncomfortable silence. Dominick stared at him with a blank grin, stopping at his locker to exchange a book. Drake appeared as though he didn't want to say what he was about to say.

"Uncle Basil is moving to Shady Oaks with us."

Dominick's eyes widened as he took a step backward. He elevated his shoulders and flung his lanky arms to the side.

"No way, man!"

Drake nodded slowly, shrugging one shoulder as he leaned his head to the side.

"Yes, he's decided with the murder case and now with his house burning down, he wants a change of pace just like my parents. Mom said he'll stay with us until he gets on his feet."

Dominick shook his head in disbelief, slamming his locker shut.

"What? He is allowed to leave Austin? Isn't he a murder suspect?"

"The District Attorney had to approve the move and all but since it's only two hours away and there are no official charges filed on Basil—

"Yet!" Dominick interrupted, the word exploding out of his mouth.

Drake's face was expressionless. He stared at Dominick for a long, awkward minute as he gathered his defense.

"Dominick, I don't think so," Drake defended warily, "Since it's her brother, my mom had to sign papers that she'll notify the D.A. if his living arrangements change or if she loses contact with him for any reason."

Dominick looked ahead in astonishment, turning to stare out of the hall window. He shrugged, slowly moving again down the hallway towards their classrooms.

"You serious, man? You are going to have a murder suspect living with you. And, not to make it worse, but some people are saying he started the fire at his house to hide evidence."

Drake nodded, shifting his weight between legs as he spoke.

"He is my uncle, you know. And I highly doubt that he murdered my aunt or started a fire. She probably deserved what she got but I don't think he did it. Many people hated her. She was the criminal."

"True," Dominick agreed.

"They always suspect the husband first in these cases. There is no evidence linking him to the murder. As far as the fire goes, could be faulty wiring or maybe he left one of his pipes going when he left the house or something," Drake fumed, face reddening.

"True, I suppose. He is always smoking those pipes like Sherlock Holmes. He's so weird. And those pictures on the news make him look like a serial killer," Dominick said, his voice a shade sharper than he obviously intended.

Drake pondered the words for a moment.

"I know. I have no idea where they got that picture but he looks insane. And why are people saying he started the fire, anyway? How stupid would that be! He lost absolutely everything he owned and nearly lost his dog!"

Dominick put his hands in front of his chest, flexing his fingers upward to offer an olive branch.

"All right, maybe he didn't burn down his own house," Dominick's harsh tone melted into calm. "However, it is somewhat obvious he murdered your aunt. The IRS serves him papers at his house. Then, he discovers she lied about paying his taxes for however many thousand years. He killed her. I would have too," he stated flatly, chuckling under his breath.

"A motive doesn't make him a murderer," Drake asserted.

"He then finds she spent over 300 thousand bones on unknown credit cards in his name that she opened behind his back! Murder!"

"Again, motive doesn't mean he did it."

"I also heard that she used his credit to buy a condo on some tropical island in the Caribbean and that she planned to escape there when he figured out what she did," Dominick added bluntly.

Reaching the hallway nearest their classes, Drake lounged against the wall, crossing one leg over the other, resting his pointed toe on the ground. He dropped his backpack on the ground next to him.

"She was the jerk, just remember that. My uncle has never done anything to show he is capable of murder. He's a tool bag, but not a murderer. All of what you say is true and he is in debt for over a million dollars because of her but he didn't do it."

Dominick leaned a shoulder against the wall and faced Drake. He glanced over his shoulder to ensure nobody was listening behind him. It had become annoying for Drake to be such a source of controversy this past week since his aunt was murdered. The initial news reporter had overstepped her boundaries by reporting Basil Cross was a potential suspect in the case and was the uncle of Drake and his younger sister Briar who attended Winding Heights High School. It was unnecessary information to report, as they had nothing to do with the case.

Dominick went on, "The news lady said it was *three* million, by the way and that he might do jail time for evading taxes."

Drake nodded, rolling his eyes.

"Basil trusted her since she was a tax attorney. If my father were a surgeon, I'd trust him to do stitches on my knee if I needed it, right? Again, just because he has a damn good reason to kill someone, doesn't make him guilty," his final words were clear and distinct.

Dominick raised his eyebrows in a defensive position before dropping them to frame an apologetic gleam.

"Sorry for bringin' it up, man. I know it is a sore subject. Must be hard to have your family going through that mess."

Dominick held out his fist and waited for Drake to return with a friendly fist bump. Drake hesitated and then performed the ritual, slowly allowing a diminutive smile to invade his face.

"Thanks, Dom. I can't say I *like* the guy that much but I don't like what it's doing to my mom."

The boys stood in silence for a moment. Conversations rumbled in every direction about his arrival back in school, his uncle and the fire.

"I still can't believe you are moving, Drake. I know it's only two hours away but you've lived in Austin your whole life. How are you going to move from the coolest city in the world to a dinky town like Shady Oaks?" Dominick whined, arms outstretching in a dramatic stance.

"Shut up, Dom. I don't need you making it worse. My dad can't take it here anymore. He has to get out of police work. That last case's got him totally freakin' out."

"Oh, yeah," Dominick added abruptly, "That crazy murderer in jail sent his friend over to your house to threaten him. Didn't he say if your dad testified against him with his forensic evidence, he'd end him?"

Drake nodded, becoming more animated.

"Yeah, but not just him. The message was that my dad's entire *family* would suffer the same fate as the victim who was killed with a chainsaw, chopped up in a million pieces, and scattered in public ashtrays around town."

"Freakin' sick!"

"I know, Dom. My dad wants to get far away from forensic labs and work at some pharmaceutical research facility in Shady Oaks. It's supposed to be low stress and very laid back and he's gettin' a huge raise. I can see my parents' point for wanting to move. It just sucks for my sister and me since we grew up here. But all of this crap with my Uncle Basil *does* make moving away from Austin a little easier, to be honest. I'm already sick of everybody asking me about his case and it's only been a week. There is no end in sight!"

Dominick grimaced at the words. He had said many times he didn't want Drake to move, even tried to talk his parents out of it. They were the best of friends since they were four years old.

"How your sis taking the move? I haven't seen her or heard her loud, annoying voice in the halls lately," Dominick said, a smile spreading across his face, revealing his crooked canine tooth.

Drake's eyes narrowed and after forming a straight line with his lips, he released a heavy sigh.

"Briar withdrew a week early so she could get prepared for her new classes at Deadwood High School. She's an over achiever, she's already contacted her new teachers and got her assignments."

"What a tool!"

Drake's face turned bitter as he scowled.

"Hey, that's my sister you're calling a tool."

Dominick cocked his head to the side in a sarcastic manner. He shook his head.

"You obviously know I'm joking. I've only wanted to go out with her for years but you won't let me near her! She is a freshman now, you know! She'll be dating skeezes soon when she could be dating me!"

"'She's my sister, Dom."

"Don't care, she's hot! She has a killer bod, a gorgeous face, and that dimple on her right cheek is the cutest thing. Oh and those eyes, like honey—

"Eww, her eyes are just like mine. Gross, so you like me now? You love my eyes, Dom?"

Dominick's expression was morose. He nodded a couple of times, pausing in deep thought.

"Yeah, you two do look like you are toys made from the same mold at the factory."

"Enough. Forget it."

The bell rang and the two scurried into their classes. Dominick took off to English and Drake took his seat in the back row of his Computer Applications class. He sat next to the infamous Elizabeth Payne, known for using her external beauty to get whatever she wanted from boys. Most of the girls in school had a crush to some degree on Drake besides Elizabeth Payne. She had never showed an interest in him. Her flawless appearance intrigued him and he often spoke to her without thinking, just to see if she had changed her mind about him. Each time he engaged into a conversation with her, he regretted falling victim to the heinous persona, hidden from sight, tucked immediately under the surface.

"Hey, Elizabeth. Howz it going?" Drake inquired swiftly.

Drake scolded his brain for allowing him to speak to her again. She turned to gaze at him, sarcasm invading her face like roaches in a dirty restaurant.

"So, Drake. I heard you almost died in a fire. Like, were you trying to be a big superhero and save your uncle the murderer?" Elizabeth paused, laughing hysterically. She continued, trying to stifle her laughter as she spoke, "But then you only saved a silly dog!"

Elizabeth leaned down slightly to toss her curtain of long, shimmering black tresses, still laughing in mockery. The straight strands fell into perfect order as she slightly shook her head, staring at him with her icy blue eyes sparkling with flecks of hate. Drake paused, studying her face as he searched for a reply.

"My uncle isn't a murderer—

His chiseled face reddened, staring past her with incensed eyes.

"Whatev, Drake. Keep believing that," she interrupted, beaming from the pleasure of her callousness.

Seriously, why do I talk to this girl? She's probably the one thing I won't miss about Austin when I leave, Drake thought, swiveling the opposite direction from the feminine abomination.

For the remainder of class, Drake was silent and focused on finishing his final project. His irritation had amassed from the inquiries and hallway gossip sessions topped with Elizabeth Payne's coldhearted comments. The only attention in life he ever wanted was on the tennis courts. He had always preferred to stay far away from controversy. He would be the last person in the world to put himself on one of those disastrous reality television shows. He always felt as though selling your soul for fifteen minutes of fame was pathetic and led to a path of destruction. He was annoyed he didn't have the choice to distance himself from his uncle. For now, only the city of Austin knew about what happened. He dreaded the story of his aunt's murder hitting the national media. He wanted to be the anonymous sixteen-year-old Drake Henry, without aggravation and gossip, and with only a handful of people knowing his personal business. If the story hit national news, he was doomed to suffer the same hassle in the new town where he hoped to start with a blank slate.

The bell rang immediately after Drake finished his webpage design project. He would never see Elizabeth Payne again, his irritated expression turned into a smile spreading slowly across his face. It was time for tennis, the highlight of his day. Drake had a lot to discuss with his tennis coach about his impending move to the small town of Shady Oaks. After fending off a few queries in the hallways, Drake made his way to the tennis locker rooms where he met up with his mentor, Coach Walter.

"Hey coach—

Drake choked at the words. The thought of leaving Coach Walter and the varsity tennis team formed a stiff lump in his throat. He held back the tears at the rims of his eyes while reminding himself that men don't cry. He would miss Coach Walter nearly as much as he would his own father if he were gone. Coach Walter had been his coach since he was in the 6th grade. He followed Drake as he moved into high school. They talked about how he would see him through to his senior year and assist him into landing a spot on any college tennis team that Drake chose. Coach had his eye on an Ivy League scholarship for Drake but he preferred to stay at home and attend The

University of Texas in Austin. Either way, he knew Coach
Walter would have done anything to help him. He
wouldn't have time to build such a trusting and caring
relationship with a new coach. This sickened Drake
tremendously.

He cleared his throat and continued in a shaky
voice, "Hey coach, last day. I'm moving this weekend,
starting school at Deadwood High on Monday."

Drake slumped down on the bench next to Coach
Walter who was finishing his review of an upcoming
tournament schedule. The coach shifted his body toward
Drake, set the papers down and folded his hands. He
released a huge sigh and nodded his head slowly.

"Wow, Drake. I'm sad this day has arrived. It's not
often that I have the pleasure of coaching such a talented
young athlete. I could never replace you, ya know."

Coach Walter looked up at the ceiling and blinked
his eyes, seemingly to fight an onslaught of tears as well.

"Thanks. That means a lot. Did you ever get a
chance to talk to the tennis coach at Deadwood High
School?" Drake asked reluctantly.

The coach shook his head, slowly shrugging a
shoulder.

"I've left numerous messages on the voice mail of
the school's athletic department. I found the coach's email
address but he has an *out of office* automatic reply that
states he won't be back until next semester. It seems
there's only a varsity team and there was only one coach at
least from what I can tell. Their website isn't all that
great."

"I know, I've looked at it. It really sucks."

Drake sledged over to his locker, opened it, and
tossed the remaining contents into his gym bag.

"It's quite disturbing he's away from campus since
it's the middle of the tennis season but I looked on their
state rankings and the team's playing in 4A tournaments.

They have a couple of seniors that are battling it out for the top position in the state right now for the 4A division—

"Seniors, huh?"

Drake never had real competition in tennis, even with older boys. Even as a freshman, the seniors never beat him on the courts.

"You shouldn't have any problems being a walk on to the team and by their schedule; it looks as though there are five tournaments left. I've faxed over your records from 6th grade until now to the high school counselor's office and a few copies of news clippings so they will give you the star treatment that you deserve. Whoever the acting coach is will get it and roll out the red carpet for you, I'm sure. All coaches appreciate winners, makes them look good, and keeps them employed. I'm just glad it's a 4A school so you won't compete against us in 5A tournaments!"

Coach Walter laughed softly, patting Drake on the back. Drake shook his head and smiled, exposing his glistening teeth.

"Thanks. I can't wait," Drake said sarcastically, rolling his eyes lightheartedly.

"It will be all right, Drake. You've only got another year left after this one and then you'll be on a college team. Since you've been the Texas State 5A Men's Singles Champion both your freshman and sophomore year, you should be able to get a scholarship anywhere. Just keep it up."

"Did you ever find out what will happen with me this year by switching divisions?"

Coach Walter's face turned to stone. Drake knew he didn't want to say what he was about to say.

"Yes, unfortunately you were on track this year to compete for the state 5A title again, but since you are moving to 4A mid-season, you won't be eligible for the state championship since you didn't play a full season in either division."

Drake's knees buckled, he leaned against the lockers for support.

"That sucks."

He had never imagined he wouldn't have the Texas State Men's Singles 5A High School Championship title again his junior year. There was no higher honor for a tennis player. Someone else would have the title without earning it by defeating Drake. He always planned on having a perfect record and going to UT without question, a scholarship in hand.

"I know, but keep your head up and finish out the season with a flawless record over at the new school. You will still get looks at a 4A school especially given your past record. However, being in a small town in the middle of nowhere, you'll really have to be on point for the recruiters to remember you."

"I know, I already thought of that," Drake's eyebrows lowered, face turning sour.

"Stay off those silly skateboards too."

"I know, I know," Drake droned, numb to the coach lecturing about skateboard injuries.

Drake knew how to evade injury on the skateboard. Dominick was the one with the frequent flyer miles at the local hospital. He was reckless.

"Don't jeopardize your undefeated record no matter what. You'll be competing at a lower level and colleges would definitely think you've lost your edge and that does happen to teenagers. You *could* endanger your standings with recruiters if you go there and start losing. Good news is that your high school years will be over in a blink of an eye."

"I know. I just fear change. I don't like starting over," Drake murmured.

"Nobody does, Drake."

3- Road Trip

"Pull over at that convenience store, Dad! We won't have any food in the new house and I know y'all will take forever signing those stupid papers!" Briar whined in a high-pitched tone.

The fair-haired Ella frantically kicked her stumpy legs against her car seat adding to the chaos in the minivan. Omen strained his long furry neck from the back seat to lick Ella's face with his warm tongue. She returned with a loud giggle.

"I'm hungry too. I remember I was at the last boring paper signing when you guys bought this minivan and thought I would lose my mind," Drake added, shaking his head wanly, rolling his eyes.

"All right, all right, peanut gallery! We'll stop here but you'll have to hurry. We've only got five minutes, the banker and title company representative will be waiting for us at the new house," Ivan Henry replied, revealing his crooked, coffee stained teeth through a narrow grin.

Drake's father Ivan, a graying middle-aged chemist, had a faded athletic build with shirts snug around his rounded belly. He refused to buy larger shirts, always claiming his newest diet would drop the additional pounds. He was a philanthropist, always having change for the homeless, spending his free time volunteering for various charities around Austin. Drake could get his way most of the time as Ivan was known for being a softhearted pushover. Ivan always had his family's best interest at heart and this gave Drake undying stability in believing his father would always lead everybody in the right direction, including the impending relocation to Shady Oaks.

"Thanks dad, you're the shiznit!" Briar said, rendering her right cheek dimple with a grin through the rear view mirror.

The car ride to Shady Oaks had been only two hours but felt like an eternity to Drake. Uncle Basil wrecked his car recently and it was in the shop for an undetermined period. Basil's other car was repossessed from his driveway only two nights before as he certainly wasn't keeping up with his bills recently. Uncle Basil agreed to drive Drake's old blue Jeep behind the Henry family's minivan driven by Ivan. Drake made a deal with his sister Briar that he wouldn't stick her riding to Shady Oaks in the minivan with awkward Uncle Basil. Sunday morning, Drake pretended to be ill right before leaving Austin and Basil took the bait, jumping at the chance to drive alone as he eagerly snatched Drake's keys from his hand. Drake hoped he wouldn't smoke his pipe in the Jeep. It wasn't much of a vehicle but it was Drake's and that is all that mattered.

Drake's mother Emily drove her gold Lexus IS300 behind the others. As if someone drew a line and placed members of the Henry family on either side, Emily and Ella, Drake's two-year-old sister, were blonde, pale skinned and blue-eyed. They looked nothing like the tanned, topaz colored side of the family. Emily preferred to drive alone, an anxious driver, known for blasting classical music to calm her nerves.

Ivan waited with his turn signal on in front of the parking lot to the convenience store. Emily drove more than two car lengths behind, Basil tailing her in Drake's Jeep. The caravan pulled into the parking lot of the Shady Oaks Mart at the corner of Whispering Point Drive and Lakefront Avenue.

"What a dive!" Briar howled, grimacing at the convenience store with disgust.

The gravel popped loudly under the tires. Drake shook his head, peering out the passenger side window at the unpaved parking lot. Omen barked loudly, saliva flickering with each woof, peppered with intermittent growls as he smeared his wet nose against the van window. Ella returned with an eardrum-shattering shriek.

"Ella! Quiet down! Omen, quiet! Why couldn't that dog ride with his owner, anyway?" Ivan said loudly in a husky voice.

"Omen wouldn't get in the Jeep. He either hates the Jeep or Basil, don't know which one," Drake added.

Briar made a strong effort to calm Ella who complied with her sister's request and quieted down to a subtle whine. Drake leaned around the front seat and snapped his fingers at Omen. Looking at Drake obediently, he downgraded his bark into a low rumbling growl. Drake snapped his fingers again and Omen quieted completely, lying down on the back seat of the van.

"All right, Bee. Change your attitude. This is a small town and some things might be older than what you are accustomed. Think of these buildings as antiques," Ivan pleaded, stroking his grayed untamed coif from his eyes.

"O.M.G., if our *house* is like this, I'm so walkin' back to Austin tonight!" Briar pouted, curling her lip downward. "That's probably why you and mom refused to show us pictures of this gross house! It's bad enough I have to quit the two things I love the most, ice skating and soccer, because this dingy place doesn't have it!"

"Hey, Bee. It'll be fine. You said you were going to switch to basketball, right? They have a girl's basketball team at Deadwood High. You're pretty good at that. Also, remember how excited you were? You said your new teachers seem awesome, right?" Drake reasoned, shooting a glance at Briar with widened eyes.

Drake was uncertain if he believed his own words.

"Whatever, Drake. But I'm sure the teachers live in Deadwood City, not in this dump hole. This town is so small; we have to travel via *bridge* over Deadwood Lake to Deadwood City just to get to school! Did you know that, Drake?"

Drake's face glimmered with confusion before he continued, "No, uh, I guess I didn't realize that. Deadwood High School isn't in Shady Oaks?"

"Hey, brainiac, it's called *Deadwood* High, not Shady Oaks High."

Briar rolled her eyes, slamming her fists into her lap.

"I guess I figured since Shady Oaks borders Deadwood Lake," Drake sighed, "I suppose I'm stupid, Bee."

Drake was starting to become annoyed with Briar's negativity. He inhaled deeply and let his breath out in increments, lungs still feeling slightly damaged from his previous bout with smoke inhalation. Ivan was tense, face reddening as Briar's unbearable attitude poisoned the van.

"Don't feel stupid, Drake. Our parents conveniently left that part of the story out. Just like leaving out how *gross* this town is!"

Ivan parked the van and spun around between the front seats to glare at Briar.

"Enough! Briar, I'm not listening to this garbage anymore. This is where you live now so get used to it. We are all making sacrifices here so stop being so selfish. Let's go get some snacks," Ivan demanded angrily, climbing out of the minivan.

Briar slumped further into her seat and stared blindly out the window. Omen's head perked up and he glared out the window with midnight eyes. A growl rumbled under his breath, increasing in volume by the second. Ella's whimper transformed into a playful giggle.

"The dog doesn't even like this place!" Briar whined, frustrated.

Ivan continued in a more positive tone as he hopped out of the van and slid open the minivan door, "We're going to try out a local restaurant tonight and I'm sure it will be great but first mom and I are meeting the folks at the new house to sign the official papers. By the time we're finished, the movers will arrive to unpack the big stuff and we'll leave and get something to eat. Calm down and try to be happy! We promised you that you would love the house and nothing has changed," Ivan explained, restraining Omen's massive body by the chest while everybody exited the van.

"Yes, father. Sorry," Briar pouted, slowly ambling out onto the graveled parking lot, shoulders slumped forward, arms dangling to the side.

Emily scuffled to the other side of the van and grabbed Ella from the car seat. The group filed into the convenience store. A low level whistling resonated from behind the checkout counter. Drake inhaled the stale aroma and concluded it smelled as it looked from the outside. The crew swiftly scattered to gather snacks.

Drake tried to remember seeing one nice or relatively new structure from the time they arrived in Shady Oaks. It was an old town. In fact, everything looked to be at least forty years old. Back in Austin, he had attempted to research the town of Shady Oaks on the internet and found that only fifty people had established it in 1971. He was convinced these fifty people built the town that year and nobody had lifted a finger since.

Wanting to trust his parents, Drake held out hope for their new home. His parents had sold him on the fact that the home was over 5000 square feet and overlooked Deadwood Lake. Their previous residence in Austin was 15 years old and was a moderate 2900 square feet one story home. The family had outgrown it a while back and had discussed looking for something slightly bigger with a swimming pool prior to Ivan making the rapid decision to move the family to the small town of Shady Oaks. Ivan promised Drake a second story bedroom with open lake view windows along the wall. He also promised to buy a boat that he could park at the dock in their new backyard. It all sounded good to Drake but he now worried that the home would be as run down and tattered as the rest of the town. It would be a nightmare if his worries were true.

"Hello, sir!" Ivan addressed the clerk, placing his items beside the cash register on the counter. "My name's Ivan Henry and this is my lovely family. I'm a chemist, starting on Monday at the Bonlin Pharmaceutical Research Center over on Friar Alley."

The clerk, reclining against the wall in a worn out plastic chair, whistling an ominous tune, studied Ivan with a cold, uncomfortable stare.

Sensing the awkward tension, Ivan cleared his throat and went on, "My family and I are moving into the home on Scarlet Court. I'm told it's the only one on the court!"

The clerk slowly rose from his chair. Stringy, sparse hair trickled down onto his hollow face. He stroked his slick goatee and twirled it into a point below his chin with his thumb and index finger. His nametag read *Quentin*. Briar, with eyes widened, cleared her throat and nudged Drake. She mouthed the words *let's wait in the car*.

"Huh – huh - howdy, folks," Quentin stuttered, punching the prices of the items into the register with his bony middle finger. "Thuh-that is one nice house up on Scarlet Court. Yuh – yuh - you all will be happy there."

The clerk became animated; Ivan and Emily seemed to relax. The portly Basil dredged up to the counter behind Ivan, placing his sugary snacks onto the counter. Basil's hair, once blonde as Emily's but now grayed, had lost the fight and exposed the top of his glistening head. He had grown full facial hair but it was sparse in areas, only serving to diminish his overall look rather than enhance it. Nobody could tell Basil anything, as he knew it all, had done it all, and had tried it all. Drake and Briar certainly didn't care for Basil but he was family, nonetheless. Ivan paused to sneer at Basil as he continued to add items on the counter, expecting Ivan to pick up the tab. Drake knew Ivan didn't care for Basil either but Ivan would put up with anything for Emily, the woman he had loved since high school.

"Well, thank you, Quentin. We are excited as well," Ivan replied casually, eyes narrowed in irritation at Basil.

Upon hearing the clerk speak of their new home, Drake and Briar stalled at the front door of the convenience store, deciding in unison to eavesdrop.

"Sss-ss-so what scares you, sir?" The clerk mumbled under his breath.

"Excuse me?" Ivan replied with derision, forehead wrinkling in uncertainty.

"I...I'm just always curious to see what scares puh-puh-people. When I meet nnn-new folks, I just always ask. Sorry, don't mean to be a bother. Neh-nev-never mind," his voice turned brittle.

Briar shot a wide-eyed look at Drake who returned with a one-shoulder shrug. Ivan laughed nervously as he stared in blank astonishment at Emily.

Ivan twirled back to gaze at the clerk and replied undauntingly, "No, it's fine. Well, I suppose it would have to be ghosts. Can't watch any supernatural movies or I won't sleep for weeks."

Ivan forced an unnatural bout of laughter as Emily gazed into his eyes, a curious expression taking over her face. The clerk's mouth turned up at both corners.

"An-anything else?" the clerk stammered, watching Ivan intently.

"Well," Ivan paused. "Terminal illness would be another one," Ivan gazed at the clerk who nodded, waiting for Ivan to continue. "Being accused of something I didn't do. Maybe financial failure, not being able to take care of my family and losing everything I—

Ivan stopped mid sentence, realizing Basil was behind him, listening intently.

Emily, with Ella on her hip, nudged Ivan in the back with an elbow and attempted a cover, "My biggest fear would be losing a family member. In fact, I'm quite obsessed about it," she laughed nervously, straightening her cat eye rimmed glasses.

Quentin's cavernous face glowed with serenity as if he were floating on air.

"Anything else, mmm-mih-miss?" The clerk shifted his deep-set eyes to lock in an unsettling gaze with Emily. She looked pensively at the counter for a moment.

"I'd add *bridges* for sure. Won't go on 'em to save my life." Emily paused, releasing a nervous giggle, shifting Ella to the other side. "Then I guess I fear aging a bit—

Basil interrupted, leaning in to get a better view of the clerk, "I've got only one fear."

Quentin moved accordingly to lay his eyes upon Basil, no longer entering items into the cash register. Both Emily and Ivan turned around, gaping at Basil in unison.

"Murderers. I'm scared to *death* of sociopaths. I recently lost my wife to one."

Emily and Ivan were openly astonished at Basil's revelation. Emily glanced at her watch, and nodded at Ivan as if they needed to go. Ivan returned the nod ever so slightly.

"I cuh -cuh-can definitely uh-uh-understand that one, sir," Quentin agreed blithely.

Basil snapped his pipe between his teeth and headed for the door, lighter in hand. Drake and Briar stepped to either side of the door, allowing him to pass. Briar rolled her eyes at Drake, sticking out her tongue at Basil as he passed. Drake countered with a smile.

"An – an - anything else you can thuh-think of? Those are all fears I've heard buh-buh-b'fore," Quentin stammered.

Through a moment of uncomfortable silence, Ivan watched Quentin slowly placing the items into a paper bag, tapping on the counter in angst.

"No, that's pretty much it. Well, Quentin, what scares you?" Ivan sounded, anxious that Quentin was moving at a leisurely pace, attempting a distraction.

"Nothing scares me," Quentin bestowed a cold stare into Ivan's eyes and paused. "That will be twenty five dollars and forty two cents, please," Quentin said each word distinct and without stutter.

Ivan paid the bill as the rest of the family piled into the vehicles.

"Thanks, Quentin. Have a good one," Ivan said, picking up the bags.

"No, thank *you*, Ivan."

4- New Beginnings

Ivan steered the minivan onto Scarlet Drive. Faces glued to the van's windows, Drake and Briar anxiously anticipated seeing the family's new home. Drake dreaded the reality of seeing it as seeing it would finalize everything. He feared the house would match the rest of the town's broken down, unkempt buildings and weed-sprinkled gravel driveways.

Maybe mom and dad weren't looking at the right pictures? What if they were tricked by their realtor in Austin into buying a dump? Why wouldn't they want to see the house in person before they agreed to buy it? Drake's mind raced in a panic.

"Oh my God. I know I'm gonna hate it, Drake. I'm gonna freak out," Briar injected a sneer into her whisper, softly kicking the back of Drake's seat.

"I heard that, Bee!" Ivan bawled, pointing a strong finger in the air.

Ella let out a long-winded whine. She was at her limit of being restrained in the car seat. The dog followed Ella's wayward lead and let out a high-pitched howl.

"Briar, chill. It's fine," Drake pushed out the words, not believing them himself. "Omen, hush!"

Back in Austin, Drake had attempted to use the Google map feature to view the town of Shady Oaks but to no surprise, the town had not kept up with technology. There were no aerial maps or street views of Shady Oaks but Drake had at least a few partial graphical maps of the small town of 5155 people. His parents told him their home was the only one on Scarlet Court, at the end and dead center of the court facing the lake with a dock in the rear. As the van drew nearer the house, Drake's heart raced wildly as his stomach felt as though he had gulped nails and battery acid.

Ivan guided the van even closer, Drake catching sight of the street sign ahead, Scarlet Court, green and weathered with white lettering. Frightened of the impending letdown; he couldn't bear to keep his eyes open any longer and clinched them shut. Ivan veered to the right as Scarlet Drive dead-ended into Scarlet Court. As promised, there was only one home on the court, number 614, now dead ahead of the van. Drake barely allowed enough light to pass through his narrowed eyes in efforts to make the vision of the house a blur. A blur couldn't disappoint him. He knew that as soon as the vision of the house seared his retina, it would be final.

"Here we are, y'all! I told you!" Ivan sang in a chipper tone, coasting the minivan onto the stately circle drive.

Drake's eyes flashed open, his jaw immediately dropped. Briar released a scream from the backseat, stomping on the floor of the van, causing Ivan to slam on the brakes.

"Hey now!" Ivan shrieked. "I told you kids you'd like it! I'll accept both of your apologies now."

The minivan halted on a cobblestone driveway lined with marble tiles. Drake's eyes swished to the left to gaze at a beautiful fountain with a massive statue in the middle, probably eight or nine feet high. His eyes shifted in the sunlight to make out a stone medieval warrior dragon suited in armor raising a slain lion into the air above his head. The sparkling clear water spewed from the lion's abdomen as if it were blood, collecting in a pool surrounding the dragon. Drake thought it was the coolest thing he had ever seen.

"Sick! Twisted!" Briar shouted, frozen in awe at the fountain as she climbed skeptically of the van.

Omen erupted out of the van, frantically inhaling the new scents in the air as he pranced around the front yard.

"Nah, that's cool as hell, Bee!" Drake shouted, taking a picture of it with his iPhone and pausing to post it to his Facebook page. Within mere seconds, ten of his friends back in Austin had *liked* his post.

"Yes, it is somewhat eclectic," Ivan said, amused. "It didn't appear nearly as large in the picture! I can't wait for you to see the inside of the house. It looks like the mortgage people are here already, can't keep 'em waiting. Mom and I will only be a few minutes. I've signed a couple of these before; I know how to speed things up!"

"Can we explore the house, dad?" Briar asked politely, attitude changed drastically from before.

"Of course! You and Drake claim your rooms on the second floor. Both overlook the lake and they are about the same size. I doubt y'all will fight over it but Mom wants Ella's room to be the one on the far right next to the attic since it is smaller and only has one wall of windows," Ivan instructed, gathering his things from the van.

Drake and Briar took off running toward the house. The front of the two-story home had four massive stone columns outlining a majestic front porch. The two front doors were rounded with thick glass windows highlighting a beautiful iron spiral staircase inside in the center of the majestic foyer.

"This is awesome! We're like royalty of this town!" Briar squealed in enchantment. "It seems brand new, Drake!"

"The house definitely looks new. It doesn't fit in with this old town for sure," Drake said, trying to sound calm.

The pair burst into the home and bolted up the massive spiral staircase in the middle of the marble-floored foyer. The pleasing aroma of fresh construction filled Drake's lungs. The house was a new build. When they reached the top, they stood in the middle of an enormous room with doors in every direction.

"Massive playroom, here!" Briar purred, spinning around in the huge room with her arms extended.

"Dad said the room on the far right is Ella's," Drake exclaimed, rushing into the room to the back right.

Drake flipped the light switch and the lights slowly ignited, revealing the most overwhelming room Drake had only seen on shows about celebrity homes.

"This is AWESOME! Come see this, Briar! You won't believe it!"

Briar rushed into the room after Drake and let out a scream of excitement. The room was multi-tiered with four leather reclining theater seats on each of the three levels. The walls and carpet were jet black and deep crimson velvet drapes framed the enormous movie screen. There were numerous black speakers in the floors, walls and on the ceiling with two large speakers in the back and front of the room. Regal sconces hung on the walls at each tier with flickering fire light bulbs, tiny floor lights lining the walkway. It reminded Drake of a miniature movie theater.

"I'm going to *live* in here!" Briar detonated.

"Let's check out our rooms!" Drake blurted, racing back into the center playroom, lunging into the room adjacent to the movie theater. Briar correspondingly chose the remaining room to the far left. Drake stood in the middle and swirled around, scanning the room in awe. He was standing on the most comfortable, fluffy navy shag carpet and staring at steel-gray painted faux finished walls. His favorite NFL team was the Dallas Cowboys so the room's colors couldn't have been more perfect.

He walked to the back wall to gaze out of considerably sized windows lending to a breathtaking panoramic view of Deadwood Lake. Drake inspected the windows. They were permanently sealed, doubled paned glass. His mind catapulted him back to his uncle's house fire only five days before. He was at 5150 Rosamond Drive. He was standing at the bedroom window; sweaty fists pounding on the glass as smoke slowly choked the life out of his body, lungs tightening with every second. The feeling of helplessness took over his senses as his heart raced, smoke stinging his eyes.

"Drake!"

He gasped as his sister's voice from the adjacent room flung him back into reality. He mechanically shook the scene from his head.

"Drake! Come and see my room! This is *obviously* my room!" Briar screamed. "It is so wonderful! I love it!"

Drake took a moment to calm his senses before jetting into Briar's pink palace. Obviously, Ivan and Emily knew which room was intended for each of them. Briar's room had thick, fuchsia shag carpet and lighter pink walls that looked like satin. The back and front of her room had massive windows along the walls like Drake's back wall.

"There's your buddy, Bee," Drake said playfully, pointing to the dragon statue in the front. From this vantage point, the water streaming from the large gaping wound in the stone lion's belly could be seen clearly.

"That is so awesome," Drake mumbled.

"That's great," Briar sighed with a sarcastic tone. "I'm definitely putting my desk facing the lake. Maybe I'll put my dresser in front of that window to block the view of that hideous thing. I hope mom and dad get rid of it."

"No way! I think it's one of the tightest things about this house! That playroom is sick. Let's see if the parentals will get us a pool table or something cool in there."

"Heck yes!" Briar agreed with a glimmer of animation in her eyes. "I suppose we should check out the downstairs. There's no debate on the bedrooms, it's pretty clear where we belong," Briar assured, escaping for the staircase.

Drake followed behind Briar on the curved staircase, sliding his hand along the cold iron rail, feeling the buoyant carpet padding of the stairs with every step. Landing on the marbled tile of the foyer, Drake felt exhilarated. His home in Austin was average at best, moderately sized. His father had worked for the county as a forensic chemist. They definitely would never have been rich. They would never have lived in a house like this. Their home in Austin was nearly half the size and lacked affluent qualities like statue fountains, marbled floors or a view of a lake.

Drake and Briar stepped into the living area to the right of the downstairs foyer. They gazed at the marbled fireplace in the corner of the room. It was the largest fireplace that Drake had ever seen. He sauntered over to a light switch next to the fireplace and switched it on. He stepped back abruptly as a roar erupted from under the logs in the fireplace. The fire crackled and popped.

"That is hardcore, Bee," Drake laughed, a throaty sound, gazing at the instant fire he had created.

Briar's mouth dropped open, processing the fact that a light switch had started a fire in the fireplace.

"Hey, boy! Catchin' some rays, huh?" Drake leaned down and raked his fingers along Omen's lengthy deer-like body, his legs stretched out, revealing their lankiness.

Exhausted from the drive and the investigation of the new house, Omen was sprawled out with his head on the marble of the foyer and rear end on the white plush carpet of the living area. He had discovered a respectable strip of sunlight streaming in from the glass of the front doors and was enjoying a snooze while basking in the sun.

"I think they're in the kitchen. Let's sneak a peek, o.k.?" Briar directed, walking silently toward the voices.

The stately kitchen, with vast windows along the back wall, had the same view of the lake as the bedrooms upstairs. Emily and Ivan were busy meeting with the title company representative and the mortgage banker, papers stacked along the black granite kitchen counters. They were signing the seemingly hundreds of mortgage papers as Ella kicked her legs and screamed to break free from Emily. Drake feared anything to go wrong with the purchase, as he now desperately wanted to live in what he and Briar termed *the mansion*. The jovial house tour had swiped his memory of the dreary small town surrounding them.

Drake caught himself in a daze at the windows of the kitchen, gazing blankly at the lake. He could see the edge of the wooden dock. His dad's promises were all coming true. Turning over his shoulder, he gave Ivan a thumbs up gesture. A grin invaded Drake's face, growing so large it appeared to hurt his cheeks. Ivan winked and continued to sign papers as directed, appearing very disinterested with the bureaucratic process. Emily maintained her struggle with the frenzied Ella, doing her best to throw her signature in when instructed.

Ella, spotting her older siblings, ramped up her unruliness. Emily attempted to reason with Ella as if she would understand the ration about the house not yet being baby-proofed. Emily was over protective of Ella but for good reason. If there were anything for Ella to hurt herself with or damage beyond repair, she would find it. That was the beautiful baby Ella. A magnet for destruction.

"Let's bounce Bee, Ella's going crazy."

"You mean crazy–*er*," Briar snickered, skipping into the master bedroom suite across the hall from the kitchen.

After stepping into the master suite, Drake knew the term *mansion* was a good fit. As he imagined, the master suite was fit for royalty with exquisitely draped windows on either side of the home's second colossal marbled fireplace. The master bathroom was endless and the walk in closet was five times the size of the one his parent's had back in Austin.

"Whoa. This is tight! I don't think mom and dad have enough stuff to fill this closet up!" Drake hedged, investigating the various mahogany shelves and built in armoires of the closet.

Drake took in the robust bouquet of new construction. Briar had discovered a separate, smaller closet in the back and was inspecting it with intense curiosity.

"Oh, you're highly mistaken, Drake. Mom alone had three closets back in Austin. She'll probably be able to consolidate into one here. Dad'll be lucky if he can fit his stuff. What's this little wood closet for, anyway?" Briar said, opening and closing the door to waft the intense aroma of cedar into her face.

"I saw one on MTV Cribs before. I think it's called a cedar closet. Rich people put furs and stuff in there," Drake brooded, nodding with confidence that he knew the answer.

"So, we're rich people now, huh?" Briar smiled.

The pair laughed as they journeyed back into the foyer and into the room toward the front corner of the home on their left. This room was underneath Bee's room upstairs and Ivan had called it the study. It seemed smaller than Bee's room, the air stale. There were no windows; the walls a dark gray color, muted and flat, not trendy as Drake's faux finished walls. The flooring was black shag carpeting as the upstairs media room. Drake was unimpressed by the dowdy color scheme of the room and lack of windows.

"Let's get out of here, I hate this room!" Briar whined. "It's the only thing I don't like so far, though!"

"I'm glad that's not my room for sure," Drake said. "Dad said Uncle Basil's staying in there. Good, he won't want to stay with us very long," he laughed.

"O.M.G., Drake. So right!" Briar chuckled, shooting a double fist pump into the air.

Leaving the study, they trekked back into the foyer and stood by the spiral staircase. With one room left to discover, they crossed over to the elegant formal dining room, taking the opposing corner of the house from the dreary study. Like the study, the room lacked windows but the gold and crystal chandelier coupled with the crimson shaded walls made the room seem strangely appealing. Upon closer inspection, Drake noticed the highly textured paint on the walls had delicate metallic gold trim on the crests of the paint waves, resembling a miniature ruby colored ocean. Maybe it was real gold painted on the tips of the ridges. If it were so, Drake wouldn't have been surprised.

Ella's nonstop whining sprinkled with erratic squeals of frustration drowned out the voices that persisted to grumble from the kitchen. Ella's incessant antics for independence grew in intensity. Drake could sense by the abrupt change in speed, tone and timbre of the voices from the kitchen that his parents, as well as the bankers, were losing patience.

"What about the backyard, Drake?" Briar inquired casually, running her finger along the gold crested ridges of the walls.

"Let's check it," Drake said with a smile, heading through the foyer toward the backdoor.

The pair hopped out onto the sizeable sundeck, inhaling the fresh, earthy perfume of the lake, the picturesque flowers edging the deck nearly encircling them. The back courtyard was lush with vegetation and was surprisingly close to the lake. A flower-lined concrete pathway leading to a small beach area split into two on either side of the wooden dock.

A thick, unnatural odor caught Drake's attention as he looked over his shoulder and caught a glimpse of Basil, already enjoying the luxurious patio furniture. Lounging and smoking his fragrant pipe, Drake didn't feel as though he looked like someone who had recently lost everything. Basil raked his hand across his balding head to collect the beads of sweat and then wiped the salty liquid on his t-shirt. Basil often profusely sweated, even while at rest, and this drove Drake crazy. Emily explained to Drake on multiple occasions that it was Basil's normal reaction to stress. It was early October, a perfect eighty degrees outside with a cool breeze, no cause for overheating. Basil took a long drag from his pipe, glaring at Drake with the same ice blue eyes as Emily and Ella. An obvious genetic link just as Drake and Briar's caramel eyes were to Ivan.

Drake cringed in disgust at the sight, choosing not to speak to him. He wished Basil had stayed back in Austin. He wasn't part of the Henry family and certainly didn't fit in with the family dynamics. Drake knew Ivan didn't care for Basil and was tolerating the situation for Emily's benefit. Drake wanted to escape the drama back in Austin, not take it with them to the new place.

"Let's check out that dock!" Briar said, pointing to the dock with an extended shapely arm.

Drake, filled with anticipation of his father buying a boat as promised, dreamed of taking rides around the lake, going fishing in the early morning and water skiing whenever he felt like it. He had no idea of the costs but believed he could get a part time job and save up for a jet ski as well. Seeing the house made it all a reality. Drake missed Austin but living in this house was going to make the transition to the small town and the new school somewhat easier.

"Drake, why does Omen growl at Uncle Basil? I mean, if it is *his* dog, why does he act like that?" Briar asked, voice rising from a whisper to a normal volume as she pulled her honey colored locks from her face.

"Donno, maybe he was more of Aunt Kerstin's dog. She named him, ya know. Sometimes dogs like one owner more than the other."

"Hmmm," Briar pondered, picking up a rock and attempting to skip it across the lake.

They both took a seat at the end of the dock, swinging their legs above the water. Drake inhaled the aromatic scents of the lake, crisp, clean and fresh odor molecules permeating his nasal cavity. Expanding his lungs, it made them feel normal as they once were before the fire.

"Dominick's mom has a Chihuahua that bites his dad on the belly if he gets near her. It's hilarious."

"Maybe Omen hates that stinky pipe and his sweaty fat belly!" Briar giggled playfully, leaning down to attempt a toe dip into the water. "Why was Basil looking at us like that? Sometimes he creeps me out."

Drake slanted down to inspect the rope tied to the dock. Briar leaned back to lay her slender body flat on the dock, marinating her skin in the sun, legs dangling over the edge at the knees.

"Donno, Briar. Why do you think we didn't spend holidays with him and Aunt Kerstin even though they lived in the same neighborhood? I think I'd only been to their house once after they moved in about four years ago. Think of how bad Basil is to be around, Aunt Kerstin was ten times worse! Who could stand that hag?" Drake laughed, pausing in thought for a short moment, "Oh, I guess I went over there another time when they got the dog. I love Dobermans, had to see him."

"No doubt. I never saw the inside of their house, actually. I knew which house it was on Rosamond Street but never wanted to visit."

The back door squeaked as it flung open. Ivan stood in the doorway, peering out into the backyard at Basil and then turning toward the dock.

"Done, folks!" Ivan shouted. "Time for a Henry family meeting!"

Drake and Briar rushed toward the house. Drake couldn't help but feel irritated when he saw Basil snuff his pipe.

He said Henry family meeting. That means us, not you, Drake thought, fighting irritation.

"Wow, that didn't take long at all! Half the time as when you bought that minivan!" Drake injected humor-filled sarcasm into his words.

Emily gestured for everybody to take a seat on the floor in the living area, still struggling to restrain Ella.

"Dad knows what he's doing. We've been through it a few times," Emily laughed, straightening her cat eye rimmed glasses and finger brushing her blonde locks out of her face. "The movers just got here. We'll let them unpack and set up our things while we grab a bite to eat. And I need a break from this one, here Ivan!" Emily grumbled, shoving Ella into Ivan's arms.

The family piled into the minivan and set out to the local Shady Oaks Diner. Excitement hung thickly in the air as they enjoyed the local cuisine - cheeseburgers and fries. The red and white checkered plastic tablecloth and other cheap décor of the diner were unappetizing but the food tasted wonderful, comforting, without a calorie spared in the preparation. Drake had settled into a state of mental content with his parent's decision to move to Shady Oaks. He missed his friends dearly, especially Dominick, but was surprisingly ready to take on exciting challenges ahead. He wished Uncle Basil would move on with his life, leaving his family alone. Drake struggled to be cordial for Emily's sake but the tattered rope of friendliness was hanging on by a final waning thread.

After discussing the various nuances of the home such as how Uncle Basil would temporarily stay in the study, how the family would rally together to baby proof the home as quickly as possible and that Omen would sleep with Drake, they headed back home in the minivan. As Ivan pulled the van onto the cobblestone driveway, Briar unexpectedly liberated a shrill scream, hands cupping ears throughout the van.

As Drake frantically scanned the front of the house, the fountain snagging his peripheral vision. The water flowing from the lion's belly now appeared as blood unlike the sparkling clear cascade from earlier when they arrived at the home.

"Briar, not necessary! Hold on, stay right there," Ivan said calmly, jumping out of the car and ambling to the fountain.

"Dad, hold up," Drake shouted, throwing off his seatbelt.

It didn't take much to signal Ella to throw a fit in her car seat. Emily rushed around the van and fought to remove the seat belts as Ella kicked her legs like a nutcracker.

"It's all right, pumpkin. We're home. I know, sweetheart. They are all being naughty yelling like that!" Emily consoled the crazed toddler.

"Give me a break, Emily! That's why the kid acts like that. You've spoiled her rotten and now you've got to pay the piper," Basil mumbled, snapping his pipe between his teeth, tossing his seatbelt across his shoulder.

Ella held on to her mother by snatching tufts of her shoulder length blonde hair with her tiny fists.

"Whatever, Basil!" Emily snorted, freeing her hair by peeling the tiny fingers back one by one.

Basil dredged out of the van and skulked toward the house. He lit his pipe, openly disinterested in the fountain and the spoiled, screaming child. His balding head gleamed in the moonlight as the puffs of smoke surrounded him.

Ivan was carefully inspecting the fountain as Briar climbed cautiously out of the van and ambled out onto the cobblestone driveway.

"Look, Drake. It's deep red lighting. Either they are on an automatic timer or we just couldn't see the color during the day. There's a track of lights in the fountain pool below and there must be the same lighting in the lion's belly. That's all it is. Bee, stop being a drama queen!"

"This is hella tight," Drake shouted, snapping another picture with his iPhone and posting it to his Facebook page.

5- Deadwood High

"Let's hit it, Bee!" Drake gently knocked on Briar's bedroom door, pausing while waiting patiently for a response.

It was Monday morning and the first day of school for Drake and Briar at Deadwood High.

"I can't wait to see the school, Drake! How do I look?" Briar spun around, modeling her attire followed by a slow trace around her face with her hands.

"Let's go, stop being crazy. You always look a'ight for a girl."

They marched down the coiled staircase and into the kitchen, random boxes scattered about the room. It didn't smell like home. Back in Austin, it would have smelled like bacon at this time.

Emily was busy feeding Ella in her high chair. Ella was a notorious food hurler so Emily still fed her, coaxing her to eat by using a silly turtle face hand puppet to hold the spoon. Drake thought it was ridiculous how much his mother pampered Ella. Maybe she was over compensating since Ella was the baby of the family. Upon Ella's arrival, Drake and Briar, at 14 and 12 years old, didn't need Emily as much. When Ella arrived, Emily resigned from her lucrative career as Chief of Operations of Heinzelman Candy Company. That is when the family decided to stay in the home they had outgrown. That is when Emily's problems with nervousness and insomnia began. She became over anxious, unable to deal with simple things. Ivan reasoned it was the change of pace from a high stress career to being a full time homemaker. Whatever it was, it was too much for Emily to handle.

"You two are not going anywhere without getting breakfast! I unpacked the food for the pantry this morning and there are some mini muffins in there. I'll go to the grocery store today and buy some real food but you'll have to make it on those for now," Emily belted sternly as she made the turtle puppet dance for Ella's amusement.

Ella leaned around the turtle puppet to smile at Drake. He returned with a wave and a warm smile. She folded her fingers down in a mock wave and started to giggle.

"I'm not hungry, mom," Drake uttered, grabbing his car keys off the granite countertop.

"Neither am I," Briar shouted as she scrambled for the front door. "I'm too excited to eat!"

The two climbed into Drake's Jeep and set out for Deadwood High School. Drake had viewed the directions from his iPhone the night before and knew how to get there. Briar was right that they would have to drive over a long bridge over Deadwood Lake to get to Deadwood City. Overall, Drake didn't think it would take more than ten minutes to get to school from 614 Scarlet Court.

"So, how'd you sleep last night?" Drake asked, igniting the engine.

The Jeep engine roared, settling down into a soft rumble. In unison, they pulled their seat belts across their bodies, clicking them into the holsters.

"Well, I had to sleep on the air mattress on the floor since Dad didn't have time to put my bed together. That red light from that creepy fountain made strange figures on the ceiling. Way uncool! I'm gonna demand very heavy drapes for my front windows immediately."

Briar was animated, flinging her arms in the air as she spoke.

"Ha! I think the fountain's tight. Wish I could see it from my room! I like the view of the lake. It's sweet,"

Drake sped off down Scarlet Court, veering onto Scarlet Drive. "I wish I could open my windows but I supposed they're too big. I'd probably fall right out. I'm gonna unpack the rest of my boxes and get my room set up when we get home. I hate not having World of Warcraft and playing games on Xbox Live with my friends."

"World of Warcraft is so last week, Drake! When are you gonna give that up? As long as I remember, you've sat for hours at the computer playing that dumb game!"

Drake's face soured as he turned onto Lakefront Avenue. He took a deep breath, irritation rising.

"Shut up, Bee. World of Warcraft is tight," Drake defended hardheartedly. "Millions upon millions of very cool, awesome people play it around the world so you are calling a large percent of the global population dumb. Not cool."

"Whatever you say, bro," Briar narrowed her eyes with a cynical mock and forced a fake grin.

"Exactly," Drake turned up a corner of his mouth.

The car passed by the run down Shady Oaks Mart - the convenience store the family had stopped at the day prior upon their arrival in town. Briar gazed out the passenger window and grimaced as the view surfaced in front of her.

"By the way, the new house creaks a lot. Kept hearing noises. D'you hear anything strange last night?"

Drake pondered the question, hesitating as he scanned his memories from the night before.

Briar went on, "I guess I'm not used to the new house's noises. I had all the noises in the old house figured out."

Drake nodded, turning on Crescent Way. This was the only way to Deadwood City. He knew the bridge was ahead.

"Yeah, I guess so; I hear what you're sayin'. It sounded like squirrels or something running around the attic around 2AM. Maybe there's a nest or something up there since the house was vacant for a while. They'll probably move out soon enough now that we're there."

Drake pulled cautiously up to the Deadwood Bridge. He hesitated, slowing down to a snail's pace as he approached. It was rusted iron, worn by the sun and humidity over many years and didn't stand that far above the lake. It appeared to be in a rather shoddy state but was the only route to Deadwood City from Shady Oaks. In the top of his peripheral view, something flashed brightly. He gazed into the rearview mirror and noticed an electric blue Challenger rushing up behind them. Drake pressed the gas pedal to reach the speed limit as the Challenger offensively rode their bumper as they drove onto the bridge.

"What's that guy's deal?" Drake spoke quickly, concern peppering his voice.

He pushed on the gas pedal a little harder, slightly rising above the speed limit. It didn't look like a bridge he wanted to push the limits on. The Challenger remained seconds behind the Jeep.

"Donno but he seems to be in a freakin' hurry. Why doesn't he just pass us? There's nobody comin' the other way," Briar asked anxiously, pointing at the other side of the thoroughfare with a half polished fingernail.

The Challenger continued to follow Drake's Jeep within a hair's distance. Drake strained to see the driver but the front window was tinted dark. At the midway point of the bridge, they came upon a small island, the bridge lowering to land, forming two lanes each direction for about half a mile. Drake chose the far right lane, exhaling with reprieve at the stability of land. The Challenger also chose the right lane and continued to ride his bumper.

"Seven Point Island, huh?" Drake scoffed, chuckling at the dilapidated sign at the side of the road, glancing into the rearview mirror.

"More like seven second island, right?" Briar laughed nervously, twisting around to catch a view of the Challenger behind them.

With the second segment of the bridge only seconds away, the Challenger abruptly maneuvered a pass to the left, swerving with only inches to spare in the lane in front of Drake. As the Jeep thumped back onto the rusted iron bridge, the Challenger's tire's squealed, leaving a puff of smoke for Drake to drive through during the subsequent ascent. Through the smoke, Drake caught a glimpse of the license plate *BFDEAL*. Drake shook his head with an angered repulsion.

"Of course, a personalized plate, how lame can you be?" Drake sounded, driving cautiously through the waning exhaust haze.

"That driver has issues!" Briar fumed, slamming her hand onto the dashboard.

"Yeah, they've definitely got something up their booty for sure."

Briar tapped on the car window repeatedly as they exited the bridge and passed the official sign.

"Deadwood City, population 36,218. Wow, it's over seven times the size of Shady Oaks!"

"Yeah but both combined don't even compare to Austin," Drake replied sharply, checking the street sign, it read Castlebend Drive. He knew they had arrived.

"Well, duh, Professor Drake!" Briar grumbled, furrowing her eyebrows in mockery.

Drake veered the car onto the front parking lot of Deadwood High School, snatching up a front visitor's space. He figured of all days, he would get away with parking here. The school was moderately sized, not nearly as vast as Winding Heights High School in Austin. The architecture appeared to be inspired by the medieval era.

"Well, this isn't too shabby!" Briar sparked with excitement. "Kinda looks like a castle!"

"Looks awesome, actually. The knights in the front are hella tight!"

They climbed out of the car and walked down the sidewalk toward the school. Drake pretended not to realize that the other students were staring at them watchfully, in awe as if they'd never had a new kid at their school before. Drake had met plenty of new kids at school in Austin. He had never been a new kid but often envied them for getting to reinvent themselves in a new place. He now had that chance.

They passed through a pair of massive steel medieval knights, probably standing over ten feet high. On either side of the knights were narrow ponds that outlined the perimeter of the school. Walkways resembling drawbridges were at each entrance and Drake supposed it was the architect's rendition of a castle moat. He peered over and gazed at the huge fish swimming energetically, coming to surface to scoop up the fish feed that students were tossing in. He grabbed his iPhone, snapped a quick picture of the feeding frenzy, and then turned to take a picture of one of the knights.

"What do you want to bet that their mascot is a knight?" Briar mused, gazing at the enormous steel knight.

"Not taking that bet. I already know it is. Looked at their crappy website a while back. There's hardly anything on it but they do say what their mascot is," Drake replied in confidence, holding open the front door for Briar.

"Well, I obviously looked at it as well but didn't notice the mascot!"

Drake chuckled, surveying the front atrium, taking a whiff of the customary aroma of school served breakfast reeking from the cafeteria.

"Hey, mom said our schedules are in the front office."

"Sweet!" Briar sang, following Drake's navigation through the school.

They notified the front desk personnel of their arrival, picked up their schedules from the counselor, and after a brief orientation to the school by neurotic Principal Apple; they headed off to find their lockers. The other students were already nestled in class by the time they were released from the front office.

Briar's locker was at the opposite end of the school's from Drake because she was a freshman and he, a junior. They traversed around the halls, finding the whereabouts of each of their classes. The hallways and lockers were color coded by grade and laid out straightforward by room number. Drake wondered why they didn't think of that in Austin, as it was always difficult to find classes in his old school. Like a coddling father, Drake escorted Briar to her classroom and then headed to his first period English class.

He approached the door; double-checking his schedule to be certain that he had arrived at the right room. He slowly turned the knob and entered, twenty-five heads raised, twenty-five pairs of curious eyes focusing on him at once. He felt slightly embarrassed by making a spectacle of himself but strangely exhilarated.

A crackling voice sounded from the front desk, "And you are—

"Drake Henry. Just moved here from Austin."

The teacher at the front desk was Ms. Pepper Crenshaw. She was an elderly woman as pasty white and thin as a crumpled paper doll with a dress collar so high, it rubbed rudely against her sagging chin. Her thinned, tightly curled hair was dyed a brilliant red, her orange lipstick faded into the creases of her lips. She removed her reading glasses, put down her book and escorted Drake down the aisle; pointing a bony finger at an empty desk.

"Class, pardon me, but I would like for you to give Blake Henry a nice hello."

"It's Drake," he corrected softly.

The class rumbled a few hellos as the girl in the seat behind him struggled to remove her feet from his chair. Drake avoided eye contact with her, only viewing her feet as they escaped under the slats in the back of the chair. He sat down, putting his head down for a moment, waiting for the other students in the classroom to grow tired of staring. Drake retrieved a spiral and pen from his backpack, still avoiding eye contact with the others as he had done in the last week back in Austin since his aunt was murdered. He wasn't entirely sure his legacy hadn't followed him here. He knew he was being paranoid but couldn't help it.

"Here you go, Blake. Here's an English textbook for you," she plunked a textbook on his desk, scuttling back to her desk to grab another. "We are also reading Frankenstein by Mary Shelley. Here's your copy. Good thing we just started yesterday so you won't have far to catch up," Ms. Crenshaw's rickety voice echoed as she extended the book toward Drake with a shaky hand.

Ms. Crenshaw set off down the aisle, giving a scorned stare to each student that had his or her head up to coax them back on task.

"Hey! Nice t'meet ya!" a feminine voice whispered from behind, smooth as honey.

Drake slowly turned around and locked into a gaze with the dramatic cobalt eyes belonging to Jade Amity. Her skin was pale as snow with an impossibly perfect complexion. Her intense auburn hair, sparkling like satin, draped effortlessly around her face and midway down her back. She was stunning. He hoped she was the same on the inside but in the past, such as with Elizabeth Payne from his Computer Applications class, he had found that most beautiful girls weren't that great once he got to know them.

"S'up," Drake whispered guardedly, nodding his head ever so slightly as to not appear eager.

"Sit with me at lunch." Jade whispered, tapping on his shoulder with perfectly rounded light pink polished fingernails.

"What lunch do you have?" Drake fought the urge to allow a smile to surface.

"Uh, the only lunch juniors have here, silly!" Jade playfully rolled her eyes, punching him gently in the arm.

"Oh, my bad. My old school had four lunch periods."

Jade hesitated, candidly admiring Drake's features.

"I bet your school in Austin was ginormous! I've always wanted to visit Austin. I heard it's super awesome there."

"Mr. Henry! Miss Amity! *Shhhhhh*! You should be reading Frankenstein! It's not talkie time!" Ms. Crenshaw scolded in a quivering voice, slamming her bony fist on her desk.

The class simultaneously giggled and shot mocking glances their way.

"My name is Jade," she leaned up in her seat closer to Drake and whispered softly, he could feel her warm breath against the back of his neck. "Jade Amity. See ya at lunch!"

Drake continued to fight the smile from surfacing the rest of the period. He daydreamed about her breathtakingly beautiful exterior through his next two classes until lunch. He couldn't wait to see her again, barely paying attention in his next two class periods. He longed for her to be just as stunning on the inside, dreading to find out otherwise.

The bell finally rang for lunch and Drake set out into the crowded corridor. He found it to be an awkward change from being a hallway celebrity back in Austin to now being an unknown that could blend in with the walls. He missed Dominick by his side. He felt alone, apprehensive. He would nearly trade the negative attention of his uncle's murder case at this moment for the empty feeling he was enduring.

"Watch it, punk!" An enormous spiky haired guy in a varsity athlete's jacket scowled, shoving an unsuspecting Drake in the shoulder, spinning him off course.

It was Nigel Sage. He had accidentally bumped into Drake in the hallway. He was a senior. He glared at Drake as he ran his thick fingers across his thin chinstrap beard, framing his broad face. He was only a few inches taller than Drake but much wider. Judging by his size and the muscle definition bursting through his tight fitted Affliction t-shirt, Drake knew immediately he had to diffuse the situation at all costs. He didn't want to end up back in the hospital *and* be humiliated on his first day at Deadwood High.

"Sorry, man. Didn't see ya coming," Drake uttered politely, keeping a cool head and steadying his feet.

Nigel clenched his fists reflexively, lunging, leaning on the balls of his feet toward Drake. He glared at Drake, eyes critical. He took cavernous, measured breaths, appearing to toss a mental coin in his head as to decide whether to continue the brawl or let it go.

"Don't let it happen again or I'll have to pound that ugly mug of yours," he bellowed in a husky voice, pivoting arrogantly toward the opposite direction. "Maybe it would help ya out, though," Nigel snorted, strutting down the corridor.

Drake noticed the patches on Nigel's letter jacket and his heart sank deeply into his chest, his warm blood turning into an icy sludge, sluggishly making its way through his veins. Nigel Sage had lettered in football, soccer and *tennis*.

Drake spotted Jade Amity trotting toward him. She had witnessed the altercation with Nigel. Drake felt ill, a gaping hole punched out of his self-esteem. This would never have happened to Drake in Austin. Everybody loved and respected Drake at Winding Heights High, even the upper classmen, largely due to his accomplishments on the tennis courts. Jade didn't know that Drake and would never know that Drake. She only knew the loser Drake on his first day at Deadwood High, the one that people like Nigel Sage could dominate and terrorize.

"Hey, don't let Nigel Sage get to you. He's the punk," Jade assured, guiding Drake toward the cafeteria. "He's a senior but for the second year in a row! Rumor has it that he failed 8th grade too!" She gestured for Drake to enter the cafeteria first. "And, you definitely don't have an ugly mug! He's obviously jealous."

Drake's demeanor raised a notch as he drew in a big breath of air. Jade seemed to understand the situation with Nigel and it didn't bother her. She was defending Drake's honor, not seeing him as weak.

"Thanks. He has issues for sure. So, he still plays tennis?"

Drake had misgivings about asking for he didn't want to hear the answer if it were yes. He narrowed his eyes in nervous apprehension as he waited for her reply.

"Yeah, he's pretty much the star athlete in *all* sports here. I didn't think he was supposed to be eligible to play sports again this year since he is a *repeating* senior but somehow he managed it. Small town, I suppose."

Drake lost himself in thought for a moment. His eyebrows raised in despondency before dropping them and letting out a sigh.

"Great," he nodded ever so slightly. "I guess I'll see him again this afternoon. I'm a tennis player. I was actually the Texas 5A State Men's Singles Champion the last two years and was headed that way again this year. But—

"Lemme guess, your parents moved you to this hell hole and you're screwed," Jade interjected mordantly, giggling softly.

"Even worse. We don't even live in Deadwood City. We moved to Shady Oaks."

Jade's mouth dropped open. Drake didn't appear as though he could live in such a tattered town as Shady Oaks. Drake knew she must have been confused.

"What! Are you serious? That town is so trashy!" She immediately stopped, cupping her hand over her mouth, eyebrows raised in an apologetic stance. "Uh...sorry. Didn't mean to—

Jade's face reddened as she looked down at the lunch table.

"No, I know exactly what you mean. Thought the same thing until I saw my house. It definitely doesn't belong there. It's like the royal mansion of the town," Drake pledged, leaning his head down gaze into her eyes. "It's also brand new so you probably haven't seen it there if you hadn't been there in a while."

His expression was soothing as though to convey that she hadn't insulted him. She leaned her head up and grinned delicately.

"No, I definitely haven't seen a mansion in the town of Shady Oaks for sure. I'll have to come and see it sometime soon, then! Hey, your buddy Nigel lives over there but I thought his parents owned the only big house in town, but I suppose I'm wrong. I think his dad runs that drug plant over there."

Drake's stomach curled into an instant knot. He shook his head in disbelief.

"You are joking, right? Wow, I hope his dad isn't anything like him."

"Why d'you say that?"

"My dad started work there today."

"Well, you better stay on Nigel's good side or he might tell his daddy!" Jade said teasingly, bursting into a fit of laughter as Drake cracked a forced smile.

"Yea, I'll try. Doesn't seem like I've gotten off to a good start, though. Maybe when he sees I'm a fellow tennis player, he'll be civil. Hey, we might even become friends," Drake said optimistically, gazing pensively around the cafeteria.

"Now that, you don't want to do, Drake!" Jade chuckled.

During lunch, the euphoria of talking to Jade wiped Nigel Sage from Drake's mind. He hadn't spent time casually with a female friend since 5th grade as Dominick had monopolized his time with video games and skateboarding over the years. A large majority of girls in Austin had confessed to having a crush on Drake. He had gone on a few dates but never made a solid connection, never feeling an authentic attraction. It seemed the more alluring girls he desired to pursue either didn't feel the same about him or were the bitter-hearted ones with inner, hidden personalities like scorned goblins.

Drake was relieved to find a friend on the first day, especially an eye-catching one that seemed to be genuine. He had worried about having to sit alone in the lunchroom. He hated being alone. It humiliated him. At least he wasn't alone.

"Drake Henry, it was a pleasure to meet you. I'm sure we'll be the best of friends in no time. You'll have to find the time to invite me to your mansion! I'd brave driving over that rickety bridge to see it!"

Jade extended her arm for a handshake. Drake locked hands, feeling her velvety skin.

"You got it!" Drake exclaimed, face serene and content.

After his next two classes, it was time for tennis. Drake had mixed emotions, as tennis practice had been his favorite part of the day since middle school. It was his lifeblood, his ticket to a college scholarship. The new coach would take the place of Coach Walter. Drake never imagined his last two years of high school without Coach Walter. He was unsure of the road ahead, cautiously navigating his way into the locker room, searching for the coach's office. Only the front light was on, barely illuminating the front portion of the locker room. Drake realized he might have arrived early.

"If you are looking for Coach Edward, he's gone. But can I help you?" A diminutive voice beckoned from the back of the shadowy locker room.

"Great," Drake sighed, frustrated. "Well, my coach in Austin faxed over my records. I'm a junior and was on the varsity tennis team back at my school in Austin. I'm the 5A state champion in men's singles, have been for the last two years and was a contender again this year until I moved here. Who do I speak with about joining the team?"

Drake looked blankly into the darkness, narrowing his eyes to catch a glimpse of the body belonging to the voice. The dense smell of soured fabric and bleach saturating the air.

The voice informed, "Impressive. The coach is Nigel Sage. He's a senior. Took over for Coach Edward when he left. He'll be here any minute."

Upon hearing the name, Drake felt as though the wind was violently knocked out of his chest. He searched for a way to bring the air back as he noticed a small figure stepping out of the shadows, leaning over to turn on the rest of the lights in the locker room with his long, lanky arm. He had to be a freshman. He was dressed in athletic gear, holding two buckets full of tennis balls. The door clambered open, others piled into the locker room, scattering to their lockers.

"Thanks. Are you on the team?" Drake inquired, surveying the latest arrivals in the locker room.

"Oh gosh, no! I'm the team manager. In other words, *ball boy*. I hope to play one day but Nigel said I'll be lucky if I get to play my senior year," he drew closer to Drake, setting his buckets on the ground, lowering his voice to a whisper, "You'll see what I mean when you meet him."

Drake nodded slowly, corners of his mouth curling downward into a frown.

"I've met him, unfortunately. Why did the coach leave?"

The boy shrugged, shaking his head, grabbing a cart full of sloppily folded hand towels, wheeling it in the center of the room.

"Nobody knows. It was about a month ago. He was here every day and one day out of the blue, Principal Apple told Nigel to take over until they could hire a new coach.

She said it would probably take a year to replace Coach Edward so Nigel would have to finish out the season as the acting coach. He's the oldest and the best player, obviously."

The locker room door opened abruptly, banging boorishly against the wall. The lockers vibrated as Nigel Sage strutted into the locker room.

"Honey, I'm home!" Nigel sang obnoxiously, launching his tennis bag toward the coach's desk, peeling off his varsity athlete jacket. "Let's go, losers!"

Nervousness overwhelmed Drake. Thoughts of the earlier altercation with the brute seared through his mind. His body trembled ever so slightly. He knew Nigel would feed off his fear if he noticed. Drake inhaled deeply, drew up the courage to shake it off and approached Nigel warily.

"Uh, Nigel. My name is Drake Henry. My coach from Austin—

Drake's breaths became shallow as Nigel spun around to face him, eyes tense and angry, eyebrows angled into a furious scowl.

"I know who you are, dweeb. I've decided against my better judgment to allow you to *try out* for our team but I can't make any promises. It's too bad that we don't have a Junior Varsity or you'd definitely be trying out for that. You'll have to see if you can hang with me and my boy Gaven Phoenix. He's also new – got here 'bout a month ago and I let 'em walk on to the team without question. He had never even played tennis before," Nigel laughed sarcastically before continuing. "He's not a loser like you, though. He's at least got some guns on his arms unlike your scrawny chicken body."

As if on cue, Gaven Phoenix walked through the locker room door wearing a muscle t-shirt and mirrored sunglasses, chocolate colored hair styled in a fauxhawk. Nigel wasn't joking about Gaven's body size. He was at least the size of a professional wrestler. Drake immediately believed illegal steroids were the cause for his massive build, as a teenager couldn't possibly grow muscles that big without some chemical assistance.

"Nigel, my man!" Gaven bumped Nigel's knuckles with his fist. "Just got to school! Didn't care to attend the rest of my lame classes today but I made a freshman nerd do my homework so all's cool."

"That's my boy. He's an entrepreneur, folks! Let's head out, wussies."

As Drake anticipated, the next two hours on the tennis courts were a living hell.

6- Stranger in the Sphere

"How was school, Drake?" Briar shouted over the roar of engines and tire squeals of the high school parking lot.

Briar was lounging against Drake's car in the front. The student drivers, just released from school, were energetically setting out in their cars, diffusing in all directions as they left the school grounds.

"A nightmare. My life is over," Drake lamented, climbing into the Jeep, chucking his backpack into the back.

"What? I love it here! I'm definitely the top of my class. I am so gonna be the valedictorian! Nobody here matches me in intelligence!"

Briar danced as she opened the passenger side door.

"Well, I have two huge seniors that want to see me in misery - both on the tennis team. Doesn't look like I'll be playin' tennis here," Drake lamented, igniting the engine, shaking his head as he stared out the window.

He gazed at the steering wheel, blinking forcefully, fighting the urge to weep.

"No way! They givin' ya crap? What did the coach say? I figured the coach would have the red carpet laid out for you in the locker room! He must not know who you are then, Drake."

Briar yanked her topaz colored locks from underneath the seatbelt strap on her shoulder before flailing her arms into the air and slapping the dashboard.

"Well, the coach is history as of a month ago. He disappeared. The senior that wants to pummel my face is now the coach. My life's over. Mom and Dad cost me a college scholarship by moving me to this nightmare."

Drake clamped his jaws tightly, the muscles in his temples wavered as the main vein in his forehead pulsed with anger and frustration. He clenched the steering wheel as he knocked the car in reverse, forcing the blood to evacuate his fingers, revealing white knuckles glistening in the sun.

"Man, I'm so sorry Drake."

Drake's mind focused on the recent memory of Jade Amity and he relaxed the vice grip on the steering wheel. Taking a few bottomless inhalations, he slowly pulled the Jeep out of the parking lot. The image of Jade's beautiful features flashed in his mind, causing the corners of his mouth to curl slightly.

"It's all right, I guess. I did meet this chick, she's great. She's in my first period English and I sat with her at lunch," Drake paused for a short moment as he looked both ways before turning onto Castlebend Drive, "She's the only reason why I didn't quit school today and try to talk mom and dad into letting me finish out my junior year online."

After a minute of silence, Drake approached the Deadwood Bridge. Both Drake and Briar peered vigilantly into the car mirrors, searching for the hostile blue Challenger from earlier that morning. Nothing in sight, Drake relaxed, Briar settled into her seat.

"Sorry, Bee. Rude of me not to ask. Other than being smarter than everybody, how'd your day go?" Drake said, feigning a smile.

"I adore my teachers, of course. I fit right in like a puzzle piece with a huge group of girls. It's like I've known them forever!" Briar sparked, wrapping her arms across her body for a self-embrace. She stopped her celebration to gaze at Drake, her smile melting into sadness.

"At least one of us is happy, I suppose. That's great, Bee," Drake replied with strained sincerity.

"I'm sorry Drake."

"I'll live, Bee."

Another few minutes of silence followed as they traversed across the rusted iron bridge, speeding up on the 7 Point Island stretch and ascending back onto the second segment toward Shady Oaks.

"Hey, can we stop at the convenience store? I need some Dr. Peppers. I'm not drinking water again, I'm allergic to it. Plus, the tap water tastes like lake water. Yuck!"

Drake shot a glance at Bee and rolled his eyes. He pulled away from the bridge and onto Lakefront Avenue.

"You can't be allergic to water, Bee."

Briar smiled, revealing her right side dimple. Drake shook his head slowly and chuckled.

"I just know mom didn't make it to the grocery store as she promised. She never does things when she says and God forbid if Uncle Basil lifts a finger to help," Briar pleaded, fingers intertwined into a two handed fist.

"I know, Uncle Basil's a sloth," Drake sighed. "Yeah, I'll stop. I hope that creepy clerk's not there."

Briar laughed uncontrollably.

"You mean *Quentin!* That guy was sooooooo weird! What scares you, Drake? Huh? What makes you pee the bed, huh? And what's up with his devil-lookin' facial hair?"

Briar giggled enthusiastically as the Jeep's tires met up with the gravel parking lot of the store, tires popping the gravel carelessly into the air.

"Go, you got cash. Pick me up one," Drake commanded, pushing the Jeep into park with the palm of his hand.

"Not going by myself, Drake! You'll have to drink nasty water if you don't come in with me. I'm not gettin' ya one if you sit in the car," Briar crossed her arms across her chest in a stubborn stance, folding her bottom lip downward.

Drake grabbed the keys and begrudgingly ambled out into the parking lot.

"Following you," he grimaced.

Upon opening the door, a bell sounded from the top of the door. A gloomy whistling echoed from behind the counter, Drake knew Quentin was there. Drake darted the back way toward the drink coolers, snatching the sodas as quickly as possible in hopes of avoiding conversation with the strange man.

"Hi, Quentin! Howz it goin' today?" Briar squeaked, tapping on the checkout stand as she whizzed by.

Damn you, Briar!

"Briar, gotta get home quick," Drake said, strolling purposely toward the checkout counter.

Briar took her time selecting sodas and then sauntered over into the candy aisle. Quentin studied Drake from behind the counter. Not knowing if he should return the gaze at Quentin or pretend not to see him, Drake nervously scanned the store. Quentin rose from the white plastic chair and stood immediately in front of Drake.

"Briar! C'mon! Let's go!" Drake yelled to Briar who was bemused in the candy aisle.

"Yuh – yuh -you like the house?" Quentin said, slowly ringing up the items on the counter.

Briar finally hopped up to the counter and added her selections to the pile, throwing a ten-dollar bill on the counter for her share.

"Sure, yeah, it's great," Drake mumbled, looking at Briar as if to dare her to speak again.

Briar started tapping her foot in a monotonous rhythm. Drake steeply arched an eyebrow, willing her with his brain energy to stop. Quentin paused, placed both gaunt hands on the counter in front of him and analyzed Drake's face.

"Nuh-Nuh-Never got to hear what you are afraid of, Drake. Ssss-so, so what scares yuh-you?"

Pretending to seem dense, Drake stared blankly at the counter for a moment.

"Donno, haven't really thought about it, sir."

Drake scrunched his lips together and raised his eyebrows, shrugging his shoulders.

"Wuh-wuh- well you have to have a fear of something, ruh-right?"

Quentin paused once again to stare into Drake's eyes. Drake knew he would be in this store longer if he didn't answer him. Briar seemed amused by the line of questioning.

"I guess I fear failure," Drake hesitated as he searched for the right words. "Failure at all levels. I fear failure, being humiliated," he paused again, looking around the store as if to get ideas, "and maybe going crazy, losing it. That's about it. Uh, we're kind of in a hurry, sir."

Quentin cocked his head to the side as if to process the information. With a blank expression, he methodically turned his gaze toward Briar. She took an ardent step backward.

"Wuh-what about you, yuh-young lady?"

Briar's amused front melted into mystification. She lightly tapped on Drake's foot with her shoe.

"Me? What am I scared of?"

Briar shrugged, squaring her shoulders and shifting her weight to the opposing side.

"Yes, ma'am."

Quentin slowly resumed punching in the item prices into the cash register, keeping one scrawny eyebrow raised while he awaited for Briar to answer. Drake got a feeling that Quentin was stalling, trying to delay their departure from the store.

Briar became animated, "I absolutely hate spiders!" She extended three fingers in the air, folding the index finger into her palm with her free hand. "And I hate being in the dark and being alone," she folded the middle finger and the ring finger down into her palm, capturing both with her thumb. "Hey, why are you so concerned with what everybody is scared of, anyway?" Briar inquired in a blissful tone. "You writing a book about fears or something?"

Drake shot her a glance of protest. Feeling as though she enjoyed taunting the clerk, he wanted nothing more than to leave the store immediately. Briar returned with a slow wink, a grin spreading across her face.

"I-I-I am not afraid of anything. That's why I-I like to hear what others are. It amuses muh-muh-me."

Briar's smile faded into confusion. Drake shook his head and shrugged a shoulder toward the door. With sodas and snacks in a brown paper sack, they headed back to the Jeep.

"That dude is the freakiest! What's his deal, Drake?"

Briar bounced to the car, swung open the door and climbed in the passenger's seat.

"He must be really bored. I can't imagine sitting behind that counter in a store that maybe has ten customers all day. Don't know if you noticed but he just sits there. There's no television, no music and I didn't see anything besides that crappy chair he sits in."

"Yeah, I'd go crazy if I had to sit and wait all day like that. Remind me to never work in a store."

Drake guided the Jeep out of the parking lot, eyes peeled to the road ahead.

"Especially in Shady Oaks!" Drake added.

Drake and Briar went on about Quentin during the short stretch to 614 Scarlet Court. On a mission to prove it to Drake, Briar marched into the kitchen to inspect the refrigerator. Briar's prediction was correct. Emily hadn't made it to the store because she had been too busy chasing Ella and unpacking the smaller boxes left from the move. As usual, Ella screamed and waddled erratically around the staircase in the foyer. The family had baby proofed the home so Ella was now allowed to run free. Drake's eyes followed a familiar sound to his left. In the study, Omen was growling at something ever so softly.

"Hey, Omen! What's the matter with you, boy?" Drake hollered, strutting purposely toward the study.

Omen's sleek form faced the dark gray wall as he growled melodiously, hair rising along the midline of his back. Drake crept up behind him, assessing the drab wall, seeing nothing tangible. Upon hearing Drake's voice, the Doberman twisted around, nubbed tail swishing back and forth like a windshield wiper, growling ceasing abruptly.

"There's nothing there, boy. C'mon, let's go outside! You're probably upset because Uncle Basil's stuff smells like sweaty pipe smoke, I know."

Drake led the way for Omen to the back courtyard, spotting Basil in the same location as the day before, smoking his pipe leisurely. Omen paused on the sundeck, curling his lip backward to expose his huge canine teeth at Basil before galloping into the back yard. Drake wondered when Basil was going to look for a job and move out of their house. He wanted him to leave as soon as possible as he didn't want to start conflict. He sensed a growing tension between Basil and his father. Drake was also aware that Omen was also growing weary of his existence.

"Hello, Uncle Basil. Looks like you had a hard day, huh?" Drake spouted in a sarcastic tone, slowly meandering toward the grass where Omen was running around in circles, happy to be in the fresh air.

"If I were you, I would cut out the crass comments, kid. What I do is none of your business. I'm in no mood for it," Basil snapped, pausing to take a lengthy toke on his pipe. "If you know what's good for you, you and that stupid dog will leave me alone," he blew out a thick plume of smoke from his thin lips. "Wished the fire had taken that mutt out."

Basil's face reddened as he stood up, the sheen on his forehead turning to beads of sweat, dropping down onto his face. Drake decided to let it go for the better good of the house dynamics. He needed something positive to shift his mind in a better, more positive place.

"C'mon Omen, let's go," he tapped his leg, holding the backdoor open for Omen.

They raced upstairs to his room, Omen attempting to gain the front position with every climb up the stairs, his massive claws gripping the carpet of each stair, catapulting him to the next. Reaching the playroom, Drake looked to his left and spotted Briar busily arranging her room, singing along with songs blaring from her iPhone. Agreeing it was a splendid idea, Drake immersed himself into unpacking his room. It was the first time since he left Deadwood High School that he didn't think about the tennis team and Nigel Sage. Hours evaporated into thin air and a full moon soon raised high above the lake. Drake felt as though only minutes had passed but he glanced at his iPhone's clock and it revealed it was already 9 PM.

"This is tight! Come see, Bee!" Drake shouted enthusiastically, eager for Briar to share in his accomplishments.

Drake was thrilled to find the internet worked without a hitch. He was back on Xbox Live where he could talk to and play video games with his friends back in Austin. Dominick wasn't signed on but he connected with his other friends and soon felt more at home.

"I almost feel normal again!" His voice breathless with exertion.

Briar rushed in the room, examining the scene from top to bottom.

"Pretty sweet, Drake. It's freakin' awesome. But I found a dang spider in my room! Did you hear me screamin'? I freaked a little. I actually dented the sheetrock in one of my walls to kill it! It was a daddy longlegs. I hate those things!"

Briar shivered, stomping her feet. Drake pondered the thought for a moment and shook his head with a grin of irony.

"Of all people to have a spider in their room!" Drake chuckled. "Hey, I'll set up your computer tomorrow, I'm really tired, o.k.?"

"No prob!" Briar said airily.

Emily's voice echoed from downstairs. She announced that the pizza had arrived. Drake was shocked to hear that there was a pizza place in town. Famished from working nonstop, the two hurried downstairs to grab a plate. They both stood at the kitchen counters and gobbled down their pizza before claiming exhaustion. They stated in unison they were ready for bed.

"Drake, I apologize. I hadn't spoke with you about how school went. Sorry, Ella just keeps me so busy, I lose track of time. So, how did tennis go? The coach freak out that he landed a superstar on the team?" Emily said, holding a spoon of cut up pizza in her turtle hand puppet.

"Mom, uh, no. There's no coach. A senior in charge already hates me. Doesn't look like I'll even be on the team. It's pretty much over."

Drake folded his paper plate and slipped it into the trashcan.

"NO! It can't be!" Emily shouted, causing Ella to liberate a shrill scream.

Ella grabbed the pizza from her mouth and threw it down to the floor. Briar couldn't help but giggle as Omen wolfed it down, licking his lips in intense culinary pleasure, looking back at Ella for the next morsel.

"WHAT!" Ivan shrieked from the dining room. "Did I just hear what I *think* I heard?"

Ivan ambled to the kitchen entryway, one hand on a hip; forehead wrinkled into a maze of befuddlement.

"Yeah, Dad. Doesn't look like I'll be playing tennis at Deadwood High."

Drake shrugged, starting his journey toward the staircase in the foyer, his lips quivering at the thought.

"Not possible," Emily scoffed. "I'll contact Principal Apple tomorrow and talk some sense into her. She seems like a reasonable lady. A little high strung but reasonable nonetheless."

"I'm tired, going to bed. See ya' in the morning," Drake mumbled, heading up the stairs with Omen's paws thumping at his heels.

The night was quieter than the first. Drake figured they had scared the animals from their nests in the attic. The moon cast a glow into his room, causing shadows to dance on his back wall. He hadn't noticed them from the night before but they amused him. Omen laid flat on the bed next to Drake, his long snout on Drake's shoulder. Drake leaned up to catch a glimpse of his digital clock, bumping Omen's frosty wet nose with his warm cheek, the contrasting temperatures giving him a slight chill. It was 1 AM. He was having a difficult time drifting to sleep.

Without a forewarning, the silence broke from downstairs. Drake's eyes burst open, focusing on the shadows. He leapt out of bed and mechanically darted to his bedroom door. Omen launched himself from Drake's bed, knocking the mattress off the frame slightly as he pushed off with his back paws. He sprinted to the stairs and was out of sight within seconds, a rage of erratic barking immediately followed.

"Drake!" Briar screamed from her bedroom.

Drake dashed over to Briar's room and flipped on the light switch, a sleepy, confused expression riddling his face.

"What's going on down there?" Briar panicked, flailing her arms in the air.

Ivan was shouting, Emily was screaming and both were drowned out by Ella's continuous ear-piercing screams. Omen's barking vibrated the walls like a cherry on top of the mayhem sundae.

"Let's go, Bee. They might need help," Drake exclaimed wildly, rushing back into his room to grab a baseball bat out of his closet. He snatched a golf club for Briar and added, "Take this just in case."

They carefully sped down the darkened staircase and into the master bedroom suite where Pandora's Box had been opened.

"It was there! I saw it!" Ivan bellowed, pointing inside the marbled fireplace.

"Ivan! I didn't see anything, I'm sorry! But you startled the hell out of me and Ella!" Emily's initial voice a shout, cracking and then lowering to a normal volume.

"Can someone quiet the damn dog, please?" Ivan screamed, extending a shaking finger at Omen, whisking his head around to glare at Drake.

Drake grabbed Omen's collar, drawing him near and cradling his face with his hand. Omen gazed up at Drake, deciding to quiet his bark, slowly twitching his nubbed tail. Emily finally consoled Ella to a manageable whine.

"What happened here?" Drake inquired with angst, stroking the back of Omen's neck in order to keep him quieted. Omen decided to sit down, perched proud that Drake was giving him attention.

"Y'all all right?" Briar chimed in, face wearing a mask of unbridled curiosity.

"We're fine," Emily heaved a sigh. "Your father thinks he saw *something* come out of the fireplace and hover over our bed."

Drake raised his eyebrows and stood up, Omen glancing at him to see if he needed backup. Briar shot a look at Ivan, intrigued. Emily pulled Ella into the bed, embracing her as she slowly rocked back and forth.

"Something?" Briar said, uncertain she wanted to hear the answer.

"I saw it clearly! It started as a pale sphere of light from inside the fireplace but by the time it got to the foot of our bed, it took on the shape of a man. It had a bluish cast to it, growing in intensity, very eerie. The man rather looked familiar to me but I couldn't place him. It's not like I wanted to stare at him!"

"A dream, Ivan. It was obviously a *dream!*" Emily spouted in an irritated tone, rocking Ella back to sleep.

"Dad, it could have easily been a dream, you know. It's after 1 AM. How do you know you were awake?" Drake plowed.

"Because I'm 43 years old and I know what the difference is between a dream and reality. Kinda figured that one out when I was ten years old, you know."

Ivan closed the fireplace doors and gently climbed into bed.

"I'm going back to sleep," Emily whispered, barely audible, laying Ella in between her and Ivan in the bed. "Sorry kids, I know you have to get up early for school. Your father just had a nightmare."

7- The Invasion

"Have either of you seen your Uncle Basil?" Emily shouted, standing at the base of the downstairs staircase.

"No, mom. Haven't been downstairs today," Briar howled from the top of the staircase.

Drake hadn't seen Basil since the day before when he was lounging, smoking his pipe on the back porch.

"Bee, it's that time," Drake informed, backpack in hand.

Drake and Briar headed downstairs. Emily was in the foyer struggling with Ella to put on a dress.

"Mom, I haven't seen 'em since yesterday when I got home from school. All the cars here?" Drake asked.

"Yes. The futon couch is still put back from when I cleaned the room yesterday. That's so strange. Did you ever speak to him yesterday?"

Ella escaped and waddled rapidly around the staircase, dress hanging from one arm.

"Uh, nah. Never saw 'em," Drake lied in a panic.

"I never saw him yesterday, either," Briar reported in a confident tone.

"Let's go, Bee. We're gonna be late if we don't leave now," Drake stated emphatically, propping the front door open for Briar.

On the way to school, Drake and Briar analyzed the details of the events from the night before. They reasoned that the stress from the move, the new job and house as well as having to live with a mooching murder suspect had collectively caused their father to hallucinate in the middle of the night, causing him to believe he was not dreaming when he saw what he called a ghost. Drake pulled his Jeep into the back student parking lot of Deadwood High. Briar suddenly pointed feverishly on the passenger window.

"Whoa, Drake, look. There's that tail-gating blue Challenger from yesterday morning!"

Drake spotted the car, eyebrows rising in a scowl.

"Yeah, you're right. I remember that license plate, *BFDEAL*. Knew it was a kid. Probably an immature sophomore."

Just as the words left Drake's lips, the massive build of none other than Nigel Sage climbed out of the Challenger. A slight tinge of nausea developed at the base of Drake's esophagus, his heart picking up its pace as it rumbled erratically in his chest.

"Figures," Drake mumbled. "Let's go," Drake whispered loudly, ushering Briar out of the car.

"Man, that's a big sophomore! That guy's massive! Looks like he's about twenty-five! And he's is *hot*!"

Drake slammed his car door in frustration.

"That's my new tennis coach. You know the one that wants me dead." Drake's voice was a shade more sarcastic than he intended. "And, he's a senior. A second year senior, actually."

Rolling his eyes, he shook his head in disbelief.

"No way, that guy? Wow, you *are* dead."

Nigel strutted toward them across the parking lot, eyes narrowed, flexing his arm muscles with every step.

"Hey, punk," Nigel blasted in a booming voice. Drake stopped where he stood, Briar walking a few more steps before realizing Drake had stopped. "You drive like a granny. I shoulda known that was your stupid Jeep yesterday driving five miles per hour on the bridge. You drive about like you play tennis."

Nigel's expression grew more resentful as he watched the play of emotion across Drake's face. Drake scrambled for a second, exhaling silently and working diligently in his mind to keep his face void of emotion.

"I remember seeing your car as well," Drake fought sarcasm with all of his will, disgust flickering on his face as he spoke.

Briar took a few purposeful steps toward Nigel.

"My brother was the state tennis champion for the last two years, a-hole!" Briar challenged, hand firmly grasping her hip. "And that was at a 5A school!" Her head rocked side to side with disdain at every word.

"Well, he's lost it, he sucks now," Nigel snarled at Briar, turning to draw in close to Drake's ear. "You better get the toddler in check before I request that one of my girls ruin her day."

"Let's go, Briar," Drake said sternly, directing her toward the school.

"That guy's a jerk!" Briar whispered, struggling to keep up with Drake's pace.

"Told you."

Drake and Briar both made it to their first class with seconds to spare. Drake's anxiety over Nigel Sage quickly dissolved into tranquil happiness as he laid eyes upon Jade Amity's amazing smile.

"Well, hello there!" Drake whispered, pulling the Frankenstein book from his backpack.

"You never called and invited me over last night, Drake! I was gonna come over and see your mansion!"

Without delay, Ms. Crenshaw pounded her bony fist on her desk, startling the class.

"Sorry," Jade whispered.

"The bell has rung! I will move you two into opposite corners if I hear another peep! Everybody! Read Frankenstein through Chapter 6 and then get out your textbooks and start on the assignment on page 230," Ms. Crenshaw squawked.

Drake wrote his cell phone number and home address on a torn sheet of spiral paper and slipped it to

Jade. He watched Ms. Crenshaw carefully before swishing his head around.

"You never gave me your number, silly. Here, take this. Come over any time you like," he whispered modestly. "I'll be waiting for ya."

Drake counted the minutes until he saw Jade again at lunch. His morning classes took an eternity as he waited for the bell. He darted into the hallway and into the lunchroom and met up with Jade who was waiting for him by the line. After getting their trays of unappetizing school cuisine, they found an empty table in the back.

A booming voice echoed from the cafeteria entryway as all eyes in the room jolted to see the source. It was Nigel Sage and he was in a furious rage.

"Where is he? Where's the punk?" Nigel stormed into the cafeteria, his strong voice thundering throughout the room.

In unison, the students in the lunchroom turned quickly back around, appearing unfettered by the disturbance. Nobody in the school was crazy enough to cross Nigel Sage. This was apparent now.

"Oh crap," Drake mumbled, gazing in Nigel's direction.

Nigel spotted Drake with furious eyes from across the room. Shoving anybody aside in his direct route to Drake, he grabbed Drake by the shirt, pulled him out of his seat and shoved him gruffly against the wall. Pitiful shame surged through Drake's body as he struck the wall, pain jetting outward from the points of impact. Nigel crouched over him anxiously, eyebrows furrowed with anger.

"You had mommy call Principal Apple? Your mommy tattled on me for not lettin' you play on the team, punk," Nigel screeched in a sarcastic rhythm, spewing tiny spheres of saliva into Drake's face.

"I-I didn't know—

"You've got a real problem controlling the chicks in your family, punk. They're gonna cost you dearly one day,"

Nigel roared, poking Drake in the chest with his index finger with every word.

"Nigel, I'm sorry—

Drake wanted to disappear from the planet at an instant. Not knowing how to react because he had never been in a fight, he stared blankly into space past Nigel. Humiliation filled every space of his being.

"It's *Mr. Sage* to you, punk. I'll see ya' later on the courts. You're on the team for now but you have ball duty every day until I decide to give it back to the freshman. You should thank your mommy 'cause I was gonna demand you get a schedule change into home economics where you can learn something more your style like cooking and sewing pajama pants."

They stared at each other for a prolonged moment. Catching Drake off guard, Nigel thrust his iron hands onto his chest, shoving his trembling body forcefully to the ground before pivoting as a military officer and marching out of the cafeteria. Jade rushed over to Drake, extending a hand to pull him to his feet. Drake's face flamed red, embarrassed to be a spectacle of frailty in front of the entire junior class. Slumping his head down and hunching his shoulders forward, he dredged over to the table and reclaimed his seat.

"Sorry about that," Drake muttered shamefully, still reeking of awkwardness. "If you want to sit somewhere else, I'll understand."

He stared broodingly at the table. Jade grabbed his hand and shook it gently, flipping her deep ginger locks onto her back.

"No way, Drake! I'm sorry that you have to deal with Nigel Sage! He's unbelievably lame!" She searched Drake's eyes for agreement.

Drake shrugged his shoulder and sat upright, trying to shake off the humiliation.

"I guess I don't get why he hates me so much," Drake said in an assertive tone, staring blankly at the glossy brick wall of the cafeteria.

Drake felt a lump form in his throat.

"I told you yesterday. He's jealous! You are flawless, Drake, and he can't stand the thought of you. He obviously heard about your tennis accomplishments and he's always been the number one athlete in every sport here. Nigel is used to most of the girls dying to go out with him. He must have overheard them all freaking out over you yesterday. Since you arrived, you can't go anywhere in this school without hearing about how hot you are!" Jade exclaimed, face flushing red.

Drake raised his eyebrows in bewilderment. He hadn't noticed any other girls paying him attention besides Jade Amity.

"Really?" Drake was silent for a long moment. "I guess you nailed it as far as tennis goes. I know he knows about my championships because my coach from Austin faxed over my records along with some newspaper articles and stuff."

Jade gently grabbed Drake by the chin, stared into his pale bronze eyes, and smiled.

"Have you looked into the mirror, Drake? Your eyes are an amazing bronze color that I've never seen before. Your skin is so tan, so perfect and your hair looks like gold satin. You're perfection. You are like a Greek God! Don't tell me that you don't know your hot 'cause I will know you are lying," Jade said coyly, face turning a deeper shade of red.

Drake let out a fit of laughter upon hearing Jade refer to him as a Greek God. He only wished he had powers as the Gods had. It would take supernatural powers to get out him of this unfortunate situation with Nigel Sage.

"Thanks, Jade. You are too sweet. After only twenty-four hours, you've become an awesome friend. I don't think I'm *ugly* but I wouldn't call myself *hot*," Drake said as he blushed, instantly regretting he didn't return the complement to Jade, his inexperience with the fairer gender had peaked and come to fruition.

After two hours of pure hell on the tennis courts, Drake was finally able to reveal his talent to the team when he tied Nigel 6-6 in the last set. Nigel refused the tiebreaker. Drake knew it was because he feared Drake would defeat him. It was a cowardly move and everybody on the team knew it but nobody was brave enough to say anything.

"Bad day again?" Briar asked, climbing into Drake's Jeep.

"Feels like a rollercoaster. I definitely miss Austin," Drake said bluntly, roaring the engine.

"Yeah," Briar mumbled. Her expression sullen.

The ride home was nearly silent. Briar wasn't the positive spirit she had been the day before but Drake didn't feel like talking. Being the new kids in school was taking its toll on both of them, as they were too mentally exhausted for conversation. Drake rushed to his room, jumped on his bed with Omen, and thumbed the numbers on his iPhone corresponding to Dominick back in Austin.

"Hey Dom! Howz it going?"

"Drake! Buddy! What's up!? Howz the new school? Sorry I wasn't on Xbox last night, Mike told me you were back online but I had tons of homework and mom took my controllers," Dominick's voice resonated from the iPhone speaker.

Hearing Dominick's voice made Drake instantly realize how deeply he missed being home in Austin.

"It's pretty rough, I must admit. The town's a tiny dump, the house is an amazing mansion, and I barely made the tennis team."

"No freakin' way, Drake! How could you possibly barely make a tennis team at a 4A school or much less at any school in the U.S? House is a mansion, huh?"

"Long story. Think you can come down for a few days? Maybe next weekend or something? Your mom said she'd let you drive it at least once a month, yeah, you'll freak over this house, man."

"Heck yeah, I'll come over there. Text me the directions. Let's make it for next weekend. Any dimes there?"

Drake laughed. He missed his best friend tremendously.

"Yeah, you can say that. Already got my eye on one I met on the first day. She's probably got a hot friend, too."

"Sah weet! Wanna play Call of Duty later?"

"How about Dead Rising? I feel more like killing things for absolutely no reason."

"Sadistic. A'ight talk at ya later."

"Later, Dom."

A mood adjusted Drake swaggered into Briar's room with Omen trailing close behind. He realized he hadn't been very caring on the ride home from school. He knew Briar wasn't as cheerful as the day before so something might have happened to her at school. He wanted to make it right and be a better brother. When he approached her doorway, he observed her standing in the center of her room. She was frozen, fighting for a breath. Omen rumbled a low, guttural growl, slowly creeping into her room, sniffing at the ground wildly.

"Briar! What's wrong?" Drake frantically surveyed her room.

She pointed to the corner of the room with a shaky finger, tears of fright streaming down her face.

"Holy mother!" Drake shouted, skimming his mind rapidly to formulate a quick plan of attack.

A steady stream of tarantulas were forcing their way through gap in the baseboard onto her pink shag carpet, their grotesque hairy bodies in contrast with the feminine fibers. As they surfaced, their eight legs immediately worked in haste to scatter them under the furniture surrounding Briar. Terrified, her mind rendered her helpless, nearly speechless.

Omen barked ferociously, chasing the spiders as they surfaced from the baseboard. He mauled them with his uncoordinated paws, ripping them apart with his sharp teeth, shaking his head fiercely as their spiny legs fought back against his lips. Drake darted back into his room, grabbed a roll of duct tape from his chest of drawers and swished back into Briar's room. He started sealing the crack in the baseboard with strips of tape across the baseboard and onto the wall for support, smashing the first spiders with a hairbrush as they burst through, segmented legs wiggling around the tape.

"Briar, get out of here, I'll take care of it."

"I can't," Briar choked out the words, frozen.

"I've got it, just go!"

Briar fought to make a move and once she did, she reached top speed toward the staircase. She flew downstairs and summoned Ivan to assist Drake in the spider extermination.

After a spell, Drake, Ivan and Omen had captured all of the spiders in the room. By the time Omen was finished with them, they barely resembled once-living creatures. As far back as Drake could remember, Ivan had established a Henry family 'no kill policy' in which they were not to harm a living thing, no matter what. Ivan and Drake simultaneously ignored the no kill policy in this matter without question.

"Of all people for this to happen to," Ivan lamented, sealing the bag of dead tarantulas.

"It's almost like it can't be coincidence," Drake added softly.

8-The Impossible

"Dinner's ready! C'mon everybody, it's the first home cooked meal in the house!" Emily shouted from the dining room.

"Smells wonderful!" Ivan said, pulling back his seat and climbing aboard, over exaggerating an inhale.

Drake took in the delectable aroma pervading the air. Without seeing the food, he knew it was Chinese stir-fry night.

"Bee, you all right?" Drake asked in a concerned tone, studying her face for clues.

"I'm fine. I'm not going back in my room for a while, though. I'm sleeping down here, in the living room on the couch tonight."

Drake nodded in sympathy.

"We got all of them, Briar. That Doberman has a keen sense of smell and he's checked the room multiple times," Ivan reported sternly.

"Still not going in there. That creepy fountain shines in the room too so until you can get some professional bug people to treat the room and get me some drapes for the front window, I'm taking the couch downstairs."

"Briar, it will shine down here too, there are big windows on the front doors," Drake pointed toward the foyer's front doors.

Briar grimaced, shrugging one shoulder, turning to glare at Ivan. Emily sighed, scuffling with Ella to get into her high chair. Emily looked worn, hair pulled back in a stumpy blonde ponytail, her makeup smudged under her black cat-eye rimmed glasses.

"Mom, when are you going to stop feeding her with that puppet? It's ridiculous!"

Emily curled the side of her lip in a sardonic fashion as she gazed at Briar, raising one eyebrow as she formulated a response.

"Hey! You had your quirks too, Briar! I believe you had a pacifier until you were three years old!"

Briar scrunched her nose at Emily, inhaling deeply and letting it out with an abrupt whooshing noise.

"Not my fault you didn't want to take it away."

Briar pointed at Emily, a smile erupting on her face.

"To more important issues, has anybody heard from Uncle Basil? I'm getting extremely worried that something awful has happened to him," Emily inquired, wiping Ella's mouth clean with a baby wipe.

Silence ensued. Emily surveyed the table to find only blank stares and heads shaking slowly from side to side. Drake recalled lying to her that morning about talking to Basil the day before and instantly felt deviant, as if he had something to do with Basil's disappearance and was hiding it from her.

"Hmmmm. Maybe I should call the police?" Emily bemused, searching the table for collaboration.

"Well, it probably hasn't been long enough. He's a grown man, Emily. For all we know, he found a bar in town and is still there. Maybe he met someone?" Ivan hedged, suddenly serious, passing the bowl of fragrant, colorful stir-fry to Briar.

"Well, we have a deal with the D.A. in Austin, Ivan. Remember that? If we lose touch with him, we're supposed to call her and report it," Emily stated abruptly, her face contorting with over expression as she spoke.

Ivan paused in silence, searching his mind for the right words, a solid plan.

"Give it until tomorrow morning. If he's still not here and hasn't contacted us, we'll call the police here in Shady Oaks and the D.A. in Austin," Ivan calmed, taking his first bite of teriyaki chicken.

"I'm just so worried. He's not answering his phone," Emily mourned, forehead depressing into sadness and eyes narrowing as she gazed blankly at the carpet beneath the dining room table.

"Mom! Uncle Basil never charges his dumb phone, duh! He was always complaining about his phone dying. He borrowed mine a couple of times and got sweat all over it," Briar shrieked, getting Emily's attention away from the floor.

"Gross," Drake whispered loudly, shaking his head at Briar in disgust.

The house phone rang, vibrating the cradle. Emily threw the hand puppet down and raced to answer it.

"Hello!" she shouted anxiously, shaking her free hand in angst while she waited for the caller to respond.

All eyes focused on Emily to figure out who was on the other end of the line. Drake figured it was Uncle Basil checking in that he was at the bar and would be home later.

"Ivan, it's for you," Emily passed Ivan the phone, slumping her shoulders in defeat.

After a few minutes of a very peculiar one-sided conversation, Ivan dropped the phone in the cradle.

"Who the heck was that, Ivan?" Emily asked, sliding the turtle hand puppet back onto her hand, making it dance for Ella.

"Well, it appears as though the C.E.O. of Bonlin Pharmaceuticals, Mr. J.R. Sage, wants to see me in his office in the morning."

Emily cautiously read Ivan's face before responding.

"Is that a good thing?"

"Donno. Never met the man. The V.P. of Research hired me and is the only person I've met besides the people in my department."

"Well, with everything that has happened thus far, we're due some good luck, right?" Emily assured, trying to convince Ella to trust the puppet's spoonful of mashed potatoes.

Omen's growls rumbled methodically from across the foyer, ears pointing toward the ceiling, a line of fur down his mid-back raising awkwardly in uneven patches. Something threatened him. Omen crept into the study, methodically placing one paw in front of the other, hunching down to ready himself for battle. He had growled at the study the day before and Drake had inspected the room, seeing nothing out of order, blaming the phantom scent of Uncle Basil. The dog certainly didn't care for Basil. Drake ran up behind Omen and flipped on the lights to the study. He scanned the room once quickly, slower and more methodical the second time around the room. Finding nothing out of order, he gently pulled Omen by the collar toward the staircase.

"Let's go, boy. There's nothing in here."

Drake and Omen headed upstairs to Drake's room. Omen, twitching his nubbed tail, was always in great spirits when he was with Drake. In Drakes room, he took a spot on his bed, chewing a rawhide bone while watching Drake play online video games with his friends back in Austin for the next couple of hours. The moon crescent dangled high in the sky and Drake shut everything down and hurled into bed, Omen snuggling tightly by his side.

"You're such a good boy," Drake stroked the fur on his neck, Omen returning the love with a warm lick, his wet, cold nose grazing the back of Drake's hand.

The house became dead silent; Drake listened for the noises of which Briar spoke. Silence, nothing. He reasoned the animals nested in the attic had definitely found other accommodations, the evacuation probably hastened by Omen's presence as well. After sleeping restlessly, he thought he heard a noise, his eyes popped open and he grabbed his iPhone to check the time. Omen's head rose in the darkness, casting a large shadow of his profile on the wall. It was 2:18AM.

A door violently slammed downstairs jerking Drake's body into a full state of shock. A shrill scream echoed throughout the foyer. It was Briar.

Omen lurched off the bed and darted down the staircase. Drake grabbed his baseball bat, heart racing, mind befuddled with confusion. He had placed the bat by the doorway the last time he awoke in the middle of the night. Drake scuffled down the staircase in the dark, the stairs barely lit by the moonlight streaming through the glass of the front doors, capturing a tinge of red from the outside fountain. Ivan was already on the scene downstairs in the foyer by the time Drake arrived, swiftly perusing the walls for the light switch.

"Dad! What's going on?" Drake hollered, gripping the bat tightly.

"Hold on, Drake. I'm checking it out, stay there Briar."

Ivan flipped on all of the downstairs lights and quickly surmised the loud noise had been the study door slamming shut. It had startled Briar, causing her to scream as she had been sleeping on the couch in the living room. Ivan concluded that Basil had come home.

"Basil? That you?" Ivan hollered, tiptoeing toward the study door.

"Why would it be Uncle Basil? He wouldn't have slammed the door like that, right? Call the police!" Briar cried, leaping off the couch and taking a position closely behind her father.

"Basil! You in there?"

"Dad, Bee's right. Basil is a tool bag but wouldn't slam a door in the middle of the night and wake us up like that," Drake informed, still gripping his baseball bat, knuckles white from the strain.

"He mighta been at the pub all day. He could be drunk. Why don't you two go to bed? I've got this covered," Ivan said sternly, pointing upstairs and then toward the couch.

"Not leaving you, Dad."

"I-I'm not leaving you either," Briar stammered.

Ivan cautiously listened at the study door. Ella raced out of the master bedroom and waddled around the foyer, Emily giving her a sleepy chase.

"Go back to bed, Emily. It's Basil. He's probably been at the pub all day."

The sleepy haze rapidly vanished from Emily's face.

"Oh, Thank God," Emily gushed.

"Dad, you don't *know* it is Basil," Drake debated, grabbing Ella, handing her to Emily.

"You really think Basil's home?" Emily whispered, accepting Ella from Drake only to let her slide down her body to her feet, gripping her tiny hand. "Basil!" Her voice echoed throughout the foyer.

Silence. There wasn't a sound besides Ella's bare feet stomping on the marble to get free from Emily. Omen growled at the door causing Ella to giggle, wiggling her hand free from Emily's, she rushed toward Omen. With ears pointing high, Omen raised the mid-line of hair down his back. He snarled, hunching his back and baring his teeth toward the study door.

"Ella, no!" Emily screamed, lunging to grab Ella. "Don't pet the dog! He's upset!"

With Emily chasing after her, Ella scuttled past Omen toward the study door. She turned the knob and the door swung open to a dark room. She dashed inside, disappearing for a long second in the darkness.

"Ella, no!" Ivan screamed, darting in after her.

He flipped on the lights. Nobody was in the room besides Ella. Drake stepped inside after Ivan, noticing immediately that Basil's things were gone. Ivan extended his arms, twirling slowly around. He clapped his hands twice, landing them palms up in front of him as if he had just performed a magic trick.

"Well, that solves it," Ivan brightened. "Basil came in the house, got his stuff, slammed the door and left. I know he's your brother, Emily, but he is one of the most inconsiderate men I've ever met. I told you that he would cause nothing but trouble if he stayed with us!"

Ivan shrugged, palms out to either side of his body, lips twisting into irritation.

"It can't be, Ivan. He wouldn't do that," Emily defended, grabbing Ella and pulling her upward to seat her on a hip.

"Mom, you are blind to it because he's your brother. He *is* rude," Drake added harshly. "He pretty much threatened me yesterday when I saw him out back smoking his pipe—

Instantly, Drake regretted the words leaving his lips. His face grew expressionless as he studied his mother's reaction. Emily's eyebrows formed angry angles as she narrowed her eyes at Drake.

"What? You told me you never spoke to him!"

"Sorry," Drake paused, looking down at the ground to avoid eye contact with Emily, realizing he had just told on himself for lying about speaking to Basil. "You caught me off guard yesterday when you asked about Basil. I didn't want you to think that I was responsible for running him off."

Drake continued to hang his head low, staring vacantly at the black shag carpet of the study.

"Well did you? What did you say to him, Drake?" Emily screeched, face reddening.

"He was lounging on the back patio furniture, smoking his pipe without a care in the world. All I said was that it looked like he had a real hard day. I admit, I was being sarcastic but he told me if I knew what was good for me, I'd leave him be. So I did and that's that."

"Well, you didn't have to give him a hard time."

"Sorry, mom," Drake said in an apologetic tone, raising his head to look into Emily's eyes.

Emily took a few deep breaths and held out an arm to get everybody's attention.

"It's time for me to be honest with everybody," Emily paused, ensuring all eyes in the room were on her. "Basil's attorney called him yesterday morning and told him that the D.A. was about to file official charges on him for the house fire. They concluded the fire was arson and are following a lead against Basil. They're also working on a solid lead in the murder case but I was unclear if it was evidence on Basil or someone else. Basil wasn't in the mood to give details after the call, I must say. I didn't want to make everyone more uncomfortable to be around him so I didn't say anything to you all. I apologize."

Emily shifted her weight and leaned against the study wall, eyebrows in a defensive position, a contrite expression expanding onto her face.

"What! You withheld news like *that?* They think he burned down his own house? With the dog inside?" Ivan exploded.

Ella released a high-pitched whine at the sound of her dad's angry bellows.

"They know that *somebody* did, at least. They found accelerant residue all along the back of the house. Because he had an insurance policy, it makes him an automatic suspect. His attorney did say the D.A. is going on the angle that he burned the house down to hide evidence in the murder case," Ella revealed, outwardly apologetic for not disclosing the information sooner.

"Well, this makes it all blatantly obvious, Emily! He's fled the scene!"

Emily nodded reluctantly. She slowly strolled into the foyer and then turned around to face Ivan.

"I'm starting to reluctantly agree, Ivan. Kids, go to bed. Sorry you had to hear all of this," Emily said as she shrugged her shoulders.

Ella's whine morphed into a feverish scream. She had a way to add chaos during times of stress. In response, Omen jetted up the staircase. Drake tried to console Emily by rubbing her gently on the back as he guided her toward the master bedroom.

"It's all right, mom. I'm sorry that you have to go through this. I know he's your brother but I'm starting to think that maybe he is guilty of *something*. He just doesn't seem like an honest person. Omen doesn't even like 'em and you know dogs have a sixth sense."

"Drake! That's your Uncle Basil you are talking about. Have some family loyalty, please! Dogs are similar to people. They have those they like and those they can't stand. It doesn't mean anything."

"I'm just saying—

"Family is the one thing that you have forever. Friends, colleagues and teachers will come and go throughout life but *family* is always there for you. Don't ever forget that!"

"But if your family murders and starts fires and stuff—

"Basil hasn't even been charged yet. Now you're sounding like the others back in Austin. Go to bed!" Emily barked, pointing bluntly to the staircase.

Briar quietly sneaked back into the living area and wiggled under the blankets of the couch. Ivan nodded at Drake behind Emily's back, grabbed Ella, and walked back into the master bedroom.

"Sorry, mom," Drake said, dredging upstairs to his room.

Omen was anxiously waiting on the bed for Drake. With ears folded back, he cocked his head to the side as if to say he understood what Drake was going through.

Drake didn't have difficulty drifting off to sleep. Seeming like only minutes later, his eyes flashed open as a downstairs door slammed two times in succession, even with more vigor than before, shaking Drake's walls from the force. From what he could discern, it sounded as if it came from the same direction as the last time. The study. Drake felt around on his bed and noticed Omen had already journeyed to the scene. Drake stumbled down the stairs, joining the rest of the family in the foyer. Omen was standing by Briar, looking as confused as the rest.

"What the hell?" Drake shouted, rubbing his eyes.

Briar had tears streaming down her face and was openly restraining hysteria. Ella, for the first time, appeared calm as she clung to Emily. Emily and Ivan had already investigated the study to no avail. Nothing had changed from before. The door had slammed shut, opened and slammed shut again without anybody near it.

"There's nobody in there! There's nobody in the house besides us. What the hell, Ivan," Emily squealed, a tear surfacing on her cheek, rolling down to her chin.

Ivan stood pensively, staring at the front door, turning to study the back door.

"Has anyone touched either of the main doors since we went to bed?" Ivan asked precisely.

Everyone responded with *no*.

"Well, then I just realized that Basil *didn't* come here to pick up his things earlier."

"How do you know that?" Emily added, bemused, wiping a lonely tear from her chin.

"Because I locked both doors with the inside dead bolts before I went to bed and they're still locked."

9 – Losing Control

With only a few actual hours of rest the night before, Drake battled the urge to nod off during class. Seeing Jade had again been the focal point of his day. He refrained from mentioning what happened the night before, as he knew the questions of his uncle's case would surface and he would break the seal of his uncle's scandals at Deadwood High. In addition, he didn't have an explanation for the door slamming or his father's claim of ghostly visions and didn't want to appear crazy or unstable. He kept their conversations steered toward Jade's family, her hobbies and her childhood. He found her to be quite interesting and it was comforting for Drake to hear about someone's normal life.

By the morning, Ivan had reasoned the door slams had something to do with air pressure building up in the house that caused the door to open and slam shut. Ivan promised the family he'd analyze the physics of the air vent and the door hinges later that evening to ensure it didn't happen again the following night.

To Drake's apprehension, a fellow tennis teammate warned him in the hallway that there was an informal tennis match scheduled immediately after school. The team from Thunder Falls, a town of barely over 50,000 people, was to arrive at the Deadwood Tennis Complex for some friendly games so both teams could get ready for upcoming tournaments. Drake was annoyed but not surprised that Nigel failed to mention the scrimmage.

Drake texted both his mother and Briar to let them know he would have to go to the Deadwood City Tennis Complex which was a mile south of the school for the last class period. His mother would have to pick up Briar from school since he had no idea how long the match would take. He was certain Nigel would force him into ball duty after the match was over, a responsibility normally given to freshman who hadn't yet earned their stripes.

As he pulled into the parking lot of the tennis center and found a spot, he noticed the blue Challenger pulling up behind him, blocking his Jeep into the parking space. Nigel climbed out of the car and smirked at Drake, pushing his car alarm button on his key fob as he strolled toward the courts.

"Jerk," Drake mumbled under his breath, ambling out of the car.

Nigel passed out the schedule for the match, tossing Drake's copy on the ground at his feet. Drake viewed the schedule, written in a barely legible scrawl, halfheartedly trotting onto his court. Drake's opponent, listed as a junior, was noticeably the largest player on the Thunder Falls team. He couldn't have been only 16 years old. He was at least Nigel's age, if not older. It was inherently obvious.

The games flew by and before Drake realized, he hadn't won one game by the end of the match. His opponent was impossible. Drake had never played someone this strong or with this much talent. He didn't remember seeing this kid's name before on any state championship titles for 4A schools. This guy, if he was a junior in high school, would have definitely held the title. Drake had never played so poorly in his life but quickly blamed the lack of sleep and need for mental preparedness for the match. He reasoned that his competitor seemed so tough in comparison due to his own pitiable performance. Drake also found it nearly hopeless to play while Nigel cast insults at him from the neighboring court. He had trouble keeping Nigel out of his head during the games.

After picking up the balls and placing the buckets next to the Challenger as instructed, Drake sledged over to his car, rolled down the window, put his feet on the dashboard and settled in to wait. Ten long minutes later, Nigel strutted out to the parking lot, pausing to speak to Gaven Phoenix before arrogantly strolling up to Drake's car window. He stared into Drake's eyes, speculating, and bitterness never leaving his face.

"Hey, punk! Told ya' you sucked. Wanna quit, now? I'm sure the counselor would be glad to switch you into home economics so you can be with people that are more your style," Nigel leaned down, his glare was vicious.

Gaven Phoenix, arms folded across his chest, stood behind Nigel as a bodyguard, still wearing his mirrored sunglasses. Both Nigel and Gaven Phoenix burst into a fit of laughter, slapping each other's hands high in the air.

Drake fought to remain calm, straining to keep a blank expression on his face.

"We can't have you dragging the tennis team down, punk. We've got a pretty decent record thanks to me and my boy Gaven, here."

Gaven extended a fist to Nigel who returned with a heavy clash from his knuckles, both continuing to laugh.

"Yeah, punk! We don't want you bringing us all down with you. Why don't you just quit? You seriously suck!" Gaven bellowed, his voice gruff.

"Nigel—

Nigel interrupted abruptly, "*Mr. Sage* to you and I won't tell you again. Insubordination is a cause for dismissal from the team. The principal can't argue that."

Drake forced the words from his mouth. He couldn't hide the anger on his face any longer, eyebrows forming a deep scowl.

"*Mr. Sage,* I'm not feeling well. Didn't get much sleep. It won't happen again," Drake articulated slowly, each word clear, separate and distinct.

Drake's mind tried to calm him, his face flushed red beyond his control.

"Excuses. Wimpy, poor excuses for failure. I'm sure your father is so proud of you, tennis champ," Nigel ranted sarcastically. "By the way, how's dad doing? He was gonna meet my father today, you know," Nigel sneered, injecting as much venom into his words as he could muster. "Dad called 'em into his office!"

Drake repeated the words in his head a few times, searching for their intent, realizing Nigel's objective. Drake's blood boiled, a cloud of fury brewing in each cell of his body.

"How do you know that?" Drake spoke through his teeth, eyes narrowing into slits.

Nigel rocked back on his heels and pounded fiercely on the top of Drake's Jeep with his fist. Drake startled from the surprise but by taking deep breaths, he was able to conceal his reaction. Nigel squared off to Drake directly through the open window, his eyes piercing into Drake as he continued his tirade.

"Because I know *everything,* Drake. You never know who you mess with until it's too late. See ya later, punk."

Nigel and Gaven climbed into the Challenger, tires squealing with fury as they peeled away from the parking lot. Avoiding a drive with the Challenger across the Deadwood Bridge, Drake waited in his car for a few minutes, pulling his iPhone out of his tennis bag, he thumbed a text message to Briar. He wanted to be sure his mother had found the school and got home safely.

After sending the message, he noticed he had missed multiple text messages from Briar, all revealing that Briar had been waiting at school for Emily who never showed up to give her a ride home. Drake panicked as he tried to call his mother on her cell phone but she didn't answer. He kindled the engine, threw it in drive and raced over to Deadwood High School. As he pulled the Jeep to the front of the school, he found Briar leaning against one of the steel knights in the front of the school. She was alone.

"Bee! Did you hear from mom? What gives?" Drake shouted as Briar opened the Jeep's passenger side door.

"No idea! She was going to pick me up immediately after school and then never showed up!" Briar hopped in, swiping her seatbelt across and latching it into the port.

"That's crazy. I hope she's all right!"

Drake sped to the Deadwood Bridge, looking cautiously for the Challenger.

"Drake, do you think she's o.k.?"

"Yeah, she might have gotten caught up chasing Ella and lost track of time."

Drake reached the bridge. There was no sign of Emily thus far on the journey home or the Challenger.

"Then why wouldn't she answer the phone?"

Drake shrugged his shoulder, still cautiously surveying the road on both sides.

"You got me on that one. Maybe Ella hid her phone or something. Did you call the house or her cell?"

"I never called the house, just the cell."

"Then, there ya go. I'll try the house phone."

Drake grabbed his iPhone and tried to reach Emily at home. There was no answer. He grew anxious. As they descended onto Seven Point Island, they saw Emily's Lexus parked on the side of the road.

"Mom!" Briar shouted, pointing anxiously to the car.

"I see her. Hold on, I'll pull up next to her. Maybe her car broke down?"

Drake steered his vehicle next to her Lexus, palmed the Jeep in park and dashed over to check on Emily. Her car was empty, the doors locked. He stood meditatively, surveying the surroundings. No clues.

"Weird! She's gone. Maybe the car broke down and she got a ride home or something?" Drake posed, twisting toward the Jeep.

"Well, that would explain why she never showed up but why is she not answering her cell phone?" Briar added assertively. "Where is Ella's car seat? She wouldn't have left her at home!"

"Wherever she is, she's got Ella and the car seat."

They scrambled back into the Jeep to get home. Drake, no longer giving caution to avoid the Challenger, sped as fast as he could to 614 Scarlet Court. As he drew closer to the house, he spotted the blue Challenger parked in the circle driveway. Drake was outside of bewilderment as he gazed at the electric blue car, the license plate *BFDEAL*.

Drake halted the Jeep in front of the house with a quick screech, slammed it in park and jumped out of the driver's seat, leaving his door open, Briar trailing quickly behind. Drake sprinted up the circle driveway behind Nigel who was escorting Emily to the front door. Gaven climbed out of the backseat of the Challenger, turning around to remove Ella's car seat. Still wearing the mirrored sunglasses, he transported the car seat up the front walkway, setting it down next to Emily's feet. He strutted back to the Challenger and climbed into the front passenger's seat, turning his head in Drake's direction, conferring a smirk.

"Mom! What happened?" Drake shouted, shrugging his shoulders, palms outstretched and facing the sky.

He was bewildered. Drake's mind raced furiously, scanning for possible reasons why Nigel, the only enemy he had in this world, ended up with his mother and baby sister.

"Hello Drake, Briar! Briar, I am so sorry that I didn't make it to school to pick you up," Emily sputtered, guiding Ella into the house, releasing her to run free in the foyer.

Omen, pausing at the front door to inhale the scents and give a security check to the visitors, playfully chased her around the staircase in the foyer, Ella's giggling echoing out into the front entrance.

"Nigel was nice enough to send you a text to let you know he would be picking you up from school soon, Briar. You never texted back, I was worried!"

Briar, puzzled, snatched her cell phone from her pocket and searched for the text message. Drake peered over her shoulder to see a text from an unknown number, received on her phone only a minute prior.

Nigel replied, "Not a problem, Mrs. Henry. I was glad that we spotted your car parked on the shoulder at Seven Point Island. I am certainly glad we could render aid to you and your lovely baby daughter in your time of need," Nigel said politely, turning his back on Emily for a quick second to sneer at Drake and Briar.

"Drake, Nigel goes to your school! Have you two met?"

Drake took a deep breath, searching for the right words, nodding slowly.

"Yes, we have. Nigel is the coach of the tennis team, actually."

"Oh, you're the boy Drake's been stressing about? Drake, you are so silly! Nigel is the nicest young man! Well, I don't want to keep you any longer. Thank you again and I suppose I don't need you to pick up Briar from school now!"

"Yes, ma'am." Nigel extended a hand out to Emily, she returned, completing a gentle handshake. Emily smiled at Nigel, turning to Drake.

"Nigel took me and Ella home and then he was going to drive all the way back to the high school to pick up Briar! How nice!"

Drake was horrified that his mother was unaware of the danger she put herself in by riding in the car with someone like Nigel Sage. Drake was unsure of his motive for helping her but didn't trust the masquerade for one second.

"Thank you, Nigel. That's pretty cool of you," Drake choked out the words, swallowing a huge lump in his throat.

"This doesn't change a thing, punk," Nigel whispered in his ear as Emily turned to check on Ella in the foyer. Nigel pulled away just as Emily turned back around.

"Not a problem, Drake. See ya tomorrow at tennis! Oh, I told your mother how you did in the match today against Thunder Falls. Not sure what's happening, but maybe you can come out of this and start playing as you used to? We need ya, buddy!"

Nigel slapped Drake with a hidden force on the back. Drake tightened his jaw, a glint of anger flashed in his eyes.

"Yeah, Drake! What happened to you today? You lost every game?" Emily went on. "Thanks again, Nigel!"

Nigel scurried off to the Challenger. Drake noticed Nigel and Gaven laughing hysterically as the Challenger rolled out of the circle drive. As he turned to enter the foyer, Emily immediately started an interrogation on Drake about what had happened during the tennis match but Drake wanted to know what happened to Emily and why she was stuck on Seven Point Island. After talking about the match in detail, it was finally Drake's turn to inquire.

"So, mom. Why in the heck were you parked on Seven Point Island? Did the car break down?" Drake said, searching the food pantry diligently.

"I'm embarrassed to say this but, hmmmm, I had a panic attack. You know I hate bridges. I can't drive on them and wouldn't ya know it, I'm here a few days and have to drive on a bridge!" Emily said, tucking her hair behind her ears, shrugging in shame.

"Ah, forgot about that, mom. Sorry! So, you had a panic attack? Nothing is wrong with the car?" Drake said, shooting a glance of confusion to Briar.

"Duh, Drake! She's terrified of bridges. Why didn't we think of that?" Briar added, smacking herself on the forehead with her palm.

"Yes, it was just a panic attack. I couldn't get the courage to continue driving on the second half of that bridge once I hit that patch of land on that island. I just pulled over on the shoulder and was going to call and tell you to go get Briar but then I noticed I didn't have my phone. I left it at home!"

Drake nodded, comprehension flickering on his face.

"That explains it."

Briar raised an eyebrow to Drake.

"Then, those nice boys stopped by and picked us up. He said our house was on the way. I thought it was a tad strange that he knew who I was and where we lived but that's how things go in a small town, I suppose. It's definitely not like Austin."

Drake looked at Emily with a blank stare, barely nodding in acknowledgement.

"You and dad will need to go get the car later, o.k.? I'm going to start dinner now," Emily jazzed, opening the refrigerator door and grabbing a package of sausages.

The doorbell rang, followed by a stern knock on the door.

"I'll get it," Drake rasped, trotting to the front door.

Omen was in the foyer, barking furiously at the intruder on the other side of the door.

"Briar, can you take Omen into the study so I can open the door?"

Drake waited at the front door, holding on to the doorknob.

"Sure, C'mon Omen. Let's go," Briar said, grabbing Omen's collar and dragging him into the study, shutting the door behind them.

Drake opened the front door and two Shady Oaks police officers stood before him, one grayed and the other younger, with brunette hair gelled into spikes.

"Did you report a missing person?" The older officer inquired sternly, removing his sunglasses.

"No sir, I didn't but my mother probably did. Hold on, let me go get her. Come in."

Drake left the door open for the police officers as he dashed into the kitchen to summon Emily. Emily turned off the stove and put Ella into her walker, sprinting into the foyer.

"Hello, officers. Uh, my brother, Basil Cross, has disappeared. The last time we saw him was the day before yesterday. And then, I know this sounds really strange but—

Drake interrupted, "What she is trying to say is that he didn't say a word about going anywhere and he doesn't have a car. You probably know we are new here to Shady Oaks so he doesn't have any friends here, either."

Drake looked at his mother sternly as the older officer jotted down the information on his form. He knew the police officers would not take her seriously if she said his things mysteriously evaporated out of the room late last night while the door's deadbolts were locked. Emily seemed to realize what Drake was doing and avoided the topic.

Sitting around the dining room table, Emily divulged the details of the murder case and the fire to the Shady Oaks police officers. She explained that she had already reported him as missing to the District Attorney in Austin as she had agreed to do. Hearing the details, the police officers soon seemed disinterested in filing the missing persons report. The younger officer stated it was obvious Basil had fled from his pending charges in Austin.

The doorknob to the study turned, Briar shouting from within the room. She had accidentally locked herself and Omen inside of the room. Omen barked wildly and after a minute or two, Briar screamed and pounded her fist on the door.

"Bee, calm down! C'mon!" Drake shouted, attempting to open the door.

He searched the doorknob for a way to open the door and there wasn't a lock. The lock must have been on the inside. He tried calming Briar but she was screaming hysterically that the light went off and she couldn't see anything. Omen's barking sounded as if he were viciously attacking someone but only Briar was in the room with him.

"Briar, the lock is on the inside of the door. Feel around for it!" Drake instructed calmly, barely audible over the ruckus exuding from Omen and Briar.

The grayed police officer rushed to his car and grabbed a slender tool. He came back in and slid the tool in between the door and the frame and the door popped open with ease. He inspected the doorknob and reported the lock on the inside of the door wasn't even in the locked position. The lights flickered and then came back on in the room.

"You all right?" the younger officer bellowed at Briar in a throaty voice.

She lunged out of the room, sobbing, grabbing Drake by the neck, hugging him tightly.

"She's fine. She's just terrified of the dark. This is a new house and she probably locked herself in there by mistake and panicked," Drake said in a muffled voice. "And the dog certainly doesn't help things when he panics too."

Omen remained in the study and continued a guttural growl.

"You've probably got some sort of electrical problem. It happens a lot in new construction. They have to work out all the kinks out, you know," The younger officer stated bluntly.

The elder officer added, "That's one vicious dog, ma'am. You ought to be careful with him around the toddler. I've heard of these attack dogs turning on their owners, especially small children that can't defend themselves," the officer said, pointing brusquely toward Omen, still growling intently at the study wall.

"He's actually a very nice dog. He just hates that room. We don't know why. He gets upset when he goes in there, ever since we moved in on Sunday. He hates Basil and that is where his things were."

"*Were?*" The elderly officer abruptly asked.

Drake immediately knew he had made a mistake. He couldn't think fast enough to cover his tracks. He was frozen and stared vacantly at the officer.

"Are you saying that Basil Cross's things are gone from the house?" The throaty-voiced officer replied curtly.

Drake glanced over at his mother with an apologetic look on his face.

"Yes, Officer. His things are missing from the house," Emily grudgingly hissed through her teeth.

The spiky haired officer added harshly, "Ma'am, next time you try to file a missing person report on a family member living with you, be sure to disclose everything. The guy obviously moved out. He's running and hiding because he's guilty. Nothing sinister happened to him, trust me."

"Well, that was a big waste of time," the grayed officer said, crumpling the report as he swung open the front door.

"Sorry, mom," Drake whispered to Emily.

Emily hung her head low, shoulders slumped forward as she drug her feet toward the kitchen to finish dinner. She didn't know what to say to the officers as they left the house. Drake shut the door softly after the officers both exited into the circle driveway. Drake could sense that Emily felt hopeless now that the police would not help locate her brother.

Within minutes after the police's departure from the house, Ivan walked through the front door. During dinner, the family discussed the ordeal with the officers and to Emily's dismay, Ivan sided with the officers about Basil fleeing the charges.

After going on a journey with his father to pick up his mother's Lexus on Seven Point Island, Drake anxiously awaited his bed, hoping to get a full night's sleep.

10 – The Jester

At lunch the following day, Drake decided that he trusted Jade enough to tell her about his Uncle Basil. He filled her in on the details of the murder, the fire and his sudden disappearance, leaving out the parts of the story without explanation such as his missing things and the slamming door of the study in the middle of the night. He didn't mention that Omen had a huge problem with an unknown force in the room, either. Jade seemed utterly fascinated with the story and devised a plan to scout out the town Shady Oaks to find Basil. She reasoned, from Drake's background information, he went to the pub in the town, met a woman, and was staying with her.

"I'd really like you to come over tonight, Jade. You got plans?" Drake said, his eyes sparkling at the thought as they put up their lunch trays in the cafeteria.

"I'm there, Drake. Can't wait to see your mansion. We'll hunt for your uncle, too!"

"Sure thing! I'll be there waiting for ya!"

A slow smile spread across his face as they sauntered out into the corridor.

"Can't wait!" Jade exclaimed, pulling her beautiful auburn locks into a ponytail, prancing happily down the hallway toward her next class.

His next couple of classes felt as an eternity with the anticipation of having Jade come over later. Drake received a text message from his mother right before the bell rang, signaling time for his last period which was tennis. She instructed him to come home immediately and to get Briar out of class as well. She didn't tell him why she wanted them home but it worried him tremendously. As he pulled the Jeep up to 614 Scarlet Court, his eyes captured the scene; the police sirens were flashing their notorious red and blue.

"Ella?!" Briar shouted with angst, unsnapping her seatbelt and flinging it to the side. "Dad?!"

"Bee, calm down. Maybe it's Basil. Dad's car isn't even here, he went to work this morning," Drake reasoned calmly, parking the Jeep and scuttling out into the driveway.

"True."

Rushing into the house, they noticed two police officers working diligently in the study and in the foyer. They were dusting for fingerprints and Emily was sitting with Ella in her lap at the dining room table. It was the same two officers that had been there the night Emily attempted to file the missing person's report.

"It's *got* to be Basil," Drake mumbled to Briar, folding his car keys into his pocket.

"Drake, you and Bee come over here. The officer needs to take your fingerprints to rule yours out from what they find in the house," Emily sulked.

Emily's face was swollen, reddened. She had obviously been crying. Irritation fumed in his veins like a poisonous smoke as he thought of the hell his mother was going through for Basil.

"Why?" Drake inquired cautiously, placing a knee on the dining room chair and offering his hand to the officer.

"Uncle Basil was found."

Briar's mouth gaped open with a gasp.

"Really? Where?" Drake asked softly.

"He was found on Seven Point Island. His body came up to shore. He's dead," Emily wailed.

Ella, still in her lap, swiveled around and flung her tiny arms around Emily's neck. Emily's eyes burned into

Drake with an overwhelming intensity as tears streamed down her face. Drake, overcome with mystifying sensations, was unsure how to reply.

"What! Are you serious? He's dead?" Briar shrieked, throwing her arms around both Emily and Ella.

Drake's stomach churned, forcing nausea to emerge. His hands started a faint tremble as the grayed officer took the first finger, pressing it onto an inkpad before guiding it onto an identification card, rocking it purposely from left to right to get a full impression. Drake felt strangely saddened. He didn't think he would ever mourn for his uncle but it was the first family member he had lost. He was unsure of how to process the emotions running their course through his mind. They befuddled him tremendously. It all seemed so final.

"Mom, I'm so sorry!" Briar shouted, pulling away from her firm embrace.

Ella hung her head low as she lounged in Emily's lap, seeming to care about her mother's feelings, as she didn't put up a struggle. Ivan burst through the front door a few minutes later, the officers took turns briefing him and inking his fingerprints. About thirty more minutes of a brief interrogation by the police officers, Drake saw the officers to the door. They hopped into their cars, drove down Scarlet Court, finally turning off their flashing lights as they veered onto Scarlet Drive.

Emily sniffled, "They said it was a head wound. He was hit with something not too large but made out of a very hard material. That's all they can say for now about the weapon. Somebody attempted to dispose of the body but didn't realize the lake tides would erode the shallow grave and it would float out onto the lake. Obviously it was an amateur – at least that's what they said."

Ivan stared at Emily, donning a sympathetic mask. He winced, pulling his eyebrows together as he took the seat next to her at the dining room table.

"Emily, I know I didn't care for Basil. I might have suspected him of having involvement in his wife's murder and maybe even the fire but I wouldn't have wanted *this* for him."

"He didn't do it, Ivan. He wasn't a murderer!" Emily shrieked, sobbing, tears streaming down her cheeks.

"Dad, let's give mom some time to get it together," Drake gestured for Ivan to take Ella with a gentle nod. "Bee, stay with mom, get her anything she needs."

In the living room, Drake fired up Sesame Street on the television, snatching a few of Ella's favorite toys from the toy chest. Ivan retreated to the master bedroom as the doorbell rang. Drake hurried to the door, swinging it open. Jade Amity was standing there, smiling. Drake appeared as though he was going to say something and then thought better of it.

"Jade. I forgot you were coming over."

Drake drew in a deep breath, squared his shoulders, looking behind him to see if anybody was there. He could detect Emily's continuous sobs from the dining room, shrill Sesame Street music adding to the baffling ambiance.

"Do you need me to go? Is this a bad time?" Jade softly said, stepping backward.

Drake seemed preoccupied, taking a deep breath, shrugging his shoulders before allowing a smile to invade his face.

"No, of course not. Hold on, let me see if my dad will take my little sister," Drake stepped backward, propping the door open for Jade to enter the foyer. "C'mon in and have a seat in there," Drake gestured toward the living area, Jade slinked warily to the couch.

Emily's uncontrolled sobbing from the adjacent dining room echoed throughout the first floor of the home. Drake knew he'd have to hurry and rescue Jade as soon as possible. After depositing Ella in the master bedroom with his father, he raced back into the living area, turned off the television and signaled for Jade to follow him into the backyard.

"Look, Jade. I've got some freaked out things to tell you but where do I start?"

He gauged Jade's expression for a moment.

"What's up? Is your mother all right? She's obviously upset about something!"

Drake explained the details surrounding his uncle's murder and how the police had just finished their investigation of the house before she arrived. He divulged the details of the mysterious door slamming, Ivan's claim of a ghostly apparition from the fireplace and the fact that his sister's room was infested with spiders and she refused to go back in there. Understanding flickered on his face the moment he realized what had happened.

"I'll be right back, stay right here," Drake spurted, tapping Jade on the knee as he flung open the back door.

His face melted into a cold, icy glaze as he stormed into the dining room to retrieve Briar.

"Bee, I need to see you for a minute. It's really important."

Briar, mystified, slowly rose from her seat, face curled into a grimace of perplexity.

"Mom, you all right? Dad's in the bedroom. He has Ella. Maybe you guys could watch a movie in there and get your mind off of things?" Briar said, slowly moving her uncertain eyes to connect with Drake.

"You are so sweet, Bee. I'll do just that," Emily sobbed, rising from her dining room chair.

Drake shuttled Briar to the backdoor.

"What's up, Drake?" Briar followed him outside.

"Oh, hello!" Jade whispered loudly. "Well, I can tell by your beautiful eyes that you must be Drake's little sister. Briar, is it?"

Jade smiled politely, gazing at Briar.

"That's right! Call me *Bee*. You must be the Jade that Drake's been talking about every single day."

"Bee, enough," Drake said sternly, waving his hand into a stop motion.

Briar, wide eyed, shrugged her shoulders sarcastically, eyes frozen on Drake. Jade chuckled ever so softly.

"Let's get serious here. I've just realized something major, Bee. We have to discuss this before we tell mom and dad, though. We don't want to pile on any unnecessary stress if we don't have to right now."

"What's going on, Drake?" Bee demanded, taking a seat on the deck.

"Yeah, let's hear it!" Jade added.

"Bee, keep a clear head, K? I'm going to ask you some questions and you have to answer them correctly."

"Shoot," Briar said, staring blankly.

"Remember the first time that we met Quentin in the convenience store?"

Briar nodded.

"Yes, clearly. It was only last Sunday."

Drake held out his hand flat in front of his chest.

"Remember the question he asked mom and dad?"

"Of course, then he asked us the same weird question the next day. What kind of stuff scares you or something like that. He's a major creep!"

Jade studied Briar, turning to gaze curiously at Drake.

"What did mom say? How did she answer his question?" Drake asked carefully.

"Hmmmm," Briar pondered the question for a moment.

"I need you to remember *exactly* what she said. I know what she said but it's important that we get it right," Drake said, each word distinct.

"I don't know what this matters!?" Bee shouted, eyebrows pulled up in a way that looked frustrated rather than confused.

Drake spoke through his teeth, "Just tell me!"

"Mom said she was scared of losing family members—

"Check. Now what did Dad say?"

Briar paused, searching for the answer.

"He said...*uh*....that he was scared of ghosts and stuff—

"Check," Drake interrupted abruptly for the second time.

"He also said he was scared of not having enough money and mom was scared of bridges and getting old," Briar added, shoulders hunched upward in a posture of bewilderment.

"Alright two out of three checks," Drake added sternly. "What about Uncle Basil?"

"He said he was afraid of killers or something—

"He said *murderers*, sociopaths," Drake gazed deeply into Briars eyes, "Check."

Briar cocked her head to the side and with a blank stare, processed what Drake was piecing together, comprehension finally shimmering into her vacant expression. Jade watched the exchange meticulously.

She added slowly, "and then the next day, I told him I was afraid of spiders, being alone in the dark and you told him you were afraid of failure and humiliation. Check, check, check."

Briar's expression transformed into a sub-zero gape, not a muscle twitched in her body.

"Can I ask what the hell you guys are talking about?" Jade interjected.

Drake pivoted toward Jake and nodded abruptly.

"Jade, this creep at the convenience store asked each member of my family what they were scared of when we went in there to buy snacks and stuff."

Jade shrugged, eyes widening in frustration.

"Sooooo, this means what?"

Drake paced leisurely across the deck.

"Well, nearly all of those things have coincidentally happened to us. Let's take my mom first. She said she was afraid of losing a family member and my Uncle Basil was murdered."

Briar became animated, also standing up and pacing opposite Drake.

Briar continued, "Basil had told that man he was afraid of murderers and well, he was murdered."

Drake raised an index finger, ceased pacing for a short moment.

"My dad's fear was ghosts and as I told you earlier, he claimed that he vividly saw a ghost come out of the fireplace and hover over him. My dad is definitely not the type to make up stuff. He's a scientist," Drake exclaimed, a convincing tone of voice. "He's creeped out by the thought of ghosts but I didn't really think he believed in them."

"Well, maybe the door slamming is also part of this ghostly trip too?" Jade said.

"You might be on to something!" Drake ruminated, stomping silently on the deck.

"But how would Quentin get in the house and make ghosts appear?" Briar questioned, plopping back down onto a patio chair.

"You know, you're right. Impossible," Drake said, taken aback for a moment.

Drake drew in a long breath, sighing.

"But he definitely could be responsible for my uncle's murder for sure. He asked the question. He knew the answer. He must have done it."

Jade shook her head in disbelief.

"Wow. You should maybe tell your parents then," Jade said.

"Maybe not, Drake. Think about it. There's no way he could have put the spiders in my room, lock me in the dark study, or caused the door slamming. And those are all coincidental things that *happened* to match our fears.

They'll say the murder is a coincidence as well," Briar debated, flailing arms in the air to strengthen her position.

Drake lost himself in thought, pausing in an awkward long minute of silence.

"You're right, Bee. We should investigate first. Jade and I were gonna scope out the town for Uncle Basil anyway so let's switch it to a murder investigation. Let's start in the study where he was staying."

"Deal!" Briar responded abruptly.

The trio crept silently by the master bedroom, overhearing Ivan's story about how the C.E.O. of his new workplace at Bonlin Pharmaceuticals called him into his office earlier at work and demoted him to a lowly reagent specialist. This means he would be making solutions for the other chemists to use in their research. Ivan explained the job was at the level of a high school student. Emily, outwardly angry at the revelation, accused Ivan of not telling her everything about what had happened at his work, saying that things like that just don't happen for no reason. Ivan insisted it had as he had only been working there a few days, not enough time for anything to go wrong enough to be demoted.

"It seems like a perfect time to get out of here," Drake said with a strained whisper, entering the foyer. "As we planned, let's check out the study before we hit the town. That's where Uncle Basil was staying and where his things disappeared from."

Briar tapped on Drake's shoulder to get his full attention, whispering loudly, "Financial failure was one of dad's fears that he told Quentin, by the way. Check."

Concern glinted briefly in his honey eyes turning into denial as he shook his head in disagreement.

"There's no way the greasy convenience store clerk got to Nigel's dad and convinced him to demote dad. I think that *I* might have had something to do with dad's trouble at work," Drake uttered remorsefully, pointing to his chest with a crooked thumb.

"Nigel's dad, huh? Makes sense, Drake. Nigel probably convinced his dad to mess with your dad at work. That guy is such an unbelievable jerk, I'm sure his dad is the same as he is. He had to learn it from somewhere," Jade added in a loud whisper as they reached the door to the study.

Once in the study, they searched the room for clues. The two officers had already investigated the room but Drake had noticed they didn't spend a lot of time in there, focusing more of their investigation in the foyer and kitchen. Briar searched the crevices of the black suede futon couch as Drake investigated the baseboards of the room. Jade inspected the items hanging on the wall such as the shelves holding Emily's antique knickknacks.

"This thing is odd," Jade picked up a bronze figurine of a jester from the shelf on the wall.

The jester statue was about ten inches tall and solid with a marbled base covered in tiny painted golden balls. The jester's face was depraved and he held a ball in one hand and a baton in the other. Drake never liked the jester as it gave him a creepy feeling in the pit of his stomach.

"Let's see it," Drake replied, extending his arm out to take the figurine. "Yeah, this creepy guy was in our old living room back in Austin."

Briar nodded as she looked over at the jester, cracking a petite smile. That's when he saw it. The police must have missed it. There was blood. The bottom marble base of the figurine had a thin layer of white felt; the corner was discolored from what appeared to be dried, hardened blood. Drake's expression turned sullen, dark. He spun around to face Jade, eyes critical.

"Jade, you probably should go," Drake said, placing the jester back onto the shelf and pointing to the foyer. "I don't think we should investigate anymore tonight," Drake whispered, ushering Jade to the front door. "I'm not feeling that well."

"Drake, are you serious?" Briar whispered loudly.

"*Shhhh*, Bee. I just think dad will wonder where we are. With mom upset and all, it's just not a good time. Plus, I think I need to get some sleep, I'm feeling light-headed all of a sudden. Sorry, but we will tomorrow at school."

"It's all right, Drake. I completely understand. I'll see you tomorrow," Jade said with a cautious smile.

Drake escorted Jade to her car and watched her drive down Scarlet Court.

11 – The Changeling

The next morning, Drake was anxious to speak to Jade in English class. He rushed into the room right as the bell rang, pulled out his books from his backpack and placed them onto his desk.

"I am so sorry about last night," Drake turned his head to the side to whisper loudly to Jade.

Jade leaned up in her seat and spoke into Drake's neck.

"I completely understand, Drake. You're going through a lot right now. It was probably not a good idea to leave with your parents so upset like that."

He smiled in deep satisfaction. She wasn't angry with him.

"I saw something, you know," Drake admitted, still speaking in a restrained whisper.

Jade grabbed Drake's shoulder from behind and gently squeezed.

"What?"

Ms. Crenshaw puffed her tightly curled crimson locks with her bony palms as she stood upright at the head of the class.

"Mr. Henry and Miss Amity! In each corner, immediately. Bring your books with you and read while facing the wall. These will be your new seats until I decide to change them," Ms. Crenshaw scorned, throwing the rest of the class into a contained round of laughter.

During lunch, Drake explained that his friend Dominick would be driving to his house from Austin and would stay the weekend with him. He encouraged Jade to come over as well and for Dominick's sake, told her that she could bring a friend if she wanted. They planned to discuss the case and continue their investigation of the murder and the ongoing occurrences in the home. Drake explained that it would be best if he showed her what he saw on the bronze figurine the night before instead of describing it.

With no tennis practice on Fridays, Drake was able to get home in time to meet Dominick. He waited restlessly in the living room, watching out the window for Dominick's burnt orange Chevrolet Camaro. Within ten minutes of waiting, the engine roar halted on the driveway followed by two stern beeps of a car alarm, car door clambering shut. Drake popped up from the couch and lurched outside into the driveway. Dominick was in a daze at the front door, mouth gaping open wide in astonishment. A smile erupted on Drake's face. He was at ease, he felt as if he were home again, back in Austin. Seeing Dominick quickly unveiled intense feelings of missing his hometown, his old friends, coach and school.

Dominick energetically scoped out Drake's new home, speechless throughout most of the tour. He told Drake that he had *under* exaggerated the magnitude of the coolness of the new house. However, Dominick agreed with Drake's assessment of the run down town of Shady Oaks. He mentioned that he stopped at the Shady Oaks Mart convenience store on the corner of Whispering Point to grab a soda on his way over.

"No, you didn't stop there. Tell me you are joking, Dom!"

"I stopped and got a soda, stop freakin'."

Drake gazed at him, concern riddling his eyes.

"Did you talk to anybody while you were there?"

Dominick's face grew confused, bending down to pet Omen on the head.

"Uh, no. Some muscly dude obviously on 'roids wearing mirrored sunglasses was there. He didn't say a word to me," Dominick defended, shrugging his shoulder and shifting his head forward, surveying Drake. "Why do you care who I talk to at convenience stores, anyway?"

"I guess Quentin is off work today then."

"Quentin?" Dominick mumbled, arms extended to the side, questioning. "You already know someone that works there?"

Drake shrugged the question off and finished the tour with Dominick, ending the adventure in Drake's new bedroom. Here, Drake had just enough time to fill in the details of what had happened in the week since he left Austin. He told Dominick about the strange events in the home and with his family as well as the details that he knew of his uncle's murder. He avoided talking about the jester figurine; still unsure if he wanted to reveal it as it could implicate someone in the house as a murderer.

The front doorbell rang. Drake raced down the stairs to answer it, Bee beating him to the door. It was Jade Amity. She was alone. Omen paused at the top of the stairs, waiting to get a view of the person on the other side of the door before turning to go back into Drake's room.

"Hey, Jade! Coming to hang with Drakey again?" Bee teased, tossing her light brown tresses over her tanned shoulder. "Maybe today he won't freak out and send you home without a warning."

Drake gently pushed Briar aside, stepping in front of her, opening the door wide for Jade.

"Hello Jade, ignore her. Come on up. My friend Dominick's here," Drake said, double-checking the front patio to be sure Jade didn't bring a friend with her.

Jade and Drake made their way upstairs and joined Dominick. Bee trailed behind, stepping into her room for the first time since the spider incident. Dominick kept looking over Jade's shoulder for another girl to enter the room but soon realized she had come alone. He glanced over at Drake, disappointment in his expression. Drake acknowledged, nodded, jetting to the playroom.

He shouted towards Briar's bedroom, "Hey Bee, we're going to talk about Basil's case so if you want to join us—

"Thought you would never ask, Drake," Bee exclaimed, darting into Drake's room.

Dominick cracked a smile. Drake knew Dominick had always had a crush on Briar but forbid him to go near her. Briar had made comments of a mutual attraction for Dominick over the years but Drake had told her he would never stand for it. He figured he would make both of them happy for now while they were under his close watch.

"I've decided to reveal to all of you what I found in the study yesterday."

Jade, concern in her eyes, stared in anticipation. Drake pulled out the bronze jester from his drawer and turned it so everyone could see the blood stain on the corner.

"Is that blood?" Bee shrieked, hands cupping her gaping mouth. "You took that from the study and are hiding it in your drawer?"

"*Shhhhh,* Bee. Keep it down! We don't want mom and dad to hear us!" Drake barked, placing the jester back into his drawer and shutting it.

"Drake, what do you think it's from? Your uncle's murder?" Jade inquired, a perfect eyebrow arched in curiosity.

"I can only assume so. The cops said he was hit with something in the head that wasn't too big but was made out of a hard material. Well, that thing fits the description. It's heavy as hell and happens to have blood on the corner of it. I suppose the cops missed it yesterday."

Briar gasped, looking at the drawer with a caustic expression, abruptly shaking her head.

"Do you think dad killed Uncle Basil?"

Drake's expression turned hesitant.

"Donno. You know that mom didn't do it. That's obvious."

"Is it, though?" Briar replied curiously.

His face twisted into a new expression. Uncertainty.

"All I know is that this might be the murder weapon and I am definitely not handing it over to the police. If mom or dad killed Uncle Basil, I'm sure it was self-defense. If Basil murdered my aunt and caught his own house on fire with his dog inside, he is capable of anything."

Dominick clapped his hands briskly, grabbing Drake on the shoulder with a strong hand.

"I told you he was a murderer and an arsonist! You used to defend that loser, Drake!"

Drake pulled away quickly, rolling his eyes.

"You think he meant to burn up Omen in the fire, Drake?" Briar inquired, plainly disturbed, her face twisting into a look of disgust.

Drake winced. Omen, hearing his name, raised his head to look at Briar.

"I know he did. The D.A. was about to charge him with the arson. Basil told me he wished Omen burned up in the fire the last time I saw him on the back patio. I thought it was a strange thing for him to say at the time, but that was before I knew the fire was officially an arson. The dog was shut into the bedroom and the front door of the house was open. If someone else started the fire, what would their motive be to kill the dog? Why not let him go?" Drake debated in a flat voice.

Briar took a few shallow breaths.

"Wow. That's intense," Briar replied.

"Are you dropping the convenience store clerk as a suspect, then?" Jade asked, gazing intently at Drake.

Drake puckered his lips in thought.

"Not exactly. I have no idea how long this jester statue has had this bloodstain. It could have been there before we moved into this house so it might not have anything to do with Basil's murder."

Briar's face relaxed into relief.

"That thing was in our house in Austin since before I was born, I'm sure. And how do you know that's even blood, Drake?"

"I'm not positive it's blood. I'm not ruling out the convenience store guy or anybody else in this town, either. We need to investigate and see if we can find something. Let's find that clerk and see what he is doing now. He shouldn't be that hard to find in this small town."

Dominick sat up from the bed, sprang to his feet and addressed the group.

"I disagree, Drake. I think we need to investigate your house, thoroughly. The clues are all here in the house, not in the town!"

Drake shook his head and inhaled a deep breath, letting it out slowly.

"The cops were here for hours, Dom. They'd have found the evidence if it were here!"

"You said the jester was on the shelf. They missed it, right? So they suck as investigators. I watch CSI; I know what I'm doing," Dominick argued, flicking his dreads away from his face and repositioning his knitted beanie.

"Maybe they didn't miss it. If they found it, they could have tested it and found it wasn't blood, you know. It's not like they were sharing their investigation with us."

"We're going to investigate this house thoroughly when we get back and that's that," Dominick demanded harshly, marching into the playroom toward the staircase.

"All right, I agree. But let's first hit the town. Mom and Dad will know what we're up to if we start investigating the house now," Drake reasoned.

The group set out on foot to investigate the small town of Shady Oaks. They tried tracing Basil's possible final route, looking for clues along the way. Drake knew that Basil often hung out at the pubs on 6th Street in Austin so he figured it wouldn't have taken him long to find a hang out in Shady Oaks. They found logic in the line of thinking that Basil could have received the call from his attorney and immediately left the home on foot to find a pub.

They also discussed the possibility that he and Emily could have gotten into a scuffle over turning himself in to the police. Maybe the argument ended with her hitting him in the head with the bronze jester figurine? However, they couldn't figure out how she could have disposed of his body in the shallow grave by the lake, especially while taking care of Ella. The only way that it could have happened is if Ivan was involved. In either case, Drake and Briar decided it was best to leave that lead alone and keep the murder weapon hidden.

After thoroughly searching the town for leads in the case, Dominick received a phone call from his parents. Drake found it curious that he only spoke in yes, no or o.k.'s. When he got off the phone, his demeanor had noticeably changed.

"I have to go home," Dominick stated emphatically, pursing his lips.

"Tonight? What? Are you joking?"

Dominick's face was blank.

"Mom wants me to drive home before it gets too late. She's changed her mind. I can't stay the weekend."

Drake raised his hand in front of Dominick, sighing forcefully.

"Did she hear about my uncle's murder on the news or something?"

Dominick shrugged, pausing in thought.

"Not sure."

Drake stomped his foot, thrashing his arms into the air, frustrated.

"Dominick! You were on the phone with her for over five minutes. What did she say to you? Why do you have to leave tonight?"

Dominick's face altered as Drake watched carefully. The confidence wavered in his expression, first showing doubt and then skepticism before he calmed into a confident façade. Drake knew that Dominick was struggling with his emotions.

"Look, Drake. I don't know. I've just got to go home," Dominick scoffed, striding purposely in front of the others.

The teens made their way back to 614 Scarlet Court. Dominick was silent the entire walk home. Jade's curfew was quickly approaching. She leaned over to Drake and kissed him softly on the cheek.

"See ya tomorrow?" she winked, pulling him in for a swift embrace, her perfume delicately filling his nasal cavity.

"Absolutely. Call me later."

Jade nodded, hopped into her red Honda Prelude and waved at the group before driving off into the night.

"Dom, are you certain you have to leave? What is wrong? Is there anything I can do?" Drake pleaded, eyes searching Dominick's.

Dominick continued to ignore Drake, only responding to him with subtle shoulder shrugs. As they approached Dominick's Camaro on the driveway in front of the house, he pivoted, strolling toward Briar. He leaned down toward Briar's neck, appearing to kiss her before bounding into his car and peeling away down Scarlet Court. Drake searched for something that he could have said or did wrong to make Dominick angry. He and Dominick had never had a cross word in all their years of friendship. This awkward tension had no precedent.

"Bee, did Dom just kiss you?" Drake queried, face contorted in confusion.

"No. He whispered in my ear."

Briar was solemn, staring vacantly at the ground.

"Well, what did he say?"

Briar sighed deeply.

"Get out of that house."

12 – Broken Kiss

Drake trusted his dad had figured out the problem with the slamming study door. Ivan was a forensic chemist but had double majored in physics in college. Ivan's repair seemed to have worked, as the house remained silent in the hours of darkness. The Henry family would finally be able to get some much-needed rest. That is, everybody besides Drake.

Drake found himself waking throughout the night, awaiting further chaos from downstairs even though nothing out of the ordinary had happened in a couple of nights. Drake had become paranoid of the night; insomnia brewed in his veins. Drake's constant stirring was contagious as he kept Omen on point, constantly popping his ears up and snarling for no apparent reason during the night.

Drake awoke to the comforting smell of breakfast lurking from downstairs. He kept his eyes shut for a full minute to pretend he was back in Austin and it comforted him. Omen, smelling the same savory aromas, jumped off the bed and waited at the door for Drake. Bee finally gave up the downstairs couch to sleep in her room, making it through the night. Drake felt proud of Briar for getting over her fear.

"Hey, sleepy head! I smell breakfast!" Drake shouted into Briar's room.

"I know, I smell it too! Feels like we're back in Austin, right," Briar exclaimed, tumbling out of bed and stumbling behind Drake to the staircase.

Omen led the way downstairs and into the kitchen. Just as Drake turned the corner, Emily slammed the phone in the cradle, in a daze she stared at the wall blankly. Drake took the cue and took over with the sizzling bacon in the frying pan.

"Mom, you all right?" Briar said, concerned.

"Yes, Bee. I'm fine," Emily whispered, pushing Omen out of the walkway.

Ivan walked into the room cradling Ella in his arms. He placed her in the high chair and walked over to confer a kiss on Emily's forehead.

Noticing something wasn't right, he inquired, "Emily, what's the matter?"

Ivan grabbed her shoulders gently, massaging while he awaited her reply. Emily snapped out of the trance and glanced at Ivan, face wearing a mask of puzzlement.

"They found some fingerprints on the black plastic that was found in the shallow grave that Basil was buried in."

Drake swished his head toward Emily, eagerly awaiting for her to continue.

"Great news! Did they make a match?" Ivan replied apprehensively.

The house grew silent, only the sound of bacon sizzling in the background could be heard as Emily drew together her thoughts.

"Yes, they did. His name is Gaven Phoenix. He's a senior at Deadwood High School."

Drake slammed the spatula down, swallowed an instant lump in his throat and choked before he could muster a reply.

"Mom! He was the guy with Nigel! The one that brought you and Ella home!"

Briar, wide eyed, slammed her hands on the kitchen counter. Emily turned her head abruptly toward Drake, locking into a mutual gaze. She studied his face for a moment before continuing.

"Yes, I know, Drake. They said that Gaven has a strong alibi. He was at Nigel's house the night Basil was murdered," Emily sighed.

Drake argued, "But his fingerprints were on the plastic!"

Emily nodded, her expression turning timid. Briar and Ivan turned their heads as if they were watching a tennis match.

"They know that the plastic came from Deadwood High School. The bolt of plastic sheeting was in the landscaping shed. There was a match to the patterns in the plastic and Gaven's fingerprints. They use the plastic sheeting at the school to keep weeds out of the flowerbeds—

"Gaven's not the gardener!" Drake interjected.

"Let your mother speak, Drake!" Ivan replied sternly.

"Gaven told the police he was in the shed earlier in the week and might have touched the roll of plastic when he retrieved a pair of pruning shears. He's in a Theater Stage Prop class and they were trimming rose bushes to be used on stage for one of the scenes in Alice in Wonderland."

Drake released a huge breath of air.

"He's a liar! Nigel is covering for him. I knew those guys were up to something bigger than being bullies," Drake roared, shutting off the stove and removing the bacon from the pan, placing it onto a paper towel. "But why would they want to kill Uncle Basil?"

The family was quiet during breakfast, solemn. There was a looming awkwardness about Basil's murder case and the newly uncovered evidence. Drake felt torn from the jester figurine he had uncovered in the study and now with Gaven Phoenix tied to the crime, he couldn't have been more confused. He tried to call Dominick on his cell phone a few times since he left the house but Dominick wasn't answering his phone. That wasn't like Dominick.

Jade came over later that afternoon. Needing to unwind, they enjoyed a few movies in the upstairs media room. Drake avoided talking about the murder and Dominick's strange behavior. He felt better giving his mind a rest from the tumultuous happenings in his life.

"Sit over here," Jade whispered playfully, scooting over slightly on her theater seat, patting the empty space she created.

Without hesitation, Drake lunged off his chair and flew over toward Jade. He took her hands into his and gently pulled her up from the chair. He hurled himself into the seat and guided her slender body onto his lap. His heart fluttered in anticipation, breathing became rapid. His eyes adjusted in the darkness into a gaze with hers, her skin flickering from the light radiating from the movie screen. He gauged her expression for a minute, unsure if she felt the same about him or if she simply wanted to sit together as friends. Figuring he would take the chance, he tenderly slithered his hands around her waist.

"Is this what you wanted?" he asked softly, pulling her body in closer, inhaling the honeyed floral and seductive musk emitting from her skin.

"This is exactly what I wanted," she leaned down and stopped within an inch from his lips, her arms braced against the chair.

Drake lifted his chin to study her incredibly perfect face, heart pounding an irregular rhythm. His rapid breathing became erratic as he anticipated Jade's lips touching his own. Jade looked as if she wanted to say something but Drake couldn't wait another second. Leaning forward, he felt every bone in his body dissolve the second their lips met. He tightened his grip around her waist and the lines of her body met his own as he reclined the chair into a horizontal position. Her sweet-scented hair brushed soft as silk against his cheek as she outlined his face with her velvety hands, sliding down both sides of his neck to caress his muscular shoulders. Drake needed this desperately.

"What y'all watchin'?" Briar busted in without warning, door clambering open, allowing an awkward stream of light to divide the room.

At an instant, they broke free from each other's clutches, awkwardly rising the chair into an upright position. Drake's face soured as he sighed quietly in frustration, still breathing sporadically. Jade quickly jumped into the adjacent theater seat, smiling with a contrasting look of surprise on her face. Drake leaned over, grabbed the remote that had fallen to the floor, pretending as though he had been searching Netflix for new movie releases.

"Donno, Bee. Just lookin' for a movie."

"Sure you were, Drake," Briar laughed as she ambled into the theater room, lunging behind the counter to peruse the candy selection.

Drake raised his eyebrows at Jade, outwardly apologetic and highly defeated, he slumped his shoulders.

"You know what, Drake," Jade said softly, glancing at the illuminated screen of her phone. "I didn't realize it's almost 6 o'clock. My mother told me to be home for dinner. We had out of town guests arrive today and I haven't even been home to say hello," she added with resignation, tapping Drake's knee.

Jade hopped off the theater chair, raising a sculpted eyebrow in disappointment, pouting her lips. His eyes narrowed and jaws tightened, shooting a quick grimace at Briar.

"Really?" He swallowed a lump in his throat.

"Yeah, walk me to my car, all right?" Jade swiveled around to face Bee who was taking a seat in the middle row, candy bar in hand. "Hi and Bye, Bee!"

Briar waved goodbye and smiled, tearing open the wrapper of her chocolate bar.

"Bye, Jade!"

Lips stretched into a straight line, Drake shrugged away from the theater seat. With shoulders hunched forward, he reluctantly shuffled forward, trailing Jade out of the media room. Before leaving the room, he shot Briar another dark scowl flickering with resentment. She countered with a nonchalant shoulder shrug and grabbed for the remote, unaffected.

"I really almost forgot about it, Drake. You wouldn't want me to get grounded, right?" Jade challenged coyly, scurrying down the staircase.

As they approached her car, Jade spun around and threw her arms around his neck, laying her head against his chest, his heart barely recovering from its arrhythmia only moments before.

"Of course I don't want you to get in trouble. Then I can't see your beautiful face," he whispered, pouting his bottom lip ever so slightly.

Drake wrapped his well-built arms around her waist, the same irregular cardiac rhythm surfacing once again. Her hand brushed softly against his cheek. She trembled ever so softly.

"See you soon," Drake added, smoothing her silky hair.

Drake closed his eyes and leaned down to meet her soft lips with his own once again. This kiss wasn't as cautious as the one before as she voraciously memorized every contour of his back with her hands. Drake yearned for this moment to never end.

"Have to go," Jade said in a smooth voice, pulling away abruptly.

She beamed at Drake, the fountain light gleaming dimly from her skin. He tried to gasp but his voice had no sound. He studied her as she climbed into her car. His brow furrowing as he watched her Honda disappear down Scarlet Court.

I can get used to that, he thought, hurrying back into the media room.

13 — Wrath

Briar was enjoying her candy bar in the middle row as she watched television on the big screen. After a few minutes, Drake stormed into the media room to confront Briar.

"Thanks, Bee. You've got great timing," Drake said sarcastically over the rumble of the surround sound.

"Like I knew, freak!" Briar defended, shoving a piece of chocolate into her mouth. "This is a common room, Drake. It's not your apartment or anything, you know. You are lucky it was me and not mom that caught you guys."

Drake shrugged, plunking down into the seat beside Briar. Bittersweet, the first kiss with Jade happened at that very spot only minutes prior.

"Wanna watch a movie?" Drake choked out the words begrudgingly, Omen had trailed him into the media room, finding the right spot to lie down on the black shag carpet.

Briar laughed, raising her eyebrows with enthusiasm and responded, "Sure but I'm not sitting in your lap."

Drake gave Briar a humored scowl, snatching the last piece of her chocolate bar. After about an hour into the action movie that they finally agreed upon, Ivan stuck his head into the theater and instructed them to come downstairs for a family meeting.

The family situated around the dining room table. Ella was in her high chair, occupied with taking apart a television remote and Omen perched next to the table as if he were a member of the family. Emily and Ivan had written down everything that happened the past week and the fears they disclosed to the clerk in the convenience store. They had pieced together the same stratagem as Drake and Briar did before with Jade but with one main difference. They didn't tie the events to just Quentin. Ivan believed it was the *house*.

"Dad, you really think this *house* heard what we said to Quentin and that it enjoys freaking us out? I thought scientists didn't believe in the supernatural," Drake said, inclining his head toward Ivan.

"I can't explain everything, Drake. Scientists deal in tangible facts. These are tangible occurrences. One fact is obvious. What we said in the convenience store that day is coming true. I mean, there are a few things that have happened that weren't discussed that day, but the house somehow knew Briar was deathly afraid of spiders and being alone in the dark."

Briar slapped Drake gently on the arm and nodded.

Briar cleared her throat to get Ivan's attention and replied, "Uh, Dad...me and Drake went into the store on Monday and that guy asked us what we were scared of too."

Ivan shot a hard stare to Briar.

"What?!" Ivan roared, taking in a stern bolus of air through his nostrils, eyes bulging, forehead wrinkled like an elephant's butt.

"What did you say to him?" he said every word slowly, distinct.

After Briar and Drake divulged what they had told Quentin, Ivan and Emily's faces were void of expression. The family sat in silence for a long minute.

"This makes the case even stronger then," Emily blurted, cautiously looking around at the house.

"We can't talk here," Ivan added quickly. "Let's go to that diner and finish this conversation."

At that moment, the front and back deadbolts locked on their own and the study door slammed shut. Drake immediately felt his heart bursting to escape his chest. Stumbling to catch his breath, he stood up from his chair. Omen scurried into the foyer, anxiously surveying the room, growling aimlessly. Briar shuttled next to Emily, grabbing her arm. Ivan rushed to the front door and tried to open it and it wouldn't budge. Ivan worked on the deadbolt for a few minutes to no avail.

"Mom! Look!" Briar shrieked, pointing to a stream of brown, furry spiders scurrying through the white marbled foyer.

Briar started to wail with fright, jumping onto the dining room table as Emily struggled to calm her. Ella added to the chaos with shrieks and screams. Ivan took control of the scene.

"Drake, take Briar upstairs to your room. Omen and I will take care of the spiders. Emily, take Ella in the master bedroom and put on Sesame Street for her. I'll only be a moment."

Drake hesitated.

"Dad, you sure?"

Ivan put up a stern hand in front of Drake.

"Drake, go."

Omen was already battling the spiders one at a time, ripping them apart through a concerted effort of his uncoordinated paws and sharp teeth. Ivan darted into the kitchen and grabbed a roll of paper towels and a plastic bag. As he threw a paper towel on a spider, he stepped on it and gathered it into a bag, also collecting Omen's spider carcasses.

Drake and Briar made it to the top of the staircase when he heard a voice coming from the door leading to the attic. It was muffled, but it sounded slightly like Jade's voice. He knew it couldn't have been Jade. He saw her drive away.

"Drake, you hear that?" Briar whispered loudly, straining to hear the noises coming from the corner of the playroom.

"Yeah, that's the door to the attic. Maybe someone is trapped in there?"

Briar's expression turned hesitant. She cautiously took a few steps towards the attic door next to Ella's room.

"Do you think it sounds like Jade?" Briar asked, scanning the floor nervously to make sure there were no spiders upstairs.

"I was kinda thinking that. Hold on," Drake darted into his room.

"Briar, help!" The faint voice within the attic muttered.

Briar reacted without thought, opened the door, stepped in and felt around for the light switch. The door slammed shut behind her.

"Wait!" Drake shouted, sprinting to the attic door with his baseball bat in hand.

It was now silent on the other side of the attic door. Briar was mute. The strange feminine voice was silenced. Drake frantically turned the doorknob but it was locked from the inside. He calmly instructed Briar to unlock the door but she failed to respond.

"Hold on, Bee. I'm going to get Dad."

Drake hurried downstairs to find Ivan, motionless in the foyer, spiders dancing around him. Omen was still working feverishly to destroy the spiders but the numbers were growing without Ivan's help.

"Dad, what're you doing!?" Drake screamed, dashing down the staircase.

Ivan held the bag of spider carcasses against his chest as he stared at something with great focus within the study. Lips pursed, he slowly lifted his hand towards Drake. The study door was wide open. As Drake got to the bottom stair, he saw a brilliant bluish light radiating from within the study. Drake moved slowly into the Foyer, dodging spiders on the marbled floor with each step. As Drake studied the light, he was horrified to see it was formed into a humanly shape, nearly appearing as a hologram, flickering as an old movie reel. Ivan's father had died a few years back and the light formed a strong likeness to him. Drake's illuminated grandfather was standing there, barely moving, staring back at both of them.

Drake broke the silence, "Dad! Briar is stuck in the attic and I don't know what to do!"

Drake's heart pulverized him internally. The study door slammed shut once again, knocking Ivan back into reality.

"Mom has all the keys to the house, she's in the master bedroom," Ivan directed, strangely calm.

Drake, feeling as though he could lose consciousness, raced into the master bedroom. Ella was on the bed watching her favorite episode of Sesame Street and Emily was in the master bathroom. She was standing at the mirror writhing in anxiety as she gazed into her reflection.

Drake approached her cautiously, "Mom, I need the key to the door to the attic upstairs. Briar accidentally locked herself in and she's not responding to me."

Drake marched into the bathroom and stood next to Emily. He looked at her before slowly turning toward the mirror at his mother's reflection. She was only forty years old and prided herself on looking much younger than her age. Gazing into the mirror, she now appeared to be in her late fifties. Through the reflection, his mother had aged tremendously.

"Mom?" Drake gazed fixedly.

"Drake, what is happening to me?" Emily touched her face, staring in horror into the mirror.

Emily's face was transforming, aging rapidly, now appearing as though she was a seventy-year-old woman. Drake looked at his own reflection in comparison. He was still only sixteen. It was beyond Drake's comprehension how his mother was aging so quickly before his eyes. He turned to look at her, outside of the mirror reflection; she was still a young looking forty year old.

"Mom, it's not real! Don't look into the mirror!" Drake demanded, pulling her away from the mirror, yanking her hands and guiding them in front of her face.

Emily looked down at her hands. They looked normal to her; she was no longer an elderly woman. Snapping out of her stupor, she dashed around Drake and into the bedroom to check on Ella who was still watching the television.

"Drake, you said Briar is in the attic? I've got the key to the door here in the drawer," Emily said, scrambling through the assortment of keys and reading the tape labels. "Here ya go, hurry! Briar is probably freaking out!"

Drake retrieved the key and raced toward the staircase. The study door was still shut and his father had resumed the spider extermination along with Omen who seemed to be enjoying himself as he ripped the spiders apart.

"Almost got it, Drake. I'll be up there to help with the attic door if you need me," Ivan said, stomping on another paper towel, face twisting into repugnance with each stomp.

Drake made it to the door and shouted for Briar. Silence broken, he now heard her crying uncontrollably. He knew she was all right; he relaxed accordingly. Shoving the key into the lock, he turned the key and the door snapped open. Briar was crouched down, flush against the wall.

"Oh my God, Drake," Briar sobbed as she lunged toward Drake, grabbing his neck and squeezing tightly. "I hate this house!"

After Briar released Drake, he shouted into the attic while holding onto the door.

"Anybody in there?"

"No, that creepy voice stopped as soon as I got locked in there. Sorry, I couldn't respond. I just froze when the lights went off," Briar wept, grabbing onto Drake's shoulder and pulling him in for a hug.

There was no response from inside the attic. The mysterious voice was silenced. After hugging Briar, he gently pushed away and grabbed his iPhone, noticing a missed text message from Jade. She had made it home. It hadn't been Jade's voice in the attic.

"*Hmmmmm*," Drake paused, looking into the dark attic. "Let's go downstairs. Dad and Omen pretty much have taken care of the spiders."

Drake locked the attic door and headed toward the staircase, Briar followed cautiously. By the time Drake and Briar got downstairs, the spiders were gone. Omen was lying on the living room floor by the couch, exhausted from the battle. Drake surveyed the front and back deadbolts and they were no longer in the locked position. The study room door was slightly ajar but Drake didn't see a bluish light inside. He didn't want to see the light.

"Time for bed, folks. I think we should call it a night, don't you?" Ivan sounded, tossing the plastic bag into the large trash bin in the garage.

"We are actually going to sleep in this place again, Dad? Are you joking?" Briar shrieked, placing a rigid hand on a hip.

"Of course, Briar. It's fine. Mom called the exterminator a few days ago and made an appointment. He'll be here Monday morning and will take care of the spider infestation once and for all!"

Briar's eyes widened in horror. Drake tapped her on the arm and stepped in front of Ivan, pointing sternly toward the study door.

"Dad, there was a *ghost* in the study! I saw it and I know you saw it!"

Ivan shrugged, shaking his head.

"Oh, that thing? Nah...it was light from the fountain the front. Didn't you notice I changed the lights in the dragon statue to blue? Briar hated the red lights, thought they looked like blood," Ivan chuckled.

Upon hearing Drake's revelation about what was in the study, Briar warily peered into the study through the partly opened door from about five feet back. Deciding to cease her investigation mid stream, she dashed over and stood next to Drake in the foyer.

"Dad, there are no windows in the study!" Drake contested.

"Drake, stop being so dramatic! There are large windows in the front doors and the light waves bent and refracted into the study. Go to bed and stop acting crazy!"

14 – Doubts

Briar refused to sleep by herself and easily talked Drake into allowing her to sleep with him and Omen. They stayed up for a while talking about what had happened in the house, with no resolve, until they both passed out from mental exhaustion.

The next morning, Drake arose before Briar and Omen. Reflecting on the night before, he thought deeply about each incident as a separate entity, fragmenting the details and giving them a thorough analysis. Ivan could have been right; each event had a somewhat rational explanation and when all put together, it could have simply seemed overwhelming.

Drake stumped shortly on one thing, however. He had trouble comprehending how his mother and he both viewed her face aging in the mirror. He eventually worked out that it was a case of poor lighting. As Emily panicked and moved her face, her reflection might have only appeared to age. He remembered hearing the girls at school discuss how the lights in the gym locker room made their faces appear purple and veiny. He reasoned this must have been the same type of issue.

During the incident, Drake was stressed out about Briar being locked in the attic and had just seen a ghostly apparition of his grandfather in the study. The mirror, as well as the blue light from the front fountain refracting into the shape of his dead grandfather could both have been a mere hallucination from stress.

Drake also reminded himself that his mother was on a daily medication for anxiety. For the first time, he wondered if he had inherited the trait. He questioned his sanity for a spell before deciding to go along with his father's line of thinking. It was just a bad night of unfortunate events and everybody had overreacted and behaved in an overly dramatic manner.

"Bee, you up?" Drake whispered loudly.

Omen was wedged perfectly in between them in the bed. His pointed ears popped upright. He raised his head and placed his long snout on Drake's leg.

"Hey, boy! Good morning!" Drake stroked the fur of his snout, he returned with a long, warm lick on Drake's arm.

Sunday morning was more than peculiar. Ivan seemed like he had morphed into a new person. He was in great spirits and no longer believed in the theory of Quentin in the convenience store having anything to do with the events in the house. When it was brought up by anybody, he said it was absurd and forbid it to be mentioned again.

After a spell, Drake whispered to Briar that they had to find somewhere safe to talk. They crept out to the end of the dock in the backyard, undetected.

"Bee, what is up with Dad? How can he think one-way last night and then do a 180 like that? It's like he is possessed," Drake said, surveying the backyard to ensure they were alone.

"No idea. When we had our family meeting, he was the one with the ideas and theories about the house and how Quentin was somehow involved. Mom seemed to go along with whatever he said but still seems freaked out about Basil. It's like she can't deal with all the stress."

Drake nodded, eyes flickering with understanding. Briar sat down at the edge of the dock, dangling her feet above the water.

"She does take pills for stress, you know," Drake reminded Briar, taking a seat next to her.

"Exactly. Even with the pills, she still gets freaked out!" Briar said, eyebrows rising, creating creases in her forehead. "Maybe she forgot to take them?"

"Donno. But when you were stuck in the attic, Dad saw something. I know he did because he stopped killing the spiders and was staring at it. It was a ghost. Don't think I'm crazy but it was Grandpa Henry. He was standing very clearly in the study."

Briar blinked, astonished.

"What?!"

Drake's voice turned papery thin, "Yes, I saw it clearly and it definitely wasn't the lights reflecting from the dragon fountain statue in the front. I've been trying to make myself believe that it was, but I just can't anymore. I saw him clearly!"

Briar cocked her head to the side, locking into a knowing gaze with Drake, swinging her legs above the water in a faster pace.

"Drake, you think this house is haunted, don't you?"

Drake puckered his lips before tightening them together in a straight line. He stared at the water for a moment before responding, angst in his expression.

"I don't believe in that stuff but I don't see how you can argue otherwise."

"What can we do? Since Dad thinks everything is fine, it's not like he'll move us out of here or anything."

Footsteps sounded softly behind them on the dock. Drake glanced over his shoulder. They belonged to Emily.

"Mom's coming. Follow my lead, o.k.?" Drake whispered as Emily approached.

"Can I speak to you two for a second?"

"Where's Dad?"

"He's giving Ella a bath. Thought I could sneak away for a moment."

"Sneak away?" Briar whispered derisively.

Emily crouched down next to them on the dock, legs folded to the side, covering them with her long satin robe.

"Dad's acting strange. Something happened to him last night," Emily reported bluntly.

"I know! We were just talking about that!"

"And I've got something to tell you two but I don't know how to say it."

Drake and Briar waited patiently as Emily hesitated.

"Just say it, Mom!" Briar shrieked with a whisper.

Emily studied the back yard as if she thought someone followed her. When she felt comfortable enough to continue, she leaned in closer to Drake and Briar.

"I found something on the floor in the study after Basil's things disappeared. I didn't know what to do about it so I took it and hid it in the secret compartment in my dresser drawer. After the police investigated our house, I placed it back on the shelf in the study," Emily spoke rapidly, turning to survey the surroundings, pausing at the windows at the back of the house.

"The bronze jester statue?" Drake said boldly.

"Yeah, that's it," Emily stated flatly.

Her expression melted into bewilderment, outwardly shocked.

"We already know about it," Drake replied bluntly.

"You knew that I hid it and put it back?" Emily said, eyebrows pushed toward the midline of her face.

"No, didn't know that. But I know it is a possible murder weapon," Drake said pointedly.

Emily cocked her head to the side and analyzed Drake. She turned to Briar to see her reaction to the revelation. Her eyes flickering between the two, she tensed.

"Drake, did *you* murder Basil?" she whispered calmly, shoulders rose and squared with her chest.

Drake's eyes widened as he processed his mother's question. She had asked him if he was a murderer.

"Of course not, mom! We did our own investigation after the cops left that night. I discovered the blood stain on it and just thought the cops missed it."

Emily's dropped her shoulders, her facial muscles relaxed, easing into a calm expression.

"Right, that makes sense," Emily said airily.

"You found it on the floor," Drake paused, mulling over the news. "Well, that makes even *more* sense. It's definitely the murder weapon then."

"Mom, who do you think did it? Dad?" Briar asked softly, looking cautiously around the yard.

"Not sure. Your father hated Basil. He fought about allowing Basil to live with us. He desperately wanted Basil to stay in Austin but I didn't have the heart to tell him no. I suppose I still thought of him as my protective older brother that he once was and then with the fire and all, I couldn't just leave him there with nowhere to stay. You know, me and Basil were a lot like you two when we were young."

Briar chuckled, rolling her eyes.

"Oh, great, Drake. You'll be Uncle Basil one day. Get prepared to be bald with a big belly and stink like sweaty smoke."

Drake shook his head violently, rolling his eyes at Briar.

"Don't think so, Bee," Drake gently punched Briar on the arm.

"Not nice, you two!"

Emily pivoted around to check the backdoor of the house and then continued, "Uncle Basil and your father exchanged words not too long before Basil disappeared. Your father was upset that Basil hadn't made an effort to look for a job."

The back door swung open.

"*Shhhhh,* he's coming," Drake whispered loudly.

"Emily!" Ivan projected from the backdoor.

"Over here, Ivan!"

"Where is Ella's hair shampoo?"

Ivan was cradling Ella, naked with suds falling from her body.

"Use the baby wash. It goes on her body *and* her hair!"

They waited until Ivan and Ella went back into the house before they continued.

"But if Dad killed Basil, what does Gaven Phoenix have to do with it? I don't buy that his prints were on that black plastic 'cause he got some pruning shears from the gardening shed at school."

Emily shrugged.

"Innocent until proven guilty, Drake. You shouldn't always think people are lying."

Drake stared, uncomprehending.

"Mom! Gaven and Nigel are not good guys."

"Drake, they seemed very nice to me."

"They have you totally snowed."

Briar interjected, "Drake's right, mom."

Emily let out an arduous sigh.

"Is dad trying to set up that creepy man from the convenience store or something? If he did it, maybe he's trying to pin it on that guy?"

"Well, I kind of thought that last night when he was so adamant about that clerk having something to do with Basil's murder based upon what we told him we were afraid of that day in the store. I mean, it makes sense on the surface but other than you two, the only one that *could* have murdered Basil is Ivan if the jester figurine is the weapon. So why would he say this?"

Drake paused, deliberating his thoughts in his mind before he spoke.

"As an alibi. As a lead for the police, maybe. He also doesn't realize we know about the jester statue having blood on it and being on the floor in the study after Basil disappeared. He definitely doesn't think the police know," Drake pointed out.

"But mom, you are not going to turn Dad over to the police, are you?" Bee asked cautiously, still swinging her legs above the water.

"No, not for now, at least. That's why I hid the jester figurine after I found it. I want to give him time to be honest with me. But in the end, I'm not sure if I can live in the house with a cold blooded murderer."

Something on the lake caught their attention and the conversation paused. A silhouette of a man in a canoe crept up from distance, paddling deliberately in their direction.

"That looks like fun, doesn't it Drake?" Bee mused.

"Fun. I barely remember what fun was like!" Drake returned, suddenly cheerful.

"Wait a minute," Emily uttered. "That guy looks familiar."

Waiting patiently, the three watched attentively as the canoe drew near. Drake recognized the man as he reached the dock. It was Quentin from the convenience store. Emily stood up, adjusting her robe.

Emily whispered, "I'll go get Dad."

"Huh-how are yuh-you folks doing in the new house?" Quentin stammered, tossing his paddle in the canoe and holding on to the dock rope.

Drake looked at Briar with concern. Emily quickly excused herself and jogged toward the house.

"We're fine, I guess," Drake responded guardedly.

Quentin paused as he surveyed the back yard, waiting for Emily to enter the house. He stared at Drake for a moment and then shot his eyes to Briar.

"Huh – huh - heard there are a lot of spiders this way. Yuh - your ma and pa should call ssss-someone out to do some bug spraying around the way," Quentin warned, keeping his small, hazel eyes affixed on Briar.

"Well, Quentin," Drake hesitated for a moment. "We've got to go now. Got a lot to do today. Still unpacking, you know,"

Drake stood up and turned toward the house, clearing his throat for Briar to follow his lead.

"Suh-saw you with juh-juh- Jade Amity the other night. Sh-she's a looker, huh?"

Drake paused to allow Briar to get in front of him. He gently nudged her to walk toward the house before turning back around to look at Quentin.

"Yes, she is. Stay away from her," Drake hissed.

"See you later, Drake," Quentin replied, letting go of the rope and pushing off from the dock.

They walked at a brisk pace to the house. Once inside, they peered out the windows to see if Quentin was leaving in his canoe. He paddled in the same direction from whence he had come. Drake knew he was at his dock with a purpose but he didn't know what it was.

15- Black & Whites

Mondays were always difficult for Drake to get motivated to go to school but the anticipation to see Jade Amity was enough to make him hurl out of bed as soon as the alarm sounded. He had only communicated with her once for a brief moment since she left his house on Saturday. He found it tough to get their first kiss out of his head, replaying it constantly in his mind as he stared blankly into space. He had only chatted to her on Skype for a minute on Sunday night as she had out of town relatives staying at her house.

As Drake walked into his English class, he was bummed to find that Jade wasn't at school. He immediately panicked, thinking something had happened to her. Thoughts raced through his mind about what Quentin had said to him the day before by the dock. Quentin had seen her with Drake. He knew her name. How would a convenience store clerk from Shady Oaks know a teenager from Deadwood City? He grew angry with himself for not questioning it sooner. If Quentin did have something to do with Basil's murder, he could get to Jade. Drake grabbed his iPhone and thumbed a text furiously to Jade.

Throughout the day, Drake obsessively checked his iPhone for a return text message from Jade. Nothing. He wished he had gotten her address in Deadwood City so he could drive over to her house to check on her. He pulled up Facebook on his phone. She hadn't posted a status update since the night before. Drake felt sick to his stomach. It was time for tennis and his day couldn't have been going any worse.

As he dredged up to the locker room, he spotted Gaven Phoenix. Gaven handed something to a figure in the shade. Drake ducked behind a dumpster and scooted along the wall to get a better view. He knew he was too far to hear them but figured he could at least see what Gaven was doing and to whom he was speaking. As he poked his head around the dumpster, he recognized the man with Gaven. It was Quentin from the convenience store.

Drake was in a daze. It was too much to process seeing these two people at Deadwood High School having a conversation. How were they linked? One had fingerprints linking him to his uncle's murder and the other had an even more perplexing link. The puzzle pieces were adjoining around the edges but with one big middle piece missing including the motive. Uncle Basil didn't have money, power, or anything that anybody wanted. If these two were involved, had they been in Drake's house? Did they use the jester figurine to murder Basil? But why? Drake's mind was a whirlwind as he pressed his body against the wall, looking intently at the exchange.

Drake glanced over to the right; the tennis team was filing out of the locker room and heading to the courts. He sneaked the back way into the locker room and hurriedly got dressed, grabbing his racquet from his locker. He was the last one to arrive on the court. None other than Nigel was waiting at the gate to greet him.

"Thirty laps in the football stands, punk. Hit it," Nigel commanded with an icy grimace, sticking his iron hand abruptly in front of Drake's face.

"What? Why?"

Nigel reddened. He grabbed Drake by the shirt, shoving him backward; he landed agilely on the balls of his feet with a low thud.

"Because I said, punk. You are late and those are the rules. There is a tennis tournament against Wild

Flower High School this weekend and I need everybody disciplined. Hit it or you will sustain further punishment. From me, personally."

Gaven Phoenix, strutting arrogantly up to the tennis courts, stopped to glare at Drake, his face tense and confident. He spun around to Nigel and burst into a fit of laughter, Nigel joining in raucously. Drake grabbed the gate, slammed the door and shuffled forward along the pathway towards the football field, his head bent forward, his shoulders slumped.

"And don't come back to practice today. By the time you are though, we will be too," Nigel chafed sternly.

Drake was humiliated as he ran up and down the bleachers of the football stadium. He knew that many classrooms in the back of the school had a vantage point to see the bleachers and many students witnessed his ridiculous punishment. He contemplated quitting the tennis team but talked himself into playing the weekend's tournament. He had to redeem himself with his team and continue his undefeated record. He hadn't lost a tournament his entire high school career. After all, Coach Walter had advised him that his years in college would be the most fun years of his life and high school, often a harrowing experience, would be over in a blink of an eye. In order to get a college scholarship, Drake needed tennis. His grade point average was certainly average as well as his class ranking in Austin at exactly the 50th percentile. He had only minimally tried in academics, as he knew tennis was his ticket to wherever he wanted to go, at least until now.

After the laps, Drake couldn't wait to get home. He had checked his iPhone about a hundred times and still no message from Jade. He contemplated calling the police but knew it would sound silly since he didn't even know if she was home and possibly, she had been too sick to attend school.

The bell rang. Drake, sweat pouring from his pores, sprinted to grab his things from the locker room and made his way to his Jeep in the parking lot. Briar was there waiting with a pleasant grin on her face.

"Ready to go home, Bee?"

Drake tossed his stuff into the back seat and fired up the engine.

"Absolutely! I hate Mondays! I'm so tired!"

"How was your day otherwise?"

He maneuvered into the parking lot aisle, trying not to be the last in line.

"Decent. I found this one guy from China in my Algebra class that might also be a contender for Valedictorian. He wasn't here last week because he was at a UIL event. At least I've got some competition, though," Briar said, pressing her face against the window.

Drake shook his head in incredulity, pulling onto the Deadwood Bridge.

"I wished that was my only worry."

Briar twisted her head to look at Drake, glint of inquisitiveness sparking in her eyes.

"What's wrong big brother?"

"Jade wasn't at school and hasn't texted back. She hasn't posted on Facebook, either," he said, face sullen.

The car was silent as they drove over the bridge. Briar was deep in thought, seeming to search for Jade's location as if she had a GPS in her head. She suddenly became animated and slapped the dashboard, Drake startled, gasped for a quick breath as he clenched the wheel tightly.

"Didn't you say this morning she had family in town?"

"Well, yeah, so?"

Briar took in a deep breath, rolling her eyes. Drake winced, preparing himself for an impending tongue-lashing from Briar.

"Duh, Drake! Maybe she is doing something with her family! Or, she *could* be sick, duh! Give the girl a break, smother king!"

Drake nodded, considering the idea.

"You know, you're probably right. I'm just being paranoid."

As Drake and Briar drove up to 614 Scarlet Court, he noticed a police car pulled up into the circle drive, lights flashing but void of sirens. Drake and Briar jumped from the Jeep and rushed into the house.

"Drake! Briar! It's Ella!" Emily exploded, rushing to give Drake a forceful hug, tears gushing down her rosy, blotched cheeks.

Drake peeled off his mother's arms and stepped backward. Emily was nearly unrecognizable. She had been crying for a very long time and her cheeks were red and swollen as plump tomatoes. As she stood, she gasped for air methodically. Like a glitch in the Matrix, the same two police officers from before were dusting for fingerprints and searching for evidence.

"Ella is gone!" Emily wailed, yanking Briar in for a strong embrace.

The grayed police officer scuffed over to Drake, aggressively introducing himself as Officer Charles Nelson. Drake had seen the officer during the investigation of his uncle's murder.

"Young man, I need to speak with you immediately."

"Sure," Drake replied, ambling over to the dining room table.

A ripple of panic flowed through his body as he remembered the jester figurine. His mother had put it back on the shelf in the study. He knew the police would find it this time. Drake believed his mother to be far too scattered to remember to hide it again. His father would certainly be implicated in his uncle's murder. He wavered, nearly losing consciousness from the intense pressure. He blinked forcefully and shook his head a few times to disconnect the stress as he grabbed his seat across the table from Officer Nelson. Officer Nelson was staring with intent at Drake's every move.

"Is something wrong? Something you need to get off your chest?"

"Uh, sorry. No, I'm fine," Drake fought a surge of panic.

Officer Nelson continued to stare at Drake until he was completely still and void of expression.

"Your two year old sister, Ella Henry, was taken from the home a few hours ago. Do you know anybody who might be responsible? Have you seen anything strange around the house lately or spoken to anyone that you found to be odd in any way?"

Drake's face turned a putrid shade of sea green under his russet skin.

"Yes. I don't know if mom already told you –

The officer held up a stern hand.

"It doesn't matter what she has told us, I need to hear your story."

Drake searched for the correct words as he gazed down at the dining room table. He took a bottomless breath, exhaling slowly.

"Well, yesterday, a man named Quentin that works in the convenience store came up to our dock in a canoe. He knew things about us. I have a feeling he has been watching us. And then, I saw him at our school talking to a student."

Officer Nelson gave Drake a cold stare, seeming to process the information before arrogantly shaking his head and slamming a hand on the table.

"I know Quentin," Officer Nelson returned brightly, smile spreading across his face. "I've actually known the guy a long time. You say he was over at Deadwood High School talking with a student today? How can that be when I saw him at the Shady Oaks Mart just this morning? Nobody else works at that store, you know."

Drake recalled Dominick said he had stopped by the Shady Oaks Mart on his way to Scarlet Court. He clearly remembered Dominick describing a well-built person that appeared to be on steroids wearing mirrored sunglasses was working in the store that day. That is not how you would describe Quentin. Could it have been Gaven? An assortment of thoughts battled in Drake's mind. Drake decided to proceed cautiously with the officer. He had seen a few movies where the police were corrupt in small towns. He started to believe this might be the case.

"Maybe I was mistaken. I saw someone that looked like Quentin today. Probably nothing."

The Officer studied Drake, narrowing his eyes.

"So you still contend that Quentin came to your dock yesterday in his canoe?"

Drake paused, gritting his teeth, hands clenching.

"Yes, sir. He was canoeing in the lake and came over to our dock."

"What did he say that seemed odd to you?"

"He said he knew there were a lot of spiders around our house."

Officer Nelson laughed, looking around for his partner.

"Hey! This young man thinks that Quentin kidnapped his sister because he knows there are spiders around here!"

Both officers cackled, nearly hysterically.

"Wow, everybody knows this part of town is infested with spiders. You live out in the country by the lake, kid! It's spider heaven!" The younger officer added sarcastically.

Both policemen laughed uncontrollably for a period while Drake anxiously waited. He wanted to finish the interview as quickly as possible. He realized the police officers weren't going to help them. He knew it would be up to him and Briar to find his sister.

16-The Message

Once the police officers set out to their car, Drake dashed into the study to see if his mother had taken care of the jester figurine. It wasn't on the shelf. He rushed into the master bedroom where he found Emily on her bed, sobbing while holding a pillow tightly as if it were Ella.

"Mom, we'll find her. Me and Briar will find her," Drake assured, rubbing his mother on the shoulder tenderly.

"Drake, it's impossible!" Emily moaned, tears streaming down her inflamed face.

Emily took off her glasses and tossed them onto the nightstand.

"No it is not! I'm sure that Quentin is responsible for all of this. We'll go to the convenience store and tell him we know he did it. We can follow him to his house!" Drake pleaded, Briar standing immediately behind him, nodding.

"Forget it. Let the police do their job. It's what they do best," Emily wept, blowing her nose wildly with a tissue. "And stay away from that crazy man! I can't lose anyone else!"

Drake leaned in, tapping Emily on the shoulder.

"Mom, one more thing. You hid the jester statue again, right? I didn't see it on the shelf in the study," he whispered.

"Didn't touch it, Drake. I forgot all about it." Emily sat up for a moment, put the pillow behind her on the bed and paused her sobbing. "I don't even care anymore, let the police have it. That reminds me, tell your father to wake me when he *finally* gets home. I called him as soon as I found that Ella was missing but he was too busy at work to come home. I don't get it."

Drake furrowed his eyebrows, turning his head to the side in amazement.

"Ella is missing and Dad's not coming home until later?" he hissed through his teeth.

"No way, mom," Briar hissed.

"I took a pill to get me to sleep, now just go. Leave me be," Emily whined, throwing her head down on the pillow and pulling the comforter over her head.

Omen jumped up on the bed and took a spot immediately next to Emily. Drake knew Omen would take care of his mother.

"Let's go, Bee. Give mom some time alone. Let her get some rest," Drake said brusquely, gesturing for Briar to leave the master bedroom.

They walked out into the living area and hopped on the couches.

"We can't let any more time go by. If the same person that killed Basil has Ella, they might kill her too," Briar pleaded, eyes locking with Drakes, her face hard and rigid.

"Don't even think that way, Bee. But you are right, we can't lose any time. Let's go to the convenience store and talk to Quentin," Drake uttered, nodding in encouragement.

They jumped in Drake's Jeep and sped off to the convenience store.

"I wished I knew where Jade Amity lived. I know she lives in Deadwood City but she never gave me her address!"

Drake grabbed his iPhone, checking his text messages. Nothing from Jade.

"Still haven't heard from her?"

"No. She still isn't posting anything on Facebook, either. She usually posts at least three status updates per day."

"While she is at school, mostly, right?" Bee posed, curving her mouth up on one side.

"Well, I suppose so."

"So that means she either isn't bored or she is sick and sleeping so stop worrying so much about it!"

They pulled up to the convenience store and saw a hand written note hanging on the door. The lights were off. Drake charged the door.

Gone for the day. Be open again tomorrow.

"That proves it!" Drake stammered, storming back to the car, furious. "You remember that policeman saying Quentin was at work today? I think they're in on it with him!"

Drake slammed the car door shut, twisting the key in the ignition with vehemence.

"What do we do now?"

Drake sighed forcefully, banging his fist on the steering wheel, upper lip curling back on his teeth.

"Ugh! What can we do? I had hoped to speak with him and then follow him home!"

Drake's iPhone rang, vibrating with his favorite song. He had assigned this song to his best friend Dominick. Drake scrambled to answer the call.

"Hello?"

Briar anxiously awaited, listening intently to Drake's every word.

"*I heard Ella is missing. That's awful, man.*"

"You heard about it already? Hey, I've been trying to call you. Why haven't you answered your phone or been on Xbox Live?"

"What, Drake? What did he hear?" Briar inquired impatiently.

"Hang on, Dom," Drake said, putting the phone aside.

"He knows about Ella. It made the news."

He put the phone back to his ear, pointing an index finger at Briar.

"The reporter said there's an Amber Alert on her across the state of Texas. I think that means that everybody in the state is looking for her. They showed Ella's picture too. What the hell happened?"

"Donno, Dom. Hey, I've wanted to ask you something. Why'd you tell Bee to get out of the house before you left that night? And why haven't you answered my calls?"

Drake awaited his answer, Briar leaning in close to hear Dominick's reply.

"Dominick?"

Drake looked at his phone and saw the call had disconnected. He tried to call Dominick back and he didn't answer.

"Maybe his phone died?" Drake said, perplexed.

"Well, what did he say? Why did he call? Because he saw a story on the news?" Briar burst with questions.

"I'll admit. Dominick sounded strange. Like it wasn't really him but I know it was his voice. I can't explain it but he nearly sounded robotic, as if he read a script."

"But what did he say?"

Briar's face turned into a mask of excited bewilderment.

"Told you already. He heard it on the news that Ella had been kidnapped from our house this morning."

"But why was he calling then? Just to tell us he knows?" Briar shrugged her shoulders, waving her arms wildly with every word.

"He said everybody in the state is looking for Ella and he heard it on the news back in Austin. I feel a little better about the cops doing their job but the whole thing is downright overwhelming. Let's get back home."

Ivan was home by the time they arrived but it was the normal time for him to be home. He certainly didn't take off work early. Emily had woken from her nap and prepared a quick dinner. He was tidying up the kitchen and Emily was setting the dinner table. Emily looked much better than before and had finally stopped crying.

"Hey, Dad. It's an absolute nightmare about Ella," Drake lamented, face sullen, shoulders slumped.

"Oh, they'll find her. Don't you worry," Ivan assured in a jovial tone.

Briar glanced at Drake, locking into a gaze of mystification.

"How can you be so sure?" Drake questioned guardedly, studying Emily as she mysteriously smiled at Ivan.

"She probably wandered out while your mom was taking a bath. Emily thought she was taking a nap but she probably got up and went exploring. It's not like she wears a dog collar so it will take a little time for someone to figure out who she belongs to. I expect her to be home later tonight or in the morning."

"Your father's right," Emily grinned, putting the dinner plates down at the table.

"I see you are feeling better, mom. That wasn't a long nap!" Briar pointed out, glancing back to Drake, her face twisting into unease.

Briar's phone vibrated. She looked at the screen and then shot a look of panic to Drake. They made it through dinner and Drake couldn't wait to get alone with Briar to hear about what she had seen on her phone.

During dinner, Emily was in good spirits considering her two-year-old child was still missing. Ivan behaved strangely, as he had before, not seeming concerned about Ella's appearance. Compared to earlier in the day when the police were in the house, Emily wasn't that upset about Ella, either. She made a few statements that she was sure that the police would find her and she'd be returned home safely soon enough. Drake couldn't figure out how she could be so sure given the fact that her own brother disappeared from the house and was murdered only days before.

After dinner, Drake and Briar excused themselves and adjourned upstairs. Briar told Drake the text message was a warning about the house but it was from a number she didn't recognize with a 512 area code. It was from Austin. She said she'd gather her books and meet him in his room so they'd appear to be doing homework while covertly speaking about what was going on. Ivan had forbidden further discussion about the unexplained events in the house citing that the two were getting behind in schoolwork and needed to focus on what was important.

While waiting for Briar, Drake grabbed his Xbox controller to see if Dominick was signed on to his account. Drake put on his headset and asked another friend if he had spoken to Dominick. He told Drake that he was playing Dominick in an online game of *Call of Duty* at that time but Dominick had signed on with a new gamer tag. Since he could remember, Dominick had always used the gamer tag *Domino*. Why would he change it now without telling Drake? Drake checked his iPhone to see if Jade had left a message. Nothing. He checked Facebook. She hadn't posted a status.

After about ten minutes, Briar brooded into his room, books in hand, a morose look twisted on her face. She gently placed her books down on his bed, opening them to a specified page and started reading the text. Drake inclined his head, clearing his throat to get her attention.

"So, what *exactly* did your phone say?" Drake asked, gazing pensively at Briar.

"Don't know what you're talking about, Drake. Let's do our homework."

17 - Unspoken

Drake's alarm was scheduled to go off in a few minutes. His iPhone vibrated, rattling his nightstand. His eyes flashed open as he grabbed the phone. His eyes furiously searched as his thumbs navigated to an unopened text message. He let out a huge sigh. It was Jade Amity. She had finally returned his text message.

Jade explained that her parents made her help host a retirement reception for her great aunt. Her aunt had retired from the Deadwood City Hospital where she worked as a nurse practitioner for over thirty years. That was the reason Jade had so many out of town guests at her home. She didn't have access to her computer as her grandparents were staying in her room. She had misplaced her phone soon after everybody arrived, finding it underneath her grandmother's suitcase right before sending the text to Drake. Drake instantly felt relieved that she was all right and Quentin did not have anything to do with her absence from school. Drake was slowly coming to the realization that Jade was the only one in the world he could trust.

At breakfast, his parents behaved exceedingly bizarre. It is not how he imagined two parents with a missing child would conduct themselves. He expected hysteria and crying but they were calm and collected, almost happy, never mentioning her disappearance as though it didn't happen.

Briar had transformed into the same peculiar behavior. On the way to school, as Drake spoke about

Basil's murder or Ella's disappearance, Briar tensed up and told Drake to change the subject, agreeing wholeheartedly with their parents. She said that Ella would be fine and that Quentin had nothing to do with the crime. She was a horrible actor. Drake knew either someone or *something* got to Briar or he was losing his mind. He hoped it was not the second option.

Drake meandered into English class, slow grin on his face. He gazed at Jade and as she returned the gaze, he felt as though nothing in the world would ever be wrong again. She looked even more amazing than he remembered. Her auburn hair sparkled in the sunlight, her creamy skin was flawless. Inhaling deeply, he filled his lungs with the woodsy floral musk surrounding her skin. He loved her perfume and longed desperately to kiss her subtle lips. Feeling as though he lost her served to conjure more powerful feelings than he ever knew existed. It was at this moment, he fell in love with her.

"Let's get out of here," Drake whispered to Jade, extending his hand.

He stood in the aisle, hazy eyes smiling down at her, impossible to look away, mesmerized. Jade returned the gaze with a beatific smile, pointing at Drake's seat.

"I can't just leave school, Drake. I missed yesterday! What's the deal? Can't we talk during lunch?"

Jade raised her eyebrows in an apologetic stance.

"Yeah, sorry. I suppose so," Drake mourned, smiling as he took his seat.

Ms. Crenshaw squawked from the front of the room, "Do not make me sorry that I allowed you two back in your seats from the corners. One more peep—

"I am so sorry Ms. Crenshaw," Drake spewed with false sincerity. "It was all me and I'll be quiet, ma'am," the class followed with a soft chuckle.

It was difficult for Drake to remain silent for the remainder of the period. He had too much to say. He needed a friend. He needed Jade; her absence had crippled him, leaving him vulnerable. Ms. Crenshaw kept a tight eye on them so it was impossible for Drake even to turn around to catch a glimpse of Jade's flawless features. The bell rang.

"See ya at lunch, baby," Jade said, squeezing Drake's hand into hers.

The hours felt like days until he could see Jade again. They found a secluded lunch table in the corner of the cafeteria. As soon as they set their trays on the table, Drake immediately disgorged everything that had happened since she left him in the media room. He confessed that he believed Quentin had kidnapped her the day before because of what he said to him by the dock. Jade was outraged that Quentin knew her name as she had never seen the man before. They further discussed the details surrounding Basil's murder and Drake filled her in on the facts surrounding Ella's disappearance.

"I can't believe that your mom thinks your dad killed her brother and she is keeping you guys in the house with him. Do you think your dad also did something to Ella?"

Drake placed a strong hand on her shoulder, gently squeezing.

"No. Can I be honest without you thinking I am crazy?"

Jade nudged toward him, nodding her head.

"Shoot, Drake," Jade turned her head to the side, gathering her hair behind her ear.

Drake shook his head slowly, always watching her face.

"I think it is the house. I think there is some creepy aura or some type of ghosts in there. I think they might be *possessing* my family."

Jade's face turned into a more serious expression as she stared at the table for a minute before responding.

She smiled coyly, tapping on the table.

"Actually sounds reasonable, Drake. You shouldn't go back into that house. You should come and stay with me."

Jade leaned over and gave Drake a quick kiss on the lips, not giving him the chance to kiss back. As she pulled away, his caramel eyes gazed into hers like a heat-seeking bomb locked on to a target. He fought the urge to whisk her away somewhere they could be alone.

"On second thought, I'm so tired of my house right now, I need some time away. I'll come over to your place later. I can trust that you won't allow the house demons to take my soul, right? Will you protect me, Sir Drake?"

He drew in a deep breath and smiled.

"You think I've lost it, right?"

"No, I'm just joking, really," Jade raked her hand slowly across his thigh ending with a couple of light taps on his knee.

Drake felt as though he could crumble into dust every time she touched his body. She paused, studying his face before glancing over her shoulder.

"I think you might be on to something, actually. I just don't know what. I've never been a big believer in supernatural stuff but I can see how you're running out of explanations with what is going on. I'll come over, though. You seem more than fine so maybe you are immune or there are no demons or freaky ghosts in your room."

For the remainder of lunch, Jade revealed her tormenting experience with the guests at her home and the retirement reception the day before. Exhausted from playing host to elderly family members, she said more than once how thrilled she would be to get out of the house later that evening. Drake couldn't wait until that time but had to get through his afternoon classes first. World Geography seemed like an eternity followed by a second sentence in eternity through Computer Applications. The bell rang for the last period. It was time for tennis.

To Drake's elation, Gaven wasn't there. Nigel was mild, almost pleasant, and to Drake's surprise; he allowed Drake to play as an equal team member. Drake didn't lose a game against his teammates but Nigel never offered one word of praise but rather said it was what he should have been doing all along. Drake couldn't wait to play that weekend. He knew he'd be able to prove himself in the tournament against Wild Flower High School. He wanted Jade to be there, to witness him shine at what he was infamous for back in Austin at Winding Heights High School.

The ride home from school with Briar was awkward. Drake knew her well. He sensed she desperately wanted to talk but something held her back. Whatever it was, it had a force stronger than their relationship. It baffled him; nothing had ever been strong enough to come between them.

"Briar, I know you agree with me. I know that you agreed with me yesterday about mom and dad acting weird and now you are doing the same thing," he said, his expression contorting into sadness and worry rather than anger.

Briar stared out the passenger window.

"Drake, that's not true. I've just thought a lot about it and think they are acting reasonable," Briar's voice was rough and zealous, each word distinct.

"Listen to yourself, Bee. Your little sister was kidnapped. She didn't just wander out of the house. You know mom. She is never careless when it comes to Ella. I know that if she took a bath, she locked the door of the master bedroom so Ella couldn't escape if she woke up. Something happened. Something not normal," Drake snapped, clenching his hands on the wheel as he drew in deep breaths.

Now there was anger upon his face. Briar lounged lazily against the car door with arms folded across her chest. Her eyes were unreadable. She was expressionless.

He had a sixth sense when something wasn't right. Briar sat forward eagerly, leaning forward toward the dashboard. She slapped the dashboard with a renewed sense of fervor.

"Can't we talk about something else? I got a 101 on my Algebra exam today. Nobody else came close. Second highest score was an 88. Suckers!"

Drake took a deep breath and stared, unseeingly, at the road for a long moment. Briar pulled out a tube of lip-gloss from her purse and started applying it to her lips while gazing into the drop down mirror. She grabbed a brush and fluffed her hair before tossing it back on her shoulders.

"That's awesome, Briar. Good job," Drake said absently, shaking his head at Briar for her senseless primping session in the Jeep.

The insincere conversation rollicked on until he pulled the Jeep onto the driveway at 614 Scarlet Court. The car doors clambered open and they both piled into the house. Emily was humming while she prepared dinner in the kitchen. Ivan wasn't home from work yet. Everything looked normal but it shouldn't have been normal. Ella was still missing and nobody seemed to care.

"Any word about Ella?" Drake said dryly, searching his mother's eyes, studying her reaction.

She looked up from the saucepan and said pointedly, "Nope, not a word. I'm sure she'll be home today."

Drake knew it was pointless to continue to speak to his mother or Briar. They were empty shells, void of normalcy. They were not right.

"Goin' upstairs to do homework. I have a friend coming over in a bit," Drake sighed.

He climbed the staircase and jetted toward his room. He paused to observe Omen, his only ally in the house, sniffing feverishly at the attic door in the playroom. Drake decided to leave the attic well enough alone. He never liked attics and this one had caused him unexplained anguish. If the house was haunted, the attic was definitely a supernatural refuge. Drake chose to ignore it existed. He had locked it for a reason.

"Omen, c'mon. Let's go big boy," Drake tapped his thigh and Omen snapped out of his quest and trotted softly behind him.

Drake snatched his Xbox controller and pulled up his Xbox Live account to see if Dominick was on his old gamer tag. As Drake expected, he wasn't. He tried to call him on his cell phone and his phone had been disconnected. Drake never had his best friend's home phone number, as he never needed it before. Everybody had a cell phone and checked it frequently throughout the day. He found it entirely strange that his best friend would change his gamer tag and phone number without notifying him.

As a final effort, he checked his Facebook page. Dominick was no longer listed as one of Drake's friends. He performed a search for his name and nothing came up. Had his house gotten to Dominick too? Is this why he went home in the middle of the night? Is this the reason he warned Briar to get out of the house? Drake's mind raced in a fury until he noticed Jade's update on his Facebook news feed. Jade had changed her relationship status from *single* to *in a relationship*. Drake cracked an enormous smile as the doorbell rang. He scampered downstairs and swung the door open for Jade.

"Hey, gorgeous!" Drake leaned toward her, holding on to the front door.

"No, that's you, Drake!"

"Come on up to my room if you dare."

Drake held out his hand for Jade. She took it eagerly.

"It's not the ghosts I'm afraid of," Jade giggled, clutching Drake's hand tightly as they ascended the winding staircase.

Omen was back at the attic door. He sniffed frantically at the door before releasing a barely audible whine.

"What the hell is that dog doing?" Jade asked, pausing to watch Omen's antics.

"Yeah, donno. He was doing it earlier. I think there was a nest of animals up there in the attic when we first moved in. They maybe either left or came back and Omen picked up their scent. I'm not going in there though."

Drake didn't dare mention the fact that both he and Briar had heard what sounded like her voice coming from within the attic, asking for help, and then Briar coincidentally locks herself in there and couldn't get out.

"Why, is that the ghost headquarters?" Jade smiled, throwing herself behind Drake.

Drake laughed to himself at the grim irony of thinking it was just that only moments before.

"*Shhhh,* they might hear you," Drake pressed a finger against Jade's lips playfully. "Let's just say that last time that door was opened, it wasn't a good thing. Come to my room."

Briar was standing strangely in the doorway of her bedroom, looking out into the playroom. Wide eyed, she gazed at Drake with a curious expression. Her eyes drew up to the corner of the playroom ceiling. Drake noticed there was track lighting there. It was quasi-modern and they never needed to turn it on because the playroom received the indirect light from the bedrooms surrounding it and the downstairs.

"What?" Drake echoed.

Briar's mouth turned into a straight line, gazing at the track lighting and then back into Drake's eyes.

"Nothing," Briar spun around and retreated into her room.

18 – Two Days

"What's gotten into your sister? She pretended like she didn't notice me when I saw her after school waiting for you by the tennis courts," Jade asked blithely, shrugging her shoulders, inspecting random tennis trophies from his chest of drawers.

"Wish I knew. Like I said, her and my parents are not the same," Drake rocked back on his heels.

"Your baby sister is still missing, I'm guessing?"

"Yes and mom is going about her normal routine," he added with dismal sarcasm, taking a seat in his computer desk chair.

"Bizarre," Jade said, arching an eyebrow and taking a seat on the bed next to Omen.

"So let me get this straight, Drake. You still believe that telling that freak at the convenience store somehow made your house possess your family by revealing their fears to them?" Jade questioned, her angelic face contorted into a state of confusion.

Drake inhaled deeply, squared his shoulders and faced Jade directly. He wanted her to believe him. He needed her to be on his side. The worst thing that could happen would be for her to believe he was insane and this was all an imaginary story in his head. Drake knew there would be a fine line to walk on as he divulged the details.

"Yes, Jade. I've been completely honest with what has happened here. My parents are acting like robots, like nothing strange happened here and like they don't have a missing kid! Then Briar did a 180 last night but unlike my parents, I can tell that she knows *something*. I can tell that she wants to talk but something is holding her back.

"Let's just go talk to her right now. She's in her room, right? If she is bursting at the seams, maybe I can help pull it out of her?"

"Jade, you could get whatever you wanted out of me but Briar is like a rock. I'd be the only one to break her and I've not been able to. It's hopeless for now."

In deep thought, Jade leaned back, propping herself up on one arm. Her eyes locked into him with an intensity that was overwhelming. Drake anxiously waited for her to reveal what struck her.

"You told that guy in the store you were afraid of failing, right? Being humiliated? Going crazy? Right?"

"Yeah, that's what I said to him," Drake's heart stopped for a moment while waiting for Jade to continue.

Drake was cautious, afraid she would say he had feared going crazy so it had happened to him and none of this was real.

"Well, you never asked what I would have said," she paused, a smile erupting on her face. "I hate thunderstorms. Don't laugh! I know!" Jade giggled, throwing herself back onto the bed.

"Thunderstorms?" Drake shook his head wanly, perplexed.

"Yup! Like a little kid, they freak me out! Second, is animals. I'm so afraid of being attacked by a wild animal. Rats, cats, dogs...it doesn't matter what kind of animal, either."

"You aren't scared of Omen, though," Drake uttered through a sigh, relaxing his shoulders.

He was relieved that she didn't admit that she believed he was insane.

"I know, right? I think it is because I can tell that he is in harmony with you. He seems so trusting of you as if he knows what you are thinking. He's pretty much the only animal I've not been frightened of."

Jade patted Omen on the head. He returned with a gentle lick to the back of her hand.

"He's a great dog. I can't believe my uncle hated him so much."

"Dogs have a way with knowing things. They sense when people are bad. Your uncle must have been a bad person."

"I'll say," Drake mused, rocking back on the chair.

"So back to the plan. What can we do here? Do you want to go back to the Quentin lead and see if he's back in the store? Maybe we can go talk to him? I'd like to ask how the hell he knows who I am!" Jade scoffed, pounding a fist on Drake's pillow.

A plan formed in Drake's mind. He thought if he could spark controversy between his parents over the jester figurine and Uncle Basil's murder, maybe it would break someone's silence. He decided that when Ivan returned home, he would implement the plan. He would say that his mother was afraid he had killed Uncle Basil, then, Drake would demand to know why neither seemed concerned about Ella. With Jade as a witness, one of them was bound to start talking – maybe even Briar. He let Jade in on his plan, she was eager to soak in the details.

"That sounds perfect. But what about the house? That might get everybody to break the silence about your uncle or maybe even Ella, but do you think they know the *house* is getting to them?"

Drake sighed. Jade agreed with his theory about the house. He wasn't crazy.

"Donno. Don't have a clue."

"We should investigate the house. Let's look over every square inch. You said that Omen used to bark in the study, right?"

"Yes, but that was when Basil's things were in there."

"I thought you said he did it after his things went missing."

"Maybe once or twice."

"Let's start in the study and we'll work our way throughout the house. Remember, we started investigating the study and last time, you sent me home? There will be none of that, Drake!" Jade said, eyes smiling.

"Yes, Cap'n Amity, agreed!" Drake chuckled.

"We might find more clues to the murder or to your sister's disappearance somewhere in the house. I'll tell my parents that I'm spending the night with a friend. We can't investigate the rest of the house while everybody's awake so sneak some flashlights in here and later, when everybody is going to bed, I'll hide out in here. Do your parents ever come up here to check on you?"

"I am 16. So, no."

"Perfect," Jade took a blanket off the bottom edge of Drake's bed and laid it on the floor on the other side of his chest of drawers. She took a pillow and laid it on top of the blanket. "Sounds like a plan. Let's start with the study now."

They journeyed to the study, avoiding detection by Briar or Emily. Both were busy in their own worlds, not paying attention to their surroundings. The study door was closed. Drake recalled it being open when he let Jade in the house. He was certain. He reasoned that Emily went in there for something. He turned the doorknob and it was unlocked, opening with a soft click. They crept into the room and shut the door behind them.

"It kind of smells funky in here," Jade whispered loudly.

"It's Basil. He must have stained the room with his stench. He smoked a pipe and sweat all the time. Even in an air conditioned room."

"Gross!"

Drake went straight for the corner of the room that Omen always pointed his bark. He surveyed the walls carefully.

"Drake! Over here. On the wall! It could be blood! How could the police have missed this?!" Jade shrieked in a whisper, standing on the balls of her feet to get a better look at the wall above her.

Drake's mind entered a whirlwind as he investigated the wall. There were small droplets of a dried substance, dark burgundy, contrasting with the dark gray wall. How could the police miss this? The dried drops were a tad over six feet high. Basil was 6'1". Their pattern appeared as though they were sprayed on or as if they had been cast off something. Maybe Basil's head after the jester statue struck it? How could a trained investigator miss such a thing while investigating a possible crime scene of a murder victim? Drake felt foolish for not seeing the drops before but Briar and Jade were with him the last time they investigated the room when they discovered the statue. Drake had called off the investigation upon seeing the blood on the jester and sent Jade home in a panic. They had never finished investigating the room.

"The paint on the wall looks so weird over there in the corner. You can see a faint outline of something," Jade pointed out, running her finger along the wall.

Drake ramped up the intensity of his focus on the wall, eyebrows raised to allow maximum light into his eyes.

"Holy hell, it does look strange," Drake agreed, eyes following the faint line from the baseboard to about seven feet high, over to the right a few feet and then back down to the baseboard.

It was a rectangular shape. Drake got closer and saw a depression in the sheet rock. He pressed it and something made a clicking sound. He had to step back quickly as the wall advanced a few inches. Drake and Jade both gasped from shock. Ivan's car motor hummed from the driveway. Drake glanced over his shoulder at Jade, her eyes widened in anticipation of the discovery. He could only stare, bewildered.

"It's a door. A secret door!" he whispered, unsure of what to do next.

Ivan charged into the house within seconds of his car door slamming. As if he knew what had happened, he marched immediately into the study. Drake pushed the door shut right before Ivan entered the room.

"Hello, young lady. I will need you to go ahead and go home now," Ivan demanded brusquely, eyes flickering between Drake and Jade, face wiped clean of emotion.

"Uh, Dad—

"Not up for debate, Drake. Family meeting, in my room now."

Ivan didn't have time for a discussion. Maybe he had news of Ella? For the first time, Ivan looked concerned about something. Jade nodded her head toward the front door to Drake as if she were asking if he wanted her to leave.

Drake mouthed the words *go upstairs*. Jade hung behind, waited for everybody to convene in the master bedroom, and then tiptoed quietly upstairs toward Drake's room.

Ivan glared at Emily, Drake and Briar for a long moment as they sat anxiously on the edge of the bed. He stood before them, taking a deep breath, mouth twisting. His bronzed eyes hardened as if his irises had frozen solid.

"I have some news. Some awful news," Ivan said, staring past the family before him with despairing eyes.

"What's the matter, Ivan?" Emily said dryly.

Ivan waited, studying their faces to ensure they were listening.

"I have only two days to live. The test results came back this morning and they don't know how I've made it this long. I have a rare, terminal condition. It's an aggressive neurological disease where any moment, my nervous system will shut down completely."

"What!" Terror flickered in Drake's face as he spoke.

Drake felt the room start to spin. He was boneless, weak.

"No, Dad. That can't be right," Briar said in a monotone.

Drake shot a look of panic at Briar. He studied her reaction. The expected words came out of her mouth but she was void of emotion. He glanced at his mother who had tears welling up in her eyes. Was she acting or was she truly feeling something? Drake couldn't tell.

"What was that?" Briar asked coldly, words slow and clear.

It was a thud from upstairs followed by Jade's scream. Immediately, he took off from the master bedroom for his room upstairs, not looking back.

"Jade!" he managed to choke out as he hurled himself up the stairs.

His bedroom door was locked and she was inside, screaming uncontrollably. He couldn't make out what Jade was saying through her hysterics. He searched for Omen and couldn't find him. Maybe he was inside the room with her. But if she was screaming, why was he silent? His mind turned into a mental tornado. He suddenly remembered the tool the police officer used to open the study door to release Briar. He remembered seeing a metal ruler on Briar's desk. It resembled the tool. He dashed into her room and searched frantically. Glancing over, Drake noticed his duct tape repair of her corner baseboard was bulging. Large, hairy spider legs jetted out from the silver barrier, waving aimlessly in the air. Locating the ruler, he returned to the bedroom door. Jade was still screaming in a frenzy. At least she didn't freeze as Briar did when she was frightened. He mimicked how he recalled the officer slid his tool between the frame and the door and the door popped open.

"Oh my God, oh my God, oh my God," Jade shrieked, jerking her head around to glare at Drake.

Jade was balancing on top of the chest of drawers. Two dull grayish brown opossums were at the base of the chest, faces dirty white, baring numerous sharp teeth along their snub-nosed snouts as they hissed. Drake surveying the room. The opossums turning their glowers towards him. Omen wasn't in the room. Omen would have made short work of these two.

"Where's Omen?"

"He's not here, obviously!" Jade screamed, wobbling on top of the chest as she continued to shift her weight from right to left.

One of the opossum's lunged at Drake just as he grabbed his baseball bat. Without a second to spare, he took a swing and connected with the animal's skull. The opossum sailed across the room, hit the wall and tumbled to the ground, leaving a small bloody smear trail.

"Hell yea!" Drake screamed, choking up on the bat and focusing on the other opossum.

Jade's eyes slammed shut and like a marionette puppet released by a puppeteer, she fell from the chest to the floor, legs and arms bending awkwardly in random directions. The opossum's head twitched back to Jade and immediately, it pounced on her chest, baring his teeth, staring hungrily at her neck. Drake dove and grabbed the possum by the scruff of the neck. The opossum fought fiercely to escape, thrashing violently, and gnashing its teeth as it swished its head back and forth. Drake lost his grip as it twisted around and it sunk its teeth into his wrist. Drake let out a blood-curdling howl along with assorted profanities as he stood up, opossum still clamped down on his flesh. He squeezed the opossum's body as hard as he could with his free hand. The pain from the bite seared through his arm and shimmied down his spine like razor blades. He slammed the possum against the wall repeatedly until he felt his skull give way like a cracked nut. Prying the possum's teeth away from his wrist, blood gushed like a crimson river down his arm.

"Jade!"

Drake tossed the possum by the first one he had hit with a baseball bat. It started to twitch. It was still alive and had released a foul odor into the room. Most likely, this was a defense mechanism to make its predators believe it was dead but it didn't fool Drake.

He gently shook Jade, keeping an eye on the befuddled possum coming to consciousness.

"Jade! Are you all right?"

He felt her pulse. It was rapid. He felt her breath. It was warm and recurring. He scooped her up and put her on his bed. He pressed his lips lovingly against her forehead as the opossum locked eyes with him, snout slowly opening, emitting a muted hiss.

"Wanna try me again, stupid?" Drake screamed at the opossum, grabbing his baseball bat again.

The opossum's fur stood up on end as he hissed viciously with the tone and resonance of a buzz saw. Opening his snout as far as it would go and curling his lips back extensively to reveal his yellowed, sharp teeth, the possum started advancing slowly toward Drake, blood seeping from the side of its head and matting into its fur.

"That's it, you're done," Drake exploded, raring back his bat and ending the ferocious creature's life with one swing. "Sorry, Dad, but I had to do it," Drake lamented as he remembered the Henry no kill policy.

"Drake?" Jade mumbled as she started to rouse.

"I'm here. You all right?"

She blinked her eyes slowly, furrowing her eyebrows.

"Yeah, I think so," Jade replied serenely, wearing a mask of mystification.

"Do you remember seeing Omen when you came up here?"

Comprehension flickered on her face but melted quickly into confusion. She narrowed her eyes as she sat in silence deliberating her response.

"I don't remember how I got here," she said slowly. "The last thing I can remember is your dad coming home and the rest is a blur until now. I'm sure it will come back to me in a minute."

"Jade, don't leave me. I need you," Drake's eyes softened as he spoke.

"What did your dad have to say, did he find Ella?" Jade asked, eyes searching Drake for answers.

"He is dying. Has only a couple of days to live."

19 – Broken Trust

Drake got Jade a glass of water and propped her in the bed to get some rest and recover from the trauma. After disposing of the opossum carcasses, Drake searched the house for Omen. He was not in the house. He replayed in his mind when the doors had been opened since he saw Omen last. He couldn't think of a time that Omen could have dashed out of the house. He went outside and searched the back and front of his house. He left out a bowl of dog food and a water bowl in case he had escaped and came back. He figured he could call the animal control officer in town the following day to help find him. It was a small town and at least a small town seemed to have some advantages in this situation. However, Ella was still missing and Drake was losing hope he would ever see her again.

"Drake!" Briar shouted, knocking on Drake's bedroom door.

"Hold on, Bee. Getting dressed," Drake grimaced, noticing Jade had woken up from the knocks.

With eyes narrowed and jaws tightened, he motioned for Jade to stay where she was, throwing a pillow next to her head and ruffling his down comforter to make her existence less noticeable.

"What's up, Bee?" Drake half-opened his bedroom door, standing in the middle, blocking her entrance into the room.

"Mom and Dad said to tell you goodnight. They're going to sleep. That is horrible news about Dad. I don't know if I can sleep tonight," Briar groaned in an artificial tone.

He thought she sounded rehearsed. He didn't buy her sincerity for a moment. This was the same Briar he had rode home with earlier that day that didn't care Ella was missing and had completely changed her line of thinking about Basil's murder, even refusing to speak about it.

"It is a nightmare. Not sure how to deal with it, actually. I'm going to bed. I have a lot of thoughts to sort out. See ya," Drake said rapidly, trying to sound calm.

He shut his bedroom door and the reality of losing his father flooded into his veins. He hadn't had time to process the news of his father's illness before having to rescue Jade. His father only had a couple of days to live. How would he live those days? Would he ever see Ella again before he died? Would he return to normal first or would he die as this bizarre empty shell of what he once was? The news was too much for Drake to handle. Even with Jade in his room, he didn't feel all right. Drake figured given his father's horrible revelation and Jade's traumatic experience, the middle of the night secret investigation was not a good idea. He didn't mind, he needed to get some rest.

"Good night, Drake. If you want to talk about anything, I'm here for you," Jade whispered, having moved to her palette on the floor by the chest of drawers.

Drake took a few deep breaths before he answered. He didn't want to appear emotionally weak in front of Jade. He had to fight off the intense grief that was strangling him. He turned off the lights, moonlight shining inside from the large windows along the wall.

"No, not now," he choked out the words one by one. "Good night, Jade," he tossed himself on his bed.

Drake woke often through the night, each time hoping it was all a dream or more like a nightmare. He leaned over to check on Jade each time and seeing her lying on the floor made him realize it wasn't a dream. She was there and his father had told him he was dying. There wasn't enough time. Why now? Why did his father have to leave them now? Was it some kind of weird karma because he had killed Uncle Basil? He wondered. He wasn't even sure if he would be able to talk to his father again. Life, at this moment, did not seem fair to Drake.

The morning was difficult. Drake had set his alarm for an hour prior to the normal time so he could get Jade out of the house before anyone realized she was there. She woke easily. She probably longed for her own bed.

"It's time," Drake whispered with a restrained voice.

The moonlight over the lake lit the room with a soft elegance. The sun was not due to show its face for another hour.

"Drake. I love you," Jade mumbled, narrowing her eyes in the darkness.

She said the words. He had always heard it was foolish to say those words too early. Maybe she was still asleep and didn't mean to say them. He gauged her actions for a moment before responding.

"What'd you say, Jade?"

Immediately he regretted that he pretended not to hear her.

She gazed into his eyes and smiled, "I better get out of here. I still have to drive home and get ready for school!"

Drake and Jade crept down the stairs. The house was silent. If Omen were home, he would have barked at them as he startled easily. Drake knew Omen was missing from the house and it pained him tremendously. Omen had become an extension of him, an ally.

"Hey, Drake. Wanna take a look behind the secret door in the study real quick?" Jade whispered, barely audible, into Drake's ear.

"Oh yeah, let's check it out," Drake returned in

a soft voice.

They crept up to the study door. He grabbed the doorknob and turned. It was locked. Since the door locked from the inside, Drake would have had to get the ruler from his room but there was not time. It would be too risky to keep Jade there in the house much longer. With Ivan only having two days to live, Drake didn't want a minute of it to be spent upsetting him.

"Can't, it's locked," Drake whispered, shoulders slumped as he gestured to the front door.

He quietly opened the door and realized again that Omen wasn't by his side. He would have been there if he were in the house. As he stepped on to the front porch, he saw the dog food bowl and water bowl were both full. They walked around the dragon statue in the fountain and toward her Honda Prelude. She had parked it far enough in front of their house where they knew Briar couldn't see it from her window. Drake realized Briar wouldn't be looking out her window at the fountain, nonetheless.

"Did I ever tell you that fountain kinda creeps me out?" Jade laughed, swinging open her car door.

"You should have seen it at night with the red lights. Now that was cool! Dad had to change them to blue for Briar, she ruined it," Drake grinned.

She shut her door and rolled down her window. He leaned toward her for a kiss good bye. He wished he hadn't hesitated and had kissed her before she got into the car. She grabbed a handful of his golden hair and with a forceful tenderness, pulled his head inside her car window. She traced the edges of his lips with her tongue before pressing her velvety lips onto his. His mind flew into a rage of regret. Why didn't he use the time in his room last night with Jade? She released her hold on his hair as she pulled away, starting her engine.

"I..." Drake paused. He wasn't sure if he should say the fated words so he changed direction, "I'll see ya in first period."

"Bye, Drake!" Jade returned quietly.

She pulled away and drove down Scarlet Court, Drake watching intently as her tail lights disappeared into the darkness. Drake's stomach twisted into an uncomfortable knot, felt bottomless, as if he were descending the climactic hill of a rollercoaster. With everything that happened to him in the last week, he was unsure if he could remain sane. That is, if he still had his sanity.

He dashed up to his room and quickly got ready for school. After a spell, Briar knocked on his door quietly while he was gathering his things.

"Come in," Drake said flatly.

Briar blew in like a gust of wind and whispered into his ear, "Don't trust them! Don't trust anyone!"

Drake grabbed her arm with a restraining hand, she shook him off. Drake's expression soured as he watched the frenzied play of emotion across Briar's face.

"Briar! Breakfast! Come down here now!" Emily shouted from downstairs.

Briar immediately pushed away and scampered downstairs. Drake followed apprehensively. He was afraid to face his father. He didn't want to see him ill. If he was to die at any moment, Drake was scared to be a part of it, wanting his dad to be the same as he always had been.

"Let's go, Bee," Drake mumbled, grabbing his keys from the kitchen counter.

"Drake, Bee has a doctor's appointment this morning so you go ahead and leave for school." Emily instructed, undaunted.

Briar's face reddened with apprehension and worry as she stood next to Emily.

"What do you have an appointment for, Bee?"

"Girl stuff, Drake! Now go to school!" Emily demanded, shooting Drake a stern look and pointing toward the front door.

Drake was dubious, "But mom, what about Dad? Is he going to work today? Shouldn't we stay home from school and be with him?"

"Dad's already left for work. See you this afternoon!"

20 – Bitter Victory

Thursday was emotionally straining on Drake as his sadness had numbed him. During the evening, he carefully watched his father for signs of illness but to Drake, he appeared physiologically normal. Drake assumed this type of neurological disease was so sudden; there wouldn't be outward signs of disease prior to the fatal strike. Like Drake's mother, Ivan's behavior remained peculiar. Speaking minimally of Ella's disappearance, there was no mention of the oddities in the house or Basil's murder. It was the most arduous range of emotions Drake had ever experienced in his life.

Where Jade was concerned, he struggled on the surface to be the same Drake that she had, possibly by accident, said she loved. Even around her at school on Thursday, he found it difficult to stay in good spirits with his father's impending demise taunting his mind. He found it hard to follow conversations and he knew it was draining her. Jade couldn't come over Thursday night as she was busy with a mid-semester World Geography project that was due on Friday. She had neglected the project upon meeting Drake followed by relatives staying at her home. Drake thought it was best to be alone with his father that night, nonetheless. This was supposed to be his father's last day to live. He wanted to be there for him. He hoped Ivan would finally reveal why he had acted so strangely.

Ella plagued Drake's mind. At school, during his Computer Applications class, he created missing child flyers with Ella's picture on them. Briar was waiting for him after school but she was like ice, even more than before. It was a struggle for him to watch Briar undergo something of which he had no control. He felt helpless but she was not going to break. She had always been so honest with Drake, impenetrably loyal. Whatever it was that had control of Briar was stronger than Drake could imagine. As they drove home from school, Briar begrudgingly watched Drake post his flyers on various light poles around Shady Oaks, constantly repeating that the police had her investigation under control and he didn't need to interfere.

Mysteriously, the flyers disappeared from the light poles nearly as fast as he had put them up. Later that evening, he notified his parents about the disappearing flyers and they responded that they were in close contact with the police every day and there had not been any updates on Ella's whereabouts and that was all they could do for now. They told Drake he was overstepping the boundaries by littering the town with flyers.

Drake had seen movies involving missing children and every time, the parents were hysterical and constantly on the television pleading with the kidnappers to release their child without harm. It simply didn't make sense that they were nonchalantly going on about their lives.

Friday morning gave Drake a new sense of excitement. At breakfast, his father looked to be in great health and spirits. He had made it past his two-day prediction of doom. Drake talked himself into believing the doctors were wrong about his diagnosis. If Ivan only had two days to live and the two days were up, he certainly didn't look like a man about to die.

Friday afternoon would be the first match of the tennis tournament against Wild Flower High School. Coach Walter had warned that he had to maintain his undefeated record, especially since he was moving down to a less competitive school. This was his chance to prove to everybody that he hadn't lost his talent. This was a 4A school with 4A competitors. There was no reason why Drake shouldn't win the men's singles division of the tournament. Jade was going to be there in the stands to support Drake. She stood by his side, even with his recent melancholy demeanor. He was excited to show Jade what he was known for back in Austin. He felt alive again.

At lunch, all Drake could talk about was the upcoming tournament. It gave him a sense of normalcy. He felt complete again. He no longer believed his father was sick, as he hadn't seen one sign of illness. As Ella popped into his mind, however, his emotions dipped like a rollercoaster.

Jade and Drake walked out to the back parking lot. As they approached his Jeep, they noticed the back tire was flat. He had only fifteen minutes to get to the Deadwood Tennis Complex for the start of the tournament.

"I've got a can of Flat Fixer in the back, hold on," Drake shouted, rushing around the Jeep to the back compartment.

He grabbed the can, swirled over to the flat tire and unscrewed the cap of the tire valve. He glanced over at the rubber of the tire. Multiple locations of the tire had deep gashes. It wasn't just a flat. Someone had slashed the tire, rendering the Flat Fixer useless.

"Damn!" Drake shouted, furious, the word exploding out of him.

Acid trickled through Drake's veins as he took a deep breath and stared at the ground for a long moment.

"Whoa, who would do that, Drake?"

His face was hard and bitter.

"Who do you think?" Drake said grimly. "The only person that has a vendetta against me. The only person that wouldn't be able to stand it if I won this tournament!"

"Nigel Sage," Jade said, shaking her head slowly in disbelief.

"I've obviously got a spare tire. It looks like it's only one tire he destroyed. But I won't make it in time. I'll be disqualified."

Drake sighed in frustration, tensing his shoulders, pacing.

"Let's go. My car is over there!" Jade said in a booming voice, darting across the parking lot to her Honda.

They spun away from the parking lot, making it to the Tennis Complex with a minute to spare. Nigel, with a hunch that Drake wouldn't make it to the tournament on time, had already asked the officials to remove Drake from the schedule. Drake didn't arrive late so the official penciled him back in, but facing a different opponent than he was originally scheduled. Drake jogged onto the court and was pleased to find a competitor across the court that he knew he could defeat. He laughed to himself as he saw whom Nigel was facing in the adjacent court – the exact court that Drake would have been on per the original schedule. His opponent was a beast of a man, could not have been a teen. He was larger than any opponent Drake had ever faced in 5 A matches. Karma had reared its ugly head as Nigel was about to lose his perfect record.

"Let's go, Drake!" Jade screamed from the stands, clapping her hands in excitement.

Nigel shot a glower at Jade as he snarled his upper lip. His eyes narrowed as he arched a thick eyebrow in a fury.

He jogged over toward Drake's court and with a sinister scowl he scoffed, "Hey Drake. Bet ya didn't know that Jade chick was out with Gaven Phoenix on Thursday night, did ya?" Nigel laughed, jogging back to the service line of his court.

Ice shot down Drake's spine and he could hear the blood pulsing faster in his head. He drew in a long, deep breath, trying to ignore what Nigel shouted across the courts. Drake hadn't seen Jade on Thursday night. How would Nigel know that? It could be true. It was game time.

It was all a blur. His opponent served first and the first game was over at an instant. Drake, missing from the game mentally, looked like a hacker. He kept finding himself in no man's land on the court and shanked some easy returns he would have aced back in sixth grade. His opponent was more than beatable. Drake couldn't get the image of Jade being out with Gaven on Thursday night out of his mind. The sting of betrayal seeped through his body. If it were true, Drake had nobody. Nigel's mouth stretched into a sneer as he heard the final score of the first game.

"C'mon, Drake. Let's do this!" Jade screamed, her voice, tinged with disloyalty, hurt his psyche.

Drake's eyes flashed back at Jade. He studied her, confused. She had a concerned look upon her face. She mouthed the words *I love you*, forcing a smile to burst free on Drake's face. He breathed deeply. It felt good. At that moment, he knew Nigel was lying. He didn't know how he knew he wasn't with Jade on Thursday night, but Nigel was a liar and Drake had to show whom the better tennis player was.

The announcer blasted the final score of Nigel's game. It was 6-3. Nigel lost to the beast and a glint of bliss flickered in Drake's eyes. With Drake's mind focused and a newfound contentment, he didn't lose another point the rest of the evening. He had one more day of the tournament on Saturday and was a leading contender.

Jade was waiting anxiously for him at the gate of the courts. Without hesitation, she threw her arms around him and squealed, kissing him repeatedly on the neck.

"You are awesome, Drake! Like a pro out there!"

Drake pressed his sweat infused lips against her forehead and gave her a transient kiss.

"Thank you, Jade. I kind of messed up the first game but I had to shake something out of my mind," Drake said cautiously, gazing into her eyes.

Yanking a towel from his tennis bag, he wiped the sweat from his face.

"I'm so gross, sorry," Drake apologized for his state of hygiene, eyes sincere.

"I think you smell wonderful. It's the smell of a winner!" Jade chuckled.

Nigel stormed toward Drake, his eyes burning with a ferocious intensity.

"Hey punk. Thanks for being late. See ya got to play the easy punk and I had to take on the guy you were supposed to play. Did it on purpose, didn't ya punk?"

Nigel's words swirled in his head. He was fraught with disbelief that the guy who slashed his tires was now attacking him about being late. He tried to breathe normally, needing to concentrate to say the right words.

"Nigel—

"Mr. Sage, punk. I'm about to beat your ass once and for all."

Drake shot his eyes beyond Jade. Quentin was standing a short distance behind her. He was there, at the tournament.

"Excuse me," Drake attempted to bypass Nigel to get to Quentin.

As Drake tried to pass, Nigel seized Drake by the arm and swung him around, tossing him to the ground.

"Don't ever disrespect me punk—

Drake's head smacked the concrete of the sidewalk and he fought to remain conscious, blinking his eyes furiously to keep sight of Jade. He heard her scream. Unsure if he had blacked out, he slowly scrambled to his feet. The voices surrounding him were full of energy but Drake heard them as if he were far away. As he rose to his feet, he saw Jade and Nigel in a heated discussion, the voices soon came clear at full volume.

"I'll give you some of what you got in third grade if you don't get out of my face," Nigel scoffed, clenching his fists.

As Drake came to his full senses, he lunged in between Jade and Nigel, pushing Nigel square in the chest, causing him to stumble backward. He looked around for Quentin. He was gone. Nigel, surprised that Drake had the courage to wage war, furrowed his brow; face reddening as he fought to gain balance. The anger seemed to hurl him into near convulsions as he pressed his clenched fist against his side, rocking forward onto the balls of his feet, leaning toward Drake. They exchanged static glowers for a cold minute before Jade gently tugged at Drake's arm.

The tournament director marched up to the fiery standoff. He snarled in a gruff tone that if they didn't get into their cars and leave the complex immediately without incident, Deadwood High School would be disqualified from the tournament and possibly all future tournaments.

"He's not worth it, Drake," Jade pleaded, gently guiding Drake by the elbow.

Nigel scrambled for a minute, exhaling loudly. He glared at the tournament director before turning toward Drake.

"You dodged this bullet, punk. Next time you won't have Mr. Proper Pants over there bailing you out. You and the tramp better get outta here b'fore I change my mind and blast both of you."

21 —Alone

Drake's head throbbed from the impact of the concrete sidewalk. The adrenaline had subsided, pain taking its place. He knew he still had to change his tire back at the Deadwood High School parking lot. *Briar!* Drake realized he forgot to tell Briar to arrange for a ride home from school. He also forgot to tell his parents about the tournament. He grabbed his iPhone and checked to see if he had a missed message from Briar or his parents. Nothing.

"Man, I *forgot* her!" Drake shouted, throwing his clenched fists against his temples.

"What's wrong, Drake?" Jade inquired, both hands firm on the steering wheel.

"I forgot Briar. I always take her home from school. I suppose I was so distracted with everything that's been going on and with the tournament; I forgot to mention it to anyone this morning."

"She's probably still waiting at school or she called your mother. She *is* fourteen years old."

"I know but it's not like me to flake like that. Also, why wouldn't she text me?" Drake was befuddled. Jade drove up to the front of the school, Briar was not there. They pulled in the back and Drake scanned the parking lot, his car was the only one there, and Briar was nowhere around.

"I'll call mom and see if she's heard from her."

To Drake's surprise, Emily answered the phone in a cheerful voice. Emily explained that Briar went home with a friend from school, apologizing for forgetting to tell Drake that she didn't need a ride home. After hanging up the call, he let out an arduous sigh.

"So, what's the verdict?" Jade inquired, maneuvering the Honda next to Drake's Jeep.

"Mom said Briar went home with a new friend. *She* forgot to tell *me* of all things," Drake jazzed with respite, shaking his head.

Jade's eyes brightened at the good news.

"You did awesome today, Drake. I'm so proud of you!" Jade shrieked, climbing out of her car.

Drake followed her lead, yanked the jack from the back, unleashing the spare tire from the back door.

"Thanks, Jade. That means a lot that you were there for me," Drake paused, searching for the right words, "I have something to ask you. I'm not the jealous type or anything but Nigel said something on the court today."

"What's that?" Jade said softly, eyebrows pulling together in mystification.

Drake squared his shoulders and faced Jade directly. He felt as though he had to force the words to continue, "He said that you were with Gaven Phoenix on Thursday night. Is that true?"

A look of shock spread slowly across Jade's face. She tilted her head to the side and deliberated how to respond. Drake regretted ever asking her. He now feared she would never speak to him again.

"Are you kidding me? Of course not! I told you I was working on a project that was due on Friday. You think I would lie to you? I don't even know Gaven!" Jade howled, stern eyes tightly focused on Drake.

Drake pretended for a moment to be in deep thought, he looked down at the parking lot, taking in a few shallow breaths. Shear happiness flooded through his body, his core turned weightless.

"That's what I thought. I just had to ask. Sorry for even asking you about it," Drake said, pulling her in close and wrapping his arms around her.

Jade returned the embrace, squeezing his chest tightly. She pulled away slightly, laying her head on his chest. He tightened his embrace, smiling. Drake pointed his chin towards the sky assessing the duskiness and noticed the sun was descending.

"Let's change this tire, baby. It'll be dark soon," Jade whispered, leaning up to kiss his neck.

Straining to read the old, tattered manual, Drake followed the instructions and changed the tire. He had seen Ivan do it a couple of times but actually doing it was another venture.

"Come over tonight," Drake insisted, twisting the last lug nut, chunking the manual and jack into the car.

"Only if we can go in that secret door we found," Jade chuckled under her breath. "Did you ever go in there?"

Drake had forgotten about the secret door in the study. He remembered that he and Jade had tried to look at it the morning he sneaked her out of his house but the door was locked. He hadn't seen the study door open since, but then again he wasn't looking, as he was preoccupied with watching his father.

"Of course, anything you want," Drake noted, smoothing her silky hair and outlining her chin with his bent index finger.

"Be right behind ya," Jade pushed away and jetted toward her Honda.

Drake's features melted into a mask of serenity as he roared his engine and pulled out of the high school parking lot. Jade followed behind as they coursed the bridge and up to Scarlet Court. Drake hesitated at the Shady Oaks Mart at the corner of Whispering Point Drive and Lakefront Avenue. He desperately wanted to confront Quentin about being at the Tennis Complex earlier but thought it best to keep Jade far away from him. They pulled up into the circle drive at 614 Scarlet Court. The fountain's blue lights were shining through the water as it cascaded from the lion's belly. Drake missed the red water.

Jade bounded out of her car and pranced over to Drake's car. She grabbed his hand, pulling him toward the house, outlining shapes on the back of his hand with her thumb as they walked.

"Oh my gosh, what about your father, Drake. How is he doing? Should I even be here?"

"Hey, calm down," Drake rubbed her back gently. "I don't think he is ill. I'm nearly certain the doctors were wrong, happens all the time. My father was absolutely fine this morning."

They strolled inside the house and it was dead silent, a faint smell of paint lingering in the air. His mom had been home only an hour before and his father should have been home from work already. He stepped back outside to inspect the driveway. His father's car wasn't there. He looked down at his iPhone and noticed a text message from his mother. She stated they were stopping by the police department to get an update on Ella and then going out for dinner and would be home late. She also stated that Briar was spending the night out.

"House to ourselves, Jade!" Drake said, a grin stretching wide across his face.

Jade took a fervent step backward. She studied Drake's squared jaw, up to his sharp cheekbones before moving her eyes to lock into a gaze with Drake, eyes appearing as liquid topaz. She dropped down to follow his shape, rounding his shoulders and stalling to view his t-shirt straining over his nicely developed chest. She bit her lip, embarrassed to be admiring him.

Drake lifted Jade onto his shoulder and carried her over to the living room couch. He flipped a switch next to the fireplace and the gas line underneath the fake log roared and burst into flames.

"Someone doing some painting in here?" Jade inquired.

"Donno. My mom is always doing art projects though, so probably. It's smelled like that for a day or two. Want something to drink?"

"I'll take a glass of water," Jade said, smiling timidly.

"You got it!"

Drake bounced off the couch and ran into the kitchen. He heard a few clicks in the front and back of the house. He was confused as to what Jade was doing.

"Here ya go."

Drake placed the glass of water on the end table by the couch. He glanced around the foyer and into the back of the house to determine what the noise was that he heard.

"Did you hear that clicking noise?"

"Yes. The deadbolt on the front door just locked on its own."

Drake gauged Jade's expression for a moment. Frozen, he took a few breaths before responding.

"Are you certain?" he said, inspecting both doors from the foyer.

Jade nodded zealously.

"Dead positive. I was sitting right here on the couch and just happened to be looking out the window on the door. When I heard the noise, I looked over at the lock and it twisted all on its own. You can't do that from outside can you?"

"No. It's only on the inside," Drake scanned the room. "Let me call my parents, hold on."

Thunder rumbled from outside and drops of rain dusted the front door windows. Drake grabbed his iPhone. No signal.

"What the hell? Do you have a signal on your phone?"

Jade pulled her iPhone from her pocket and thumbed around for a few seconds.

"Nope. Nothing. Maybe the storm?"

"I don't remember seeing rain in the forecast, strange."

Drake lunged to the house phone. It was dead. Lightning flashed in the windows, followed by a rapid succession of thunderclaps. The rain intensified. Jade started to tremble, face like a stone sculpture. Another boom of thunder vibrated the walls of the house. Jade started breathing rapidly, teeth gritted, hands clenched into a double fist. Drake, remembering she was scared of thunderstorms, dashed over.

"Hey, hey, hey. None of that. It's only a thunderstorm," Drake calmed, watching the tears dew up on the rims of her eyes, rubbing her back with gentle pats.

"I know, sorry for being such a baby. I've always been like this."

"But you are with me. I won't let anything happen to you," Drake said, eyes sharp on Jade's face, watching her reaction closely.

Jade, lost in thought, concentrated on the storm while Drake scurried around to find a way to get the front or back doors open to no avail. Jade suddenly rose from the couch and stomped her foot.

"Let's investigate. Let's find that door, Drake. I want to get my mind off of the storm," Jade said, lips pulling up at the corners.

Drake spun around, confused by her sudden twist. He shrugged away from the front door, gesturing for her to follow him into the study. The door was slightly ajar. As they crossed the threshold into the room, Drake noticed the paint fumes grew stronger.

"You got it," he replied serenely.

Marching straight for the wall where they had discovered the secret door, Drake felt along the painted sheet rock for the depression he had found. Nothing. The wall was smooth. They stood back, searching for the faint outline of the door. The wall had been repainted; the door was no longer there.

"You kidding me?" Drake sneered. "It was here, right? Am I losing it or something?"

Two successive thunderclaps shuddered the walls, Jade jumped close to Drake in response.

"Uh, yeah. It was right there. I saw it too, Drake. When you pushed right here," Jade pointed to a specific spot on the wall, "the door clicked and came forward."

"You positive?"

"Yes, absolutely."

"Then someone has covered up that door. But who would do that? My mom is home all day; my dad has gone to work. Why would mom do that?"

"Donno, Drake but I'm starting to feel like I'm on an episode of Scooby Doo with all these mysteries."

"DRAKE! A PIPE! LOOK!" Jade screeched, pointing to the floor behind the black suede futon couch.

"Whoa, that's my Uncle Basil's pipe!" Drake snatched it, inspecting it, cautiously smelling the residue. "Yup, that's his pipe. My gosh, if we would have found this before, we would have known he must have died in this room. That man doesn't go anywhere without this pipe. It's really expensive so it's not like he'd just go get another one."

"So that's that. The blood on the wall, the jester, now the pipe. He died here. So what does that mean?

"It means that one of my parents is a murderer."

The house phone rang. Drake shot a confused glance to Jade before taking off to answer it. He snatched the phone from the cradle.

"Hello?"

A momentary pause ensued before a voice sounded. The voice sounded official.

"Is this Drake Henry?"

"Uh, yes it is," Drake's eyebrows made a channel of confusion.

Jade anxiously stood in front of Drake, reading his face.

"This is Monty Williams. I'm the director of the Texas State Tennis Association. I've been made aware that the opponent you faced today in the first match of the tournament at Deadwood City Tennis Complex is actually not an eligible player for a high school tournament. He is only an eighth grader at Wild Flower Junior High, illegally playing up with his high school. Therefore, you are disqualified from the tournament, as there is no way for you to make up this match. There is no reason for you to attend the rest of the tournament tomorrow. My apologies, good night."

Drake's face was frozen as the phone clicked, followed by a dial tone. The front and back door deadbolts clicked as he dropped the phone into the cradle.

"What is it, Drake?" Jade asked, jaws clenched with the intensity of her concern.

The thunderstorm silenced at an instant.

"The tournament. I'm out. The guy I beat was only an eighth grader. No matter what I do, I can't seem to win. I give," Drake said, eyes hardening as he stared past Jade.

"Not true at all, Drake. I saw you play, you are a winner. I'm sure your parents can appeal to the director, right?"

"Not in time for me to play in the tournament. I'll look like I forfeited or that I was disqualified. Either way, the college scouts won't like it," Drake shrieked, slamming his fist on the dining room table.

"Drake, the doors," Jade whispered loudly, pointing to the deadbolt on the front door.

Drake dredged hastily to the door, swinging it open. The rain had ceased and it was seemingly dry outside.

22 —Toxic Rescue

"Let's get out of here. I've got someone I want to see."

Jade followed Drake into the circle driveway. She climbed into the passenger seat of the Jeep, throwing the seatbelt on before locking eyes with Drake.

"Wow, quick storm. Everything is already dry," Jade marveled, surveying the front walkway.

"Guess since it's been so warm lately, the water didn't have a chance to soak in. Donno?"

"What does the convenience store clerk have to do with this and why now? He couldn't possibly—

"He has everything to do with it, Jade! He was at the tournament. He probably set me up!"

Understanding washed over Jade's face before the mystified mask returned.

"But why?"

"That's what I've got to know."

The car ride to the store was filled with tension. Drake was focused, hands purposely clenched on the steering wheel, eyes burning intensely into the road ahead. Jade's apprehension was apparent as she stared out the passenger window, hands folded in her lap. Drake pulled into the parking lot of the Shady Oaks Mart, gravel popping, hitting the side of the car.

"What are you going to say?" Jade asked softly, glint of nervousness flashed in her eyes.

"Donno," Drake mumbled as he scrambled out of the car, "stay here."

Drake flew into the store, swinging open the front door and lunging to the front check out. He grabbed the lip of the counter, leaning over to face Quentin. Nobody was there.

"Quentin! I want to talk to you!" Drake screamed, tapping on the counter.

Rumbling followed by footsteps echoed from the back of the store. Drake anxiously awaited, eyes narrowed, jaws tightened, blood pulsing fast through his veins.

A demure elderly lady surfaced in the aisle, whitened hair teased in careless directions, papery thin skin wrinkled in large grooves. Drake gasped at the sight of her.

"Can I help you, young man?" she quavered, hands trembling methodically.

"I need to see Quentin right now," Drake responded rapidly, eyes tense and angry.

"I'm sorry, young man. I've never heard of anyone named Quentin," the woman crowed, hobbling to the magazine rack, straightening the daily papers with unsteady, frail hands.

"You are saying that a man named Quentin doesn't work here in this store? Have you been away on vacation or did you just start working here?"

The elderly lady turned around slowly, studying Drake. She shook her head in incredulity, taking a deep breath and letting out a labored sigh. Her sunken eyes smoldered with irritation as she grimaced at Drake.

"No, I've not taken a vacation in thirty years. I own this store. I'm the only one that works here. Paw died last year, leavin' me to handle everything," she scolded, narrowing her eyes, face contorting into a deepened scowl.

Drake, mystified, scoured back to the car, shoulders hunched over in defeat.

"Drake, I've got to get home. I don't want to leave you like this but can you take me back to my car?"

Drake leaned over, placing his cheek on her hair, smelling the enchanting scent of her skin, staring aimlessly at the car seat.

"Sorry. I'm sorry for acting so crazy. Just with everything going on, I think that most of all, my baby sister is getting to me the most. I kind of feel like I might lose control at any moment if she is not found."

"I can't imagine what it feels like, Drake. I don't have a brother or sister but if I did, I can imagine how much I would care for them. It must be a nightmare," Jade said caringly, stroking her fingers through his golden hair.

The remainder of the weekend was uneventful. Saturday, Drake sulked around the house, mourning the tennis tournament debacle, shooting off an email to Coach Walter back in Austin to get some sound, trusted advice. Ivan seemed healthy as a horse and Emily pretended to be working with the police in efforts to find Ella. Drake told his parents about the deadbolts locking on their own again and Ivan went on a quest to figure out the issue, even traveling to a home improvement store to purchase new locks. Briar never came home, staying the weekend with her new friend from Deadwood City. Drake believed this to be strange considering she had never spent more than one night away at a time. Drake spent some time searching Quentin on the internet in every way he could think to find him to no avail. It didn't make sense to him that the elderly lady had said she didn't know who she was when he was clearly there at the counter both times he had visited the store prior to that day.

Monday at school, Drake and Jade decided to skip English class to talk about things. They trekked over behind the football field behind the school. After meticulously lining out the details in handwritten scrawl on a spiral notebook, they concluded that Jade had revealed her fears of animals and storms while she was in the house and both fears manifested themselves while Jade was in that house. They could only explain this by pointing to the supernatural so they tabled the discussion on that until a later time. They went on to discuss Quentin and his possible involvement with the events at the house and with Drake's family as well as how the elderly store owner could have never known he was working there. They decided Quentin was definitely involved since the fears for his family revealed to Quentin at the store had also come to fruition. They were still baffled as to how and why Quentin was connected and how the storeowner didn't know about his existence. What could an absolute stranger want from them? In the end, they couldn't answer this question.

Jade settled upon the idea of calling her uncle, a long time homicide investigator from New York City, to get some advice. She stated that he often worked with psychic analysts who assisted in finding the bodies of victims when they were missing. Given that he worked with a supernatural force in his line of work, Jade believed he might be able to shed a tad of light upon the supernatural events involved with the house. She planned to meet up with Drake on Thursday at his house in hopes that she would have spoken to him by then. She assured Drake that her uncle wouldn't turn in his parents to the authorities if she divulged the details of what they had found in the house.

As Drake trudged toward the tennis locker room, he spotted Nigel Sage. He was walking backwards across the bus path, chatting ardently with a girl, a sophomore, giddy with excitement that the infamous Nigel Sage was paying attention to her. Drake shot a glance at a school bus traveling at a high speed, rounding the corner. The driver seemed preoccupied with something on the drop down mirror in front of him. Nigel, unaware of the bus's arrival, continued to shout flirty remarks across the way, the girl giggling with enchantment in return. The intersection was rapidly becoming apparent as Drake watched in horror. Even Nigel didn't deserve to be hit by a bus. As the bus straightened out to its final approach toward Nigel, Drake chucked his gym bag onto the sidewalk and soared at top speed towards Nigel, knocking him out of the way just in time as the bus drove by, both rolling in the grass next to the curb. The brakes screeched, tires scorching the pavement, the bus abruptly halted, releasing a gust of exhaust from the mufflers. A bald, middle-aged bus driver ambled out of the side door, furious, glaring at Nigel as he lay on the ground.

"Why you playin' in the street for? Why you do that? You coulda been killed! I coulda lost my job! Stay out of the streets and watch where you goin'," the angry driver howled, shaking his fist in the air.

"You all right, Nigel?" Drake waned, dusting off the dirt and gravel from his arm, ambling to his feet.

Nigel remained on the ground, a blank expression. He took a deep breath, his cold eyes on Drake, watching his every move.

"That bus...it was about to—

"I know. Thanks," Nigel interrupted Drake's apprehensive play by play, rolling over and stumbling to his feet.

On the courts, Nigel was amicable but obviously restraining himself from harassing Drake. Gaven was absent, hence the formula to Nigel being tolerable at best. Drake decided to take a huge risk at making Nigel an ally.

"Nigel, um, I know we haven't really gotten along since I moved here. I was just wondering—

"Spit it out," Nigel snarled.

"Maybe you'd want to come over after school and hang out?"

Drake winced, fearing Nigel's unpredictable response. He turned his head to the side slightly, narrowing his eyes.

"I can swing by and check out your place on Thursday afternoon. Your hot sister gonna be there?" Nigel glowered, sizing up Drake's reaction.

Drake pondered his reply for a moment, sorting through a rainbow of emotions about other males, especially Nigel Sage, having intimate feelings toward Briar.

"Yeah, she should be home on Thursday afternoon. So, you think she is hot?"

"Yeah, I'd do that."

Drake fought resentment from spreading across his face and captured a couple of quick, thin breaths.

"Oh, gotcha. Well, you know where I live. See ya," Drake chanted, brushing off toward his Jeep. "Thursday it is."

23 – Vengeance Seed

Briar wasn't waiting for him by the Jeep.

Hmmmm, no Briar again? He thought grimly, searching around the parking lot. He checked his iPhone. There was a text from her. *Gotta ride, see ya.*

Drake drove home, ambled into the house to find Emily and Officer Nelson speaking at the dining room table. They both paused to watch Drake as he whizzed by and up the stairs. He jogged up to the upstairs playroom, peeking into Briar's room. Nobody there. He hadn't seen Briar and she still wasn't home. He listened for her for the next hour. She never appeared so he shot her a text message. No reply. Emily had been making excuses that she was staying with a new best friend but Drake didn't believe the story.

Dominick's cell phone number had been changed and he still wasn't using his old Xbox gamer tag. He also hadn't logged on to his World of Warcraft online account since before he drove to Shady Oaks and with the same top level character since the first of 7th grade, he probably hadn't gone more than 1-2 consecutive days without logging on. Something was definitely wrong with Dominick and it had started while at Drake's house.

Drake grabbed his Xbox controller, finding one of his other friends from Austin, instructing them to confer a message to Dominick. He bluntly stated to tell Dominick if he claims to have been Drake's true friend for the last ten or so years, he will drive to Shady Oaks and meet him in front of his house on Friday at 6 PM. He hoped that

Dominick would come to his senses and snap out of the quest to cut Drake out of his life.

Since rescuing Nigel from the near bus hit, Nigel slowly over the next few days trended back into his old ways towards Drake. Drake wondered if he would still come by on Thursday as he promised. A pattern had ensued with Nigel. If Gaven were there, Nigel would browbeat and harass Drake. If Gaven was not there, Nigel was minimally tolerable. Drake believed if he could get Nigel away from school and Gaven, he might actually turn him into a valuable ally.

On Thursday, Drake rushed home from school and took a seat in the living room, anxiously anticipating Nigel's arrival. The doorbell rang. It was Jade. Ten minutes later, as soon as they settled in Drake's room, the doorbell rang again. Emily, speaking to Officer Nelson again at the dining room table, shouted from downstairs for Drake to answer the door.

"Who would that be? The cop is already here." Jade inquired.

"Oh yeah, forgot to tell you. I saved Nigel from being hit by a bus on Monday right before tennis. Invited him over—

"NO! You didn't invite that pig to your house. What? Drake, are you insane?" Jade's face reddened, her voice low and tense. "You saved Nigel? Why?"

"He's a human being, Jade. Of course, I saved him from being mangled or possibly killed. As far as why I invited him over, I guess I was caught in the moment and saw a way to get him off my back. If you turn your enemies into friends, you'll have no enemies."

Drake shrugged his shoulder and started for the staircase.

"Drake, it's a mistake. Nigel is evil to the core. Think of what all he's done to you since you've been at Deadwood High. There is no way he'll ever be a friend. He is jealous of you. You are the only one at that school that can compete with him in athletics. Don't answer it," Jade pleaded, fingers intertwined, shaking her two handed fist as she spoke each carefully selected word. As if on cue, a lonely tear rolled down her cheek.

"Jade, I've just got to try. I need tennis. With Nigel hating me, I will have to give up on my scholarships for college," Drake scuffled down the stairs, swinging open the door to expose Nigel, standing with arms folded across his chest.

"Hey, punk. So what's going on over here? You gonna have a party or something or are you gonna try to hit on me in your room, pansy boy," Nigel scoffed, strutting into the foyer, nudging Drake aside.

Emily continued to meet with Officer Nelson at the dining room table, giving a slight nod as Nigel walked into the foyer.

"Hey, what's up Nigel? Not really a party but Jade's here, C'mon," Drake uttered nervously, rambling up the stairs.

Nigel stomped behind Drake, chuckling with every step. Drake found his behavior unnerving, wishing he wouldn't have invited him over. Nothing had really changed, even with saving his life. Jade was appearing to be right. They reached the top of the stairs and Nigel laid eyes upon the hot pink walls of Briar's bedroom. He dashed into her room and rudely ransacked her things.

"This your hot sister's room? Whoa, check it," Nigel jeered, ambling into Briar's room and rudely sifting through her things, tossing them out of place.

"Yeah, but come in here, Jade is waiting in my room," Drake asserted, waving at Nigel to head the opposite direction.

Nigel continued to sift through Briar's things as Drake looked on in annoyance, pleading with his eyes for Nigel to sojourn. Nigel shrieked with joy as he uncovered her panty drawer. He held out a red, lacy pair followed by a black cotton pair, both boy short style. A mocking smile erupted across his face as he tucked a hot pink thong inside of his pocket.

"Hey, man. That's not cool. Put that back, Briar will kill me," Drake pleaded, shoulders slumped.

Jade strolled up behind Drake, shaking her head in disgust.

Nigel opened another dresser drawer. It was her bra drawer. Outstretching a white cotton bra in front of his face, he inspected the size and chuckled, throwing it back down in the drawer.

"Freshmen," he sneered, chuckling. "Guess I'll have to wait until next year to get at her. It'd only be a disappointment right now," Nigel continued.

Drake's impending fury was unbridled. With lips sealed, he inhaled deeply through his nostrils. He strained to remember who Nigel was and what he could do for him.

"C'mon man, let's go," Drake bellowed, pushing Jade gently toward his room, hoping Nigel would follow.

To Drake's astonishment, Nigel tailed them into Drake's room. Jade rolled her eyes fervidly as Nigel filtered through Drake's things as he had done in Briar's room. Drake wanted him to do it as he had many of his tennis trophies, newspaper articles and other accolades for Nigel to see, even to hold in his hands, forcing realization that Drake was a true tennis competitor. Nigel, upon seeing the memorabilia, abruptly hurled himself onto Drake's bed, bouncing the bed so harshly that Jade nearly popped off the edge.

"So is this all you do, sit in here, play video games while your girlfriend, or whatever you claim to be, watches you?" Nigel snappishly added, eyes widened in sarcasm, waving his bulky arms in the air.

"Pretty much, I guess. Kinda lame, huh? What is it that you do in your spare time?" Drake inquired, trying to remain polite, while in the back of his mind formulating a plan to get rid of Nigel as quickly as possible.

"We egg houses, chunk rocks at cars from the rooftops of buildings, vandalize things, terrorize homeless people with air horns. You know, fun stuff that you wouldn't know anything about," Nigel barked gruffly, yanking open his nightstand drawer and slamming it back shut.

A heavy metal song echoed from the speakers of Nigel's cell phone. He snatched the phone from his back pocket, accepted the call with his index finger, letting out a massive sigh. Drake looked at Jade wearing a mask of apology as she shook her head, blinking her eyes slowly.

"Gaven, s'up brother?"

There was silence while Gaven responded. Drake and Jade exchanged looks of frustration.

"Yeah, I'm at Drake's house. It's lame over here. Yeah, bud, come on over and liven this party up," Nigel scorned, eyebrows furrowed in resentment.

Another pause while Gaven responded. Nigel returned with a furious bout of laughter.

"A'ight man, see ya in a minute," Nigel rasped, ending the call with his thumb.

"You invited Gaven Phoenix over here?" Drake said hesitantly, staring blankly past Nigel, not wanting to hear the answer.

"No, he invited himself, I just gave him permission. He happens to be around the corner. Be here in a minute. We gotta get something going here, Drake. You are lame."

Within a minute, the doorbell rang.

"You weren't kidding. He *was* around the corner," Jade added mordantly.

"Well, don't be rude, Drake. Go get the door," Nigel hissed, curling his lip to expose his glistening white teeth, lining his chinstrap beard with his thumb and index finger as he glared at Jade.

Jade quickly responded, "I'll go with you, Drake."

"No, you'll stay here," Nigel scorned, grabbing onto Jade's arm.

Not knowing if Jade would be safe alone with Nigel, Drake hesitated at the doorway.

"Go, punk. I'm about to pound your face in memory of the good ole' days."

Drake, believing he could answer the door and return within a minute, jetted toward the staircase and bounded to the front door. He swung open the door and Gaven Phoenix was standing there, massive arms crossed on his chest. He was still wearing sunglasses; Drake started to believe he didn't even have eyes. Gaven's mouth curled up at the corners as he walked inside, pushing Drake against the doorframe.

"Where's the party?"

Emily looked up from her meeting with Officer Nelson with an anxious expression at seeing Gaven. Drake curiously watched the exchange between Gaven and Emily. Possibly something was said or happened the day that Nigel and Gaven brought Emily and Ella home from 7 Point Island. Drake didn't know what it was, but whatever had happened in the past between his mother and Gaven Phoenix was making her look very anxious now.

"Mom, you all right?" Drake ambled over to Emily, leaving Gaven in the foyer.

"Of course she is all right, young man. Carry on," Officer Nelson abruptly interjected.

Voices became enraged from upstairs. Drake couldn't make out the words but it was intense. Gaven shot up the stairs toward the voices and Drake followed immediately behind.

"What's going on in here?" Drake shouted, bounding in front of Gaven, for the first time not caring if Nigel accepted him any longer.

Jade's eyes were watered with tears, waiting to stream down her cheeks. Nigel was mocking her, turning toward Gaven to slap hands.

"Jade, you all right?" Drake asked in an uneasy tone, leaping over toward Jade.

"I'm fine. He's just a big jerk and I have no idea why you would ever invite him over!" Jade shrieked.

Nigel and Gaven snickered sarcastically in enjoyment.

"Jade, be nice. I'm sure whatever Nigel did, he didn't mean it," Drake looked deeply into Jade's eyes, caramel irises frozen into ice, burning with a growing intensity.

Drake gestured for Nigel and Gaven to take a seat. He turned back to Jade, an intensity growing in his gaze, begging her with his eyes to follow his plan.

"You guys are obviously the toughest guys at Deadwood High School, right?"

Nigel and Gaven started laughing, slapping hands and smacking their knuckles together. Gaven surveyed Drake's room as if he were looking for something in particular.

"Uh, yeah, obviously you dweeb. We could kick anyone's butt in the entire school. Probably this entire weak town as well," Nigel snapped, flexing his biceps as he felt the curvature with his free hand, flicking his eyes at Gaven for approval.

"Well, then I have a question for you," Drake brightened in a new, fresh tone of voice.

Jade was mystified. Undulating her eyebrows, watching Drake cautiously, a foreboding expression reaching the borders of her face.

"Spit it out, punk," Nigel disparaged, open palms in the air.

"If you are so fearless, is there anything in this world that scares you? You have to have at least one fear, right?"

Jade nodded ever so slightly, comprehension spreading across her face. Gaven stared pensively at Drake, outwardly befuddled at his question. Nigel raised one eyebrow, curling one lip sardonically toward his cheek.

"I'll tell you this for sure, nothing scares me," Nigel responded bluntly.

Jade's eyes sparked, she understood what Drake was doing. She approved. Drake smiled on the inside as she rubbed the tears away from her eyes, squared her shoulders and leaned toward Nigel, anxious as she awaited his response.

"There has to be *something* that freaks you out. Something? Anything?"

Nigel, confused by the line of questioning, blurted, "The only thing in the world that I freak out about is getting injured, not being able to kick everybody's ass at sports. But aint nobody big and strong enough to hurt me so I don't even think about it."

Gaven crossed his arms, finally removing his sunglasses to reveal his deep-set brown eyes, small and spaced awkwardly across his face. He had a black eye and a deep cut immediately underneath his eyebrow on the right. He nodded intently with a smile as if he too knew what Drake was trying to accomplish.

"I'm scared of being in a car accident and not being able to work out. If I don't work out, I'd lose this," Gaven spoke though his teeth, raising his t-shirt to reveal perfectly sculpted abdominal muscles. "Let's get out of here, Nigel. Time to have some fun," he smirked, jetting out of the room towards the staircase in the playroom.

"You are lame, punk. And don't forget what I said, tramp," Nigel pointed at Drake, moving to Jade as he followed Gaven out the door and to the stairs.

Upon hearing the front door slam shut, both Drake and Jade relaxed, muscles no longer locked into position.

"I told you he was no good!" Jade shrieked, slapping Drake gently on the arm.

"What was going on up here while I answered the door to Gaven? I heard you guys yelling at each other and then you were upset when I got back. Be honest," Drake said, jaw tightening in anger.

Jade's eyes flickered in apprehension. She paused, staring impassively at the floor.

"Many years ago," Jade hesitated, taking a deep breath and sizing up Drake's expression. "I was spending the night with my best friend that lived in Shady Oaks and, being a summer day, we went to the playground at the Shady Oaks Park. Nigel was there. There were many kids there, he wanted to cut the line in front of me to the slide, and I refused to allow it. Then, he attacked me. He pulled me by the hair and punched me in the face, repeatedly. I nearly lost unconsciousness but I remember him pulling out a Swiss army knife from his pocket," Jade's eyes welled up like miniature swimming pools.

Drake fell to his knees in front of her, taking her trembling hands into his, rubbing them softly with his thumbs as he stared intently into her eyes.

"Are you serious? Did he get into trouble for attacking you? He had to have, right?" he asked in a small voice.

"No, his dad owns the town of Shady Oaks because either you work at that drug company or you have a family member or close friend that does. He is known to retaliate against your friends and family at the company so everybody in Shady Oaks does what he wants. Nigel could get away with murder in Shady Oaks. If the incident had happened in Deadwood City, Nigel would have served time in juvenile detention," Jade sniffed, taking a deep breath. "It gets worse. He sliced me multiple times with his knife. I was bleeding everywhere, my clothes were torn," Jade slowly lifted up her shirt to reveal the silvery scars along her abdomen.

Drake felt the blood rush to his head, his eyes flashed and narrowed, face twisting in horror.

"Jade, if I would have known that he did that to you," Drake labored, room starting to spin from the flush of adrenaline coursing through his veins.

24 – The Bark

The following day at school, Drake anticipated going to tennis. Angst filled his core. He wanted desperately to confront Nigel Sage about what he had done to Jade in the past as well as what he had said to her in his house the day before. Drake wasn't known for starting fights but he had a cerebral threshold and Nigel had crossed it. Nigel had disrespected Jade in Drake's own bedroom, drudging up horrific past events he had done to her. Drake didn't care anymore about Nigel's size or the fact that he traveled with a henchman the size of a professional wrestler. It didn't matter anymore.

The bell rang for last period; Drake marched intently to the tennis locker room, waiting for Nigel. He was prepared to ambush him, to get the first strike. Drake's teammates filed into the locker room, their conversations were like hollow roars inside of his ear canals. Every muscle tensed in preparation for battle. It was time. Nigel always arrived at this time. Drake's heart raced with eagerness. He knew he'd be severely wounded when it was over but he didn't care. Jade had begged Drake a thousand times to forget about it, not to start a fight with Nigel, calling it a *death wish*. Minutes passed and now Nigel was late. Nigel was never late. Drake's iPhone buzzed. It was Jade Amity.

"Don't say it. I'm going through with it," Drake answered sternly.

"Drake, it's Nigel. He's been in a car accident. It happened yesterday. I just heard about it in Spanish class from someone whose mom is friends with his mom."

"What? Are you serious? When?"

"Supposedly on the way home from your house, he and Gaven were hit by a car on the driver's side. Most of Nigel's bones are crushed, he may never walk again is what they said."

A tremor pulsed down Drake's spine. He did this. He asked Nigel what his fears were while Nigel was in his house. Drake did it on purpose and now, because of his own actions, another human being's life was ruined. Drake paused, frozen.

"Drake, it's not your fault. Don't blame yourself. How could it be your fault because your house put some kind of curse on him? You didn't do it. And most of all, Nigel deserved what he got."

"What about Gaven?"

"He walked away uninjured."

Drake was in a daze. Deciding to skip tennis, he waited in the parking lot in his Jeep for Briar. The bell rang. He waited for fifteen minutes until everybody had filed out of the parking lot. No Briar. A text message popped up from Emily. *Briar has a ride. It's Friday so she is gone for the weekend.*

"Figures," Drake scoffed, peeling out of the parking lot.

He drove home, hands firmly clenched to the wheel, in deep thought about how he had nearly killed someone. Even though it was as far-fetched as his house causing the accident, Drake had knowingly asked Nigel what he was afraid of because he knew the house would make it happen. Drake needed Jade. He pulled over briefly to thumb a text before pulling the Jeep onto the Deadwood Bridge. She returned it immediately and said she was already waiting in front of his house. Drake felt an instant relief, his muscles relaxed into a normal tone. His mind freed him of all thoughts as he stared at the road ahead. Driving up to 614 Scarlet Court, he curled his mouth up slightly at the sight of the Honda in front of the circle drive. Immediately as he climbed out of the car, Jade was there, wrapping her arms around him. She was smiling, obviously pleased at the day's news.

"Drake!" she squeezed her arms tightly, leaning her head against his chest.

He kissed her on the top of the head, squeezing back, eyes shut in deep meditation.

"You seem happy," Drake outlined each word.

"Drake, you don't know how deep seeded my hatred for Nigel is. You have no idea. That guy tried to kill me! He just didn't know how to do it because he was too young and his knife was too small and very dull. He has terrorized me ever since. He is not a good person and bad people always get what they deserve. It's ying and yang, it's karma; it's not your fault."

Drake looked away, gazing vacantly into the fountain. He viewed the armored dragon as himself and Nigel as the slain lion, blood pouring out of the wounds of victory. He was the victor but now realized that winners don't always feel good about their victory. It can still feel awful even if the loser deserved what they received.

"Drake, how can your house really cause a car accident? Just think about it. It can't happen."

"You're right. Let's go watch a movie," Drake countered, cupping her chin into his hand and pulling her face upward, locking into a penetrating gaze.

Jade rose on the balls of her feet to give Drake a soft kiss with her subtle lips. Drake felt slightly disoriented by the range of emotions surging through his veins. He pulled her in, bodylines matching, as he tightened his embrace before she gently pulled away, taking his hand and pulling him toward the house.

"Great idea, let's go!" Jade sparked.

"Yes!" Drake countered, leaning down to smile at Jade.

"Hey, I finally talked to my uncle in New York City," Jade added casually, strolling toward the front door.

"Yeah, what did he say?"

"Well, I told him everything just as we discussed and don't get mad but he said your dad is most likely the one that killed Basil. He's got over thirty years experience with homicide investigations and given the facts, he said that's usually how it goes."

"My dad? A murderer?" The reality of it struck Drake like a Mack truck.

"This is interesting, Drake. He asked his psychics about the supernatural aspects of the house. He actually didn't freak out about the whole story as I thought he would. The psychics were pretty sure of one thing, Drake."

"What is that?"

"Well, they said that no matter what, a supernatural force could never interfere with a parent's love of a child. There's nothing in the world stronger than that bond and it cannot be broken or interfered with in any manner – even by supernatural forces. Second to that would be the love between siblings and so on."

"How do they explain it, then? My parents have acted like they are not concerned that their child is missing and that's a fact!"

"The *only* explanation is that she is *not* missing, Drake."

As they entered the foyer, Drake's ear caught a familiar sound, distracting him from Jade's revelation that Ella wasn't missing.

"Did you just hear that?" Drake whispered, slowly scanning the foyer, eyebrows creating a fierce angle with his eyes.

"Is it—

"Barking. I heard barking. Did you?"

"Yes, very clearly. It was in there," Jade said softly, pointing toward the study.

Drake and Jade crept toward the study, listening keenly with every step. With a hand flat on the door, he pushed it open wide, surveying the room carefully. The barking grew louder, almost like the day Drake rescued Omen in the fire at Basil's house.

"It's —

Jade interrupted bluntly, "Omen."

"He's in that secret room! But where is the door?"

"Your parents here?"

"Nope, nobody is here, the cars are gone. I'll be right back," Drake shouted, the words stern.

Drake stormed out into the foyer and into the kitchen. He clambered open the door to the garage and sifted feverishly through Ivan's tools, settling on an old rusted axe. With one hand on the axe handle, he thundered back into the study, gesturing for Jade to step backward.

"What the hell are you doing, Drake?" Jade cried out, scampering behind the black suede futon couch.

"I'm getting Omen out of there," Drake said in a belligerent tone, swinging the axe backward over his shoulder like a lumberjack.

Drake winced as he swung the axe at the sheetrock. The barking grew intense, followed by vicious growling. Drake continued to slash at the wall, hitting sheetrock and wood, causing a large gaping hole to form.

"Drake! Look!" Jade screeched, pointing to an adjacent part of the wall that had pushed forward. It was the shape of a door. The secret door had been moved.

Omen lunged out of the space, his barking subsiding into vigorous licking of Drake's hand.

"Hey, boy! What are you doing in there?"

The door pushed back on its own, sealing itself with the wall.

"I don't think so," Drake said, the words calm and cool.

He swung the axe at the secret door, finding a wooden panel with each blow. The door popped open again. Drake reached into the space, pulling the door open wide. He heard some rumbling around the corner.

"What's in there, Drake?" Jade questioned, voice shaking as she rushed up, standing behind Drake and looking around his shoulder.

"It's dark. Hold on, let me see if there's a light in here," Drake felt around the walls for a light switch. His fingers landed on a cool piece of plastic. He moved his index finger about and found the switch. He pushed it into the opposite position and a bluish white glow ensued, lighting up the area.

"What the hell is this?" Drake bawled, restless eyes darting everywhere.

It was a narrow hallway, with a long, slender desk positioned along the wall filled with stacks of papers and files. File cabinets flanked each side of the desk. Drake picked up a paper on top of one of the stacks and examined it under the light.

"Right House Production Company," Drake read the name on the letterhead aloud in a curious tone.

Jade entered the narrow hallway and stood next to Drake, looking on to read the paper he was holding.

"Drake!" a voice boomed from inside the study.

It was Gaven Phoenix. He was standing in the middle of the study, sheen of sweat glistening across his thick forehead.

Drake locked into a quick glare with Gaven before jetting further into the slender hallway, turning the corner to a larger, open room filled with television monitors and more desks. The monitors displayed the various locations in his house, including his own bedroom. Jade gasped for air at the sight, Drake pulling her arm to drag her behind him as if he were shielding her from the impending attack from Gaven Phoenix. Gaven's footsteps thundered as he stormed around the corner to join them.

"Get out of here now," he exploded, fist pounding onto the adjacent wall.

"Not until you explain what the hell this is, Gaven. Or is that your real name? Who are you and what is all of this?"

Drake struggled to conceal the fear behind his serene expression. Gaven's glare strangled the words in his throat. The room began to spin, a hollowed out roar bounced around his ear canals.

"Drake, I will give you one more chance to get the hell out of here immediately," Gaven bellowed, fists clenched, arm muscles flexed.

Drake froze, muscles rigid in anticipation of Gaven's first strike. He labored to respond despite the dizziness, his body reacting faster than his mind could realize the implications of his actions. He grabbed Jade's hand and ran further into the crypt behind the study walls, turning another corner and coming face to face with Quentin Maddox. He looked slightly different. He wore a baseball cap, looking a tad cleaner, as if he had been playing a character the times Drake had interacted with him before. He stood along a narrow walkway of desks with various equipment scattered throughout, collectively looking like an airplane dashboard.

"Gaven! Seriously?" Quentin waned, stutter absolved.

Gaven's thunderous footsteps were mounting behind them, turning the corner.

"What the hell are you doing, Quentin? I leave for a few minutes and all hell breaks loose and they're in here with you, the dog is out there? What were you thinking? Mr. Nelson is going to be pissed!"

"Do you see what he did to the wall, Gaven?"

Drake's body started to tremble. It was too much to comprehend. His mind paused, body swaying while fighting the urge to lose consciousness to get relief. He knew he had to protect Jade. He had to get her out of the situation safely at all costs.

"We will be going now. Sorry to bother," Drake said in monotone, pulling Jade in front of him and pushing her toward the monitor room.

"Wait a minute. You've seen too much. We need time to think. You are not going anywhere. Both of you have a seat. Mr. Nelson will be back soon, we need a solid plan. He freaks out when things go wrong."

"It's another Basil situation. We won't have a show by the time this is over. It will all be for nothing."

Drake hinged on the words *Basil situation*. His mind went from confusion to untainted terror.

"Basil wasn't even supposed to be here and therefore he wasn't needed. Drake is essential. Drake is *the one*."

"The time was coming anyway, Quentin. It might not be as bad as you think," Gaven said airily.

"Wuh-what is going on?" Drake stumbled, begrudgingly taking a seat at one of the desks, signaling for Jade to take the seat on the far side of him.

While Gaven and Quentin stepped aside and whispered feverishly, Drake pulled out his iPhone and dialed the numbers 911.

A device started to beep on the machine in front of Quentin. He chuckled and flicked a switch. *911 what is your emergency?* A prerecorded voice sounded.

Drake endured an instant queasiness. Quentin had answered his phone call. Quentin had been controlling his phone. His mind entered a flurry, seeking the correlation to his phone calls he had made in the house. Dominick flickered into his mind.

He looked down at his iPhone. It was nearly 6 PM. If Dominick got the message from his mutual friend Mike on Xbox Live, Dominick would arrive at the house at any moment.

25- Treacherous Past

"Drake!" a familiar voice sounded from inside the house.

It was Dominick. Drake fought through a bout of emotions as his eyes flickered between Gaven and Quentin. Dominick had arrived to 614 Scarlet Court at Drake's request. Drake realized at that moment that he might have put his best friend in mortal danger.

"Who the hell is that, Quentin?" Gaven barked, his voice husky and intense.

Gaven spitted out furiously through the monitor room and wheeled around the corner, shouting, "You miss something else, Quentin? You are supposed to monitor *everything!*"

Drake paced back and forth within his mind. Jade nudged him in panic, widening her eyes, before glancing at Quentin who seared a burning intensity into Drake's every move, shifting his eyes to Jade in random flashes. The next minute felt eternal.

"Well, lookie who's here!" Gaven said sarcastically, holding Dominick unwillingly by the elbow, dragging him around the corner toward the seat next to Drake.

"Hey, Drake," Dominick whispered as he fell into the chair.

Drake pushed to the edge of his seat, every nerve ending felt like a live wire.

"Thought we instructed you to stay away if you knew what was good for you, your family and your friend

Drake here. Were we not clear?" Gaven growled, shrugging his shoulders mockingly.

"Uh—

"That is what I thought, Mr. Botticelli. We instructed you *clearly* to stay clear from Drake including *all* methods of contact. So how did you arrive back at this house? Come on your own accord, did you? Do we need to teach you a lesson? Does ole mom and dad back in Austin need to have a little unfortunate accident?"

"No," Dominick mumbled.

"I'm very surprised your parents would allow you to break the deal like this. They must not know you left Austin."

Dominick shifted his weight from right to left, looking into Drake's eyes for the right answer. He took a deep breath. The silence seemed so much longer this time.

Clenching his teeth to concentrate, Dominick responded, "No, they don't know I'm here. Drake asked my friend Mike to give me a message over Xbox live. He said if I was ever his friend that I'd be here tonight at 6 PM. I guess I assumed it was the end of the show and it was all over."

Gaven eyed Dominick suspiciously. His mouth twisted to the side, he muttered to himself as he glared fiercely into his eyes.

"Well you guessed wrong!" Gaven bellowed, vibrating everything around him as he punched his fists into against the wall. "I told you I would contact you *myself* if and when we ever needed you again!"

Quentin interjected softly, "Hey, Gaven. We were pretty much done, you know. I don't know what kind of conclusion we decided upon but maybe we can use Dominick—

Gaven interrupted abruptly, strolled intently toward Quentin with anger intensifying in his eyes at every step. Omen crept slowly from around the corner, rupturing into a slow, menacing growl. Drake snapped his fingers at Omen who quickly retreated toward the study.

"Let me tell you one thing, Quentin Maddox. You need to remember who you are. You are nothing but a lowly criminal, a street thug that lucked into some blood money to start this production company after serving your term in federal prison for involuntary manslaughter. Mr. Nelson and me are the only ones with production experience. You *need* us and can't do this show without us. I am a leader here and what I say – *goes*. Do you understand me when I say that this show is not over?" Gaven derisively spit out every word, clear and distinct, thrusting his index finger into Quentin's bony chest with each syllable. "And we better get this straightened out before Mr. Nelson returns. He's due back in an hour!"

Quentin rolled his squinty eyes and marched off down the narrow hallway. Drake took a deep inhalation, tensing his muscles to prepare for impact as Gaven spun around and glared deeply into his eyes.

"Just because I served time for involuntary manslaughter doesn't mean it was involuntary, Gaven," Quentin mumbled. "You should remember that."

Gaven spun around and glared at Quentin before turning back toward Drake.

"Well, Drake. Since you broke all the unspoken rules, took an axe to the walls, and found out about our little lair here - let me just say that your mom and dad signed a contract, albeit it was disguised as mortgage papers but who ever reads those things, right? Nobody ever takes the time to read the tons of legal mumbo jumbo in those stacks of papers when they buy a house. They just roll their eyes and sign, sign, sign," Gaven punched Drake in the chest with each *sign*.

"I don't know what you are talking about, Gaven," Drake whispered loudly, barely choking out the words, frustrated, scared.

"If you or any member of your family breaks this contract, your father Ivan and your mother Emily will owe five million dollars to *us*, the Right House Production Company. They signed a contract to be on the show *614 Scarlet Court* – a reality show about how the inhabitants of a suspected haunted house believe that their fears are implemented by their new home. But in reality, it is *us* causing your fears to show their ugly heads because we control the house, we control the townspeople, we control *everything*. Money talks and people are easily bought. Seriously, Drake. Did you really believe that your house could cause your mother to age, your dad to see ghosts, you to fail at every aspect of your life and your sister to be infested with spiders? Seriously?" Gaven let out a burst of laughter. "Boy, America's gonna love your gullibility!"

It only took a heartbeat to comprehend the words. Drake instantly put the pieces together. It all made perfect sense. He pursed his lips, considering the situation.

"It was confusing, I admit," Drake said in monotone, glancing at Jade in the adjacent seat who had a stream of tears rolling down her cheeks. "But did you murder Basil?"

"Don't worry about that nosy moocher. He stuck his nose in where he shouldn't have. He's out of the picture and that's all that should concern you. You didn't want him here anyway and neither did your dad. We did you both a favor. He was never supposed to be here and neither was that stupid dog, wasn't in the master plan."

Turning the other direction to view Dominick's reaction to the scene, he witnessed every pigment in his skin evaporate, eyes widened and eyebrows raised toward his scalp in horror. Drake moved in front of Jade in his chair, his back ramrod straight in a defensive shield position as Gaven advanced toward him.

"Remember the tennis scrimmage against Thunder Falls?" Gaven lost himself in hysteria for a long moment before continuing, "Well, the chap you played in that match was actually a college senior! He plays for Texas Tech University! Supposed to be going pro next year! Can't believe you don't keep up with college players. I mean, I thought we'd be busted for sure; we had bets going that you'd recognize the guy. But nope, it worked like a charm!"

Drake shook his head, appalled.

"Knew he wasn't in high school. No surprise there, actually," Drake's face reddened as he clenched his fist in anger.

Quentin stomped his foot on the ground to grab Gaven's attention, "Oh, wait. Remember when Nigel slashed Drake's tire right before that tournament."

"Nigel is one of you?" Drake inquired hesitantly.

"No, of course not. He's dumber than a box of rocks and refused to follow Gaven's direction so he had to go," Quentin mumbled, removing his baseball cap to rake back his thinning straggly hair before putting it back on.

Gaven nodded, swiping the point of his chin with his thumb and index finger, "Yes, how can I forget, Quentin. Bull-headed Nigel slashed your tire, Drake, which wasn't part of our plan. You were supposed to play the opponent Nigel ended up facing at the tournament. Another Texas Tech player, by the way. You lucked out on that one! People will do anything for money and so we easily bought the tournament director. Too bad we didn't have time to switch the schedule back before the match started or you would have ruined your perfect little tennis record. You should thank Nigel for that one. Nonetheless, in the end, he got what he deserved, didn't he, Drake?"

Drake let out a laborious sigh, glaring at the floor, his jaw muscles flexing methodically as he contemplated the real meaning of Gaven's last words.

"You caused Nigel's accident," Drake hedged, his voice gruff.

"Why, no! Heavens, no! The *house* did! But by your request. You are the one who made Nigel say what he was afraid of while he was in the house. So we'll give you half credit, o.k.?"

Gaven and Quentin burst into a fit of laughter. Drake shot a gaze of trepidation at Jade, looking for a plan of escape through her eyes. Jade's face twisted in horror, her eyes tortured.

"Oh, here's another good one. It was Gaven's idea to call as the tournament director and tell you that you were disqualified from the tournament when you actually weren't! You didn't show up to the courts on Saturday and *that's* why you were disqualified!" Quentin barked, followed by ruckus laughter.

Drake's anger intensified as he glared at Quentin.

"And you, pretty little lady, how'd ya like those possums?" Gaven sniped suddenly, turning to glare mockingly at Jade. "Not sure if they were rabid or not so you might wanna get that bite checked, Drake. You were valiant the night that you saved Jade from those beasts. Jade, he's a stud; you should keep 'em. America will love Drake, everybody loves a hero!"

She looked at Drake panic-stricken, unable to speak. Drake slid slightly more in front of Jade. Sitting on the edge of his chair, he balanced his weight with his thighs, his muscles burning as if they were on fire.

Gaven subsided his laughter and continued, "Your parent's realtor in Austin that found this house, well, that was our casting producer. The mortgage banker that met up with your folks here in the house, well, that was our production assistant and the title officer was the very hot legal representative for our production company," Gaven cackled enthusiastically.

"She was actually my criminal defense attorney. Awesome attorney, I must say. She reduced the charges of my premeditated murder case to involuntary manslaughter! Now who ever can pull that off? We call her our *legal representative* 'cause it sounds more corporate like, huh?" Quentin added slyly.

Gaven shot an abrupt nod toward Quentin before turning to smirk at Drake.

"Oh, and the cops? Let's put it this way, you've never met a *real* Shady Oaks police officer! Officer Charles Nelson is actually the executive producer of this operation. He was dying to make cameo appearances in the show. The young cop, Mr. Nelson's partner, was just a hired actor, by the way, but he had you all fooled! He'll probably make it big one day and you should be thrilled to have met him. But you," Gaven strolled closer to stand in front of Drake, "You'll be infamous, Drake. You've done so well on my show. You are a producer's dream, actually."

"Yeah, right. Sorry, but I'm not into exploiting myself on television. I will never be on television. Your dumb show will never air," Drake said sarcastically. "Where are my mom and dad? Where is Ella?"

"So many questions, Drake. Show's not over. You *will* be on television, there's no way around it. It's time to end the show. You've got to give us a big conclusion. A huge melt down is what we need, maybe some self harm, something massively disastrous. We need something that will blow people's minds, as this show will be infamous."

"I'm not doing *anything* for you—

"Drake, do you really want to crash your parent's finances for the rest of their lives? What if one of them got into a horrible accident? That would be terrible, wouldn't it?"

"Tell him about my brother, Gaven. Just do it," Quentin added with angst.

Gaven stared at Quentin for a long minute and slowly, an eerie smile crept across his face.

"You'll enjoy this one, Drake. You wanna know who Quentin's brother is?"

"Sure," Drake reluctantly blurted, peering over at Quentin with narrowed eyes.

Gaven gazed into Drake's eyes with a sarcastic expression infesting his face, soaking up Drake's terror through his eyes. "Remember the last man that your father testified against back in Austin? You know, the one that caused your father to relocate your entire family here to Shady Oaks, bringing you right here to 614 Scarlet Court."

"Uh, yeah—

"Well, that is Quentin's twin brother that is now serving a life sentence because of your dad. Quentin, his brother, and all of their friends are not pleased with what your father has done. Therefore, I am confident that you'll do *anything* we want. Tomorrow night, Drake. You got to end it tomorrow night and then you can have your life back. Maybe we'll even let your family stay in this house," Gaven scoffed, turning to glare at Jade. "But you, my pretty, got to go. We're not entirely sure what we can do with your footage since your parents refuse to return our calls. We're about to pay them a visit."

Jade barely choked out the words, "But, why—

Gaven hoisted his thick fingers in the air, tapped his foot on the ground, and went on, "On second thought, don't worry. Before the show airs, we'll get a hold of them and they *will* sign the consent forms, but just in case something happens to them and we can't use your footage – you've gotta stay clear of here for now. We can't have you screwin' up the conclusion of the show."

Quentin cleared his throat in an exaggerated fashion to get Gaven's attention. He held up a bony finger in thought before he spoke, swallowing a hard lump in his throat.

"As a last resort, we could always force her to emancipate, Gaven. Then, she can sign the papers herself. Our legal representative had initially mentioned that as an option for all the minors involved in the show and said it wouldn't take long since she knows the judge very well, if you know what I mean. Then, pretty little thing there will sign anything if it means her boyfriend will live to see another day."

"That's a plan. We'll give her mom and dad a couple more days to come around before we take that route. Whatever, you can be on the show, but we need footage this afternoon of just the two boys coming up with the plan for the conclusion. For now, you need to go home and do not breathe a word about this show to anyone. Do not forget that we know who your parents are, where they work, where they shop for groceries and work out on the weekends and of course, we know where you live."

Jade lost control and broke into a restrained crying spell, cupping her hands over her face to catch the tears as she slumped her head into the recesses of her lap. Dominick looked on, helpless. Drake wrapped his arms around her body to console her. He lifted her trembling body from her seat and guided her through the maze behind the study. He escorted her to the front door, secretly whispering into her ear by disguising it as a nuzzled kiss, instructing her to meet him behind Deadwood High School the following morning at 8 AM.

26 – Terminal Plan

For the remainder of the day, Drake and Dominick, knowing every action was recorded, resumed into their normal routine of playing video games. Omen was back by Drake's side and they had been instructed by the producers to talk about how they found him wandering around outside. The story was that he must have simply escaped from an open front or back door the day Drake realized he was missing. The producers revealed to the boys that they hadn't planned on Basil or Omen moving with the Henry family and they certainly didn't like how Omen was giving away their locations so they trapped him in the production rooms with them by luring him with a piece of sliced ham. Even under the stressful pretense, it felt good to Drake to be with both of his best friends, man and dog.

Knowing there were no supernatural forces in the house gave Drake a strange sense of relief and he slept soundly through the night. The recording equipment even gave him an unexpected and ironic sense of security. Realizing that his baby sister Ella was not actually missing also offered much needed relief, even if she might have been in the hands of soulless criminals.

The following morning, Drake's iPhone alarm sounded. Without hesitation, he woke up Dominick, signaling him to follow his lead. With crumpled hair and sleepy eyes, they quietly crept down the stairs and out onto the driveway. Climbing into the Jeep, they sped away as rapidly as they could, both refraining from speaking as Drake had gestured for Dominick to remain silent.

Drake had concluded without a doubt that his dad, mother and Briar all had found out about the show at various times and this was the reason for their curious actions over the past several days. He saw through Briar and knew *something* had gotten to her. Now he knew exactly what it had been. Briar's actions of not wanting to speak to Drake in the house and while riding in the Jeep made it apparent that the producers knew what was being said within the Jeep and where the Jeep was at all times. Otherwise, Briar would have broken the seal and blabbed everything she knew about the show. If she weren't being watched, she definitely wouldn't have tried to stop Drake from putting missing child flyers around town for Ella unless someone was watching who didn't allow her to participate or maybe it was because Briar knew it was a moot point since Ella wasn't really missing.

The silent ride to Deadwood High School ended abruptly in the front of the school as Drake palmed the Jeep into park. Gesturing for Dominick to leave his iPhone in the seat of the Jeep, he tossed his own into the driver's seat, hastening around the back of the school where Jade was patiently waiting. Dominick followed his lead.

"Please tell me you have a great plan, Drake," Jade said, befuddled, shifting her weight from her left to right side.

Drake motioned for them to remain quiet and guided them swiftly to the back of the football fields.

"All right, I'm pretty sure we can speak openly here. But we don't have long as they'll know we are all here and will be here soon. Since the producers didn't get to your uncle in New York, Jade, I'm sure this must be a black spot where they can't record us."

Jade surveyed the area and nodded.

"Good point, Drake. But I'm not entirely sure that they could have gotten to my uncle. He's a pretty bad dude, been a cop for over 30 years," Jade added bluntly.

"No, *these* are bad dudes! I think they can get to just about anybody," Drake added. "Think about it. Your uncle in New York City shed some light on the fact that Ella wasn't missing and nearly ruined their dumb reality show at that point. I was just too dense to realize he was right. Don't you think that if they knew you were going to talk to him, they'd have found a way to figure out what he was going to say to you before he told you that their story line had a gigantic hole in it like that, possibly causing us to investigate other options further?"

"Yea, I guess so. You may be right. They never saw it coming until it was too late," Jade mourned.

"So, what's the plan, Stan?" Dominick said, shrugging his shoulders, flicking his dreads behind his ears.

"Tonight, I'm giving them the conclusion to the show they asked for. I am going to burn down 614 Scarlet Court."

"What?" Jade exclaimed, searching Drake's face for an inkling of sanity.

Dominick held his head low, shaking it in disbelief.

"Yes, I am going to destroy everything and put an end to this dumb show. But first, I'm going to pour massive amounts of gasoline all over the study to make sure that all of their equipment, all of their stupid files, everything is destroyed. This show will not and cannot happen. My family is not going to look like idiots on national television and my father is not going to go to jail for a crime he didn't commit. And, the last thing this world needs is for these guys becoming successful and doing this or something worse to someone else."

"Wow. Now you are an arsonist?" Dominick said.

"Guess so. I just don't see another way out of it, do you? They said they wanted a big ending. I'll give it to them. I can't imagine that these guys are that organized to have copies of their recordings at another place. I mean, they just started this production company and by the looks of what they have in those rooms behind the study walls, it appears as though everything is being stored there."

"I agree with Drake. There were filing cabinets. *Wooden* filing cabinets that would go into flames pretty easily, by the way," Jade agreed. "And with all of that equipment, it looks as though everything they need can be done there. Plus, I recognized a lot of that software in the back room. It's film-editing software. They've created a full production company and film studio in the walls behind your house, Drake. Creepy!"

Dominick was in deep thought. He nodded slowly, staring toward the clouds.

"I see no other way out, Drake. Sounds good to me. The only problem is that you'll have to do it quickly. You'll have to be sure they don't have time to stop us or put it out once it starts," Dominick said rapidly.

"What about your family? How can you be sure they won't hurt them or even murder them as they did Basil? Is it worth it? I mean, why can't you just give them what they want? It's just stupid reality television," Jade pointed out brusquely. "Nobody will watch it, anyway."

Dominick interjected, "Jade, don't forget that our families are at risk too. They know everything about us and have already threatened my parents and said they'd be in touch with your parents soon! I'd guess they have Drake's family shacked up at a hotel somewhere close by. They're obviously not at Drake's house."

"Dominick is right, Jade. We are all at risk and I understand this but this show cannot happen. I'll just claim that I was doing what the producers wanted. I won't let on that I'm doing it on purpose to ruin their show. It will just end up that way. I'm a teenager and they asked me to come up with a big ending. A fire is a big ending, right? Plus, why would they hurt my family? What good would it do them besides make them all suspects in murder cases?"

"If you blaze your house, you have to realize, you won't be able to save your stuff. Your family will lose everything," Dominick said bluntly.

"I know but I also know that they have a killer home insurance policy. Mom was bragging about how she didn't care if the house burned down like Basil's because she'd get all new clothes and stuff. Besides, it is better than the alternative."

Dominick continued, "This may work but you'll have to be careful. If you put gas in the study, you'll have to put it everywhere in the house or it will be very suspicious that you did it to kill their show. And they might even stop you once they know about the gas, you know."

Jade added in an energetic tone, "I agree, if you charge into the study and douse the room with gas and throw a match, it would be obvious what you are doing and they are likely to retaliate. If you pour gas around the house, you are obviously going to start a fire, Drake."

"Great points. I just have to figure out a good reason as to *why* we'd be pouring gasoline everywhere other than to start a fire. Well, they should be coming soon. I'm sure they don't have your car rigged since they admitted they haven't got to your parents or been to your house *yet*. Jade, can you pick up some gasoline and haul it over around 7 PM tonight but in some type of hidden containers? I'm going to come up with a plan, don't worry. Just have the gasoline there, all right?"

"Absolutely. 7 PM with gasoline in containers. We'll have to split up and drench the house all at once so put that into your master plan."

Drake suddenly became animated, jumping up and down in a restrained manner.

"Hey, I've got it!" Drake exclaimed, palms facing the sky, eyebrows arched high, widening his topaz eyes.

"What is it?" Dominick shrieked, flailing his arm.

"Haven't you ever seen how in movies and television, they bring in a priest and do a ceremony on possessed stuff? Well, if we are supposed to believe that my house is possessed and all evil and stuff, let's do a fake ceremony and dump fake holy water *uh hum* gasoline everywhere!"

"Genius! An exorcism! Sick!" Dominick slapped Drake on the arm and jumped up in excitement. "The producers will love that 'cause they can make the house freak out on us and we can act all scared."

"Jade, just follow our lead no matter what. Even if I call you, go along with whatever I say. You know they are listening and everything said will be for their benefit. No matter what, stick with this plan unless I say the words *dog food*. Pretend that the gasoline in the containers is holy water when you get to the house and say that you had it blessed at your church, all right?"

"Dog food. Got it. That's the change of plan phrase and anything said after the words dog food will be the changes. But you don't know how to do an exorcism, Drake. Are they even real?"

"Jade, it doesn't matter. We will fake it and do as we've seen in the movies. Dominick and I will find some scary exorcism movies on Netflix this afternoon and then pretend as if we're doing whatever we saw them do. It will make, *uh hum, seem to make*, for good television," Drake's voice was full of amusement.

"Got it. I'll bring the gas. Oh, I mean holy water," Jade sounded with a smile, kissing Drake on the cheek before trotting off toward her car.

Dominick nodded, a big smile spreading across his face. The plan was in place.

"Let's go, Dom, back to the house. We have all day to act as if we're freaking out about the house. Let's go watch that movie and pretend we're getting ready for the ceremony. Hey, let's call a fake priest too. They control my phone and can arrange for an actor playing a priest to show up at the house. We'll never let it get that far, though. The house will be on fire by the time the dude arrives."

"Drake, you are a genius. But hold up—

Dominick pulled Drake by the arm gently to the back of the football field before speaking softly.

"Hey Drake, do you think your dad really killed Basil or do you think they did it or was it all set up by the producers as part of the plot of the show and Basil's smoking a new pipe at some hotel pool somewhere?"

"Don't know and don't care. But if they air it and Uncle Basil is really dead, my dad will go to jail, you know. They'll plant the evidence and make him guilty no matter what. They would never take the blame. They are criminals! Criminals with the upper hand on *everything,*" Drake bemoaned, shoulders slumping toward the ground.

"No lie. We have to destroy everything."

Drake and Dominick retreated to the house, pretending to work on their plan for the upcoming house blessing and exorcism. They pretended to find the town priest in the shoddy Shady Oaks phone book left by the mortgage officer on the day of their arrival. Drake punched in fake numbers in his iPhone and pretended to call and have a conversation with the priest, requesting that the priest arrive at 8 PM, knowing the producers were watching intently and recording the conversation for their television show. This would give them enough time to start the fire prior to the actor's arrival. They followed it up with a real call from his monitored iPhone to Jade, which the producers allowed to go through, instructing her to come over to Drake's house with multiple containers of water. They told her to arrive at 8 PM. She knew, however, this was all a cover and would still arrive at 7 PM with the concealed gasoline. Then, Drake used the change of plan phrase and asked her to pick up a special type of dog food for Omen on her way over to the house before explaining that he and Dominick had called a priest that would show up to their house at 8 PM to bless the water containers that she brought with her. Jade knew that they had one hour to start the fire before the priest arrived to Drake's house once she got there. She also knew she would have to come up with a clever story about why she arrived an hour early with the water already blessed.

The boys adjourned into the media room upstairs, grabbing a handful of snacks from behind the counter. After finding an old scary movie about an exorcism on Netflix and pretending to take notes, Drake heard something at the door. He jetted into the playroom and looked down the stairs from above. It was Ivan, Emily and Briar. Ella was still not with them. Drake's mind raced. Had the production company kidnapped Ella and were they holding her for ransom so Emily and Ivan would be their drones? This was a possibility that Drake needed to know the answer to but there was no way to ask them without the producers knowing about it. This also complicated the fire. How would he ensure the safety of his family after the fire started? He would now have to coordinate the swift rescue of his family without planning it with Dominick and Jade.

Drake scampered back in the room with Dominick and filled him in on who was at the door. Dominick's eyes widened in a panic as he shrugged his shoulders ever so slightly.

Drake did his best to act his role as he whispered loudly, "how are we going to perform the exorcism with my parents here? When the priest arrives, the plan will be ruined; my dad will send him home."

Dominick studied Drake before adding, "Well, I guess we can just wait until they leave again to do it. I agree. I know your parents and they'd never let us perform the exorcism while they are home."

Drake nodded and continued, "Yeah, whatever. We can sit here and play video games for another 24 hours. That's fine with me," Drake whispered loud and clear for the hidden microphones to pick it up.

"But if they leave the house and we're alone, what time would we do the exorcism?" Dominick pondered.

"Remember, the priest and Jade are both are set to arrive at 8 PM."

"That's not long."

"Well, we'll see if we are alone and if not, we'll just chill for the night."

The boys threw themselves back into playing video games, attempting to act as normal as possible. Drake had decided against starting the fire as long as his parents were there. It was too risky. He wasn't sure what the producers were thinking by having his family come home. Normalcy, maybe? Maybe they thought Drake could bring his parents into the storyline and have them assist in the ceremony but once the boys refused it, the producers didn't have a choice but to get rid of Ivan and Emily for the night. Nonetheless, Drake wouldn't be able to tell Ivan and Emily the plan and couldn't afford for his parents to put a stop to the plan once they smelled the gasoline fumes or to give it away to the producers by accident before he could strike the match. After a while, Briar entered the room.

"Hey Drake! Hey Dominick! When did you get here? You staying the weekend?" Briar said dryly with a strained, unnatural appeal, flashing her eyes between Drake and Dominick, searching for a gleam of understanding. Neither comprehended her message, she was too difficult to read.

"I'm here for the weekend, yeah. Mom made me leave last time because I didn't clean my room before I left. This time, I'm here until Sunday. Paid my neighbor to clean my room for me," Dominick replied, a tiny smile plaguing his face.

"Though you were going to be with your new friend, Bee?" Drake inquired flatly.

"Nah, I didn't feel all too good and asked mom and dad to pick me up," Briar responded in a nervous voice. "Well, see you guys later."

"You going somewhere?"

"Nope, just to my room. Got a project to start working on."

Drake waited her out until she was in her room before he spoke. He hoped Dominick would be able to decipher his code.

"Well, I guess during the exorcism, she'll be in her room. Maybe she won't see what we are doing so she won't ask questions," Drake stared intently into Dominick's eyes and went on, "I know Briar and she wouldn't want us doing anything crazy like that so it's best if she is not involved."

Comprehension invaded Dominick's expression. He nodded twice.

"Oh yeah, I know, right. She'll stop it and our plan will be ruined. I guess we'll sit tight until your mom and dad finally leave. Wanna play Call of Duty?"

"Sure, let's see if Mike's signed on."

27 —Windows

"Hey, Drake! Drake!" Emily shouted from the base of the spiral staircase.

Drake lunged out into the playroom, stepped onto the first step and leaned down, gazing intently at Emily.

"What's up, mom?"

"Your father and I have decided to grab a bite to eat over in Deadwood City. Want us to bring you and Dominick something back?"

Drake paused, fighting a smirk. He had gotten his way. His parents would not be an issue with the fire.

"Nah, that's all right. We will take care of ourselves," Drake bellowed, darting back into his bedroom and patting Dominick enthusiastically on his bony shoulder.

"They are going to go out to eat. Now we have the house to ourselves and only have to avoid Briar during the exorcism, no biggie. Let's just chill for a bit and wait for Jade and the priest."

"Yea, good idea."

The boys sat in silence, both outwardly nervous of Jade's arrival. She would have the gasoline and she would arrive an hour before she was scheduled to, as far as the producers knew. The plan had to be implemented flawlessly. He needed to start a massive fire that couldn't be put out quickly but at the same token, make sure that Briar and Omen got out safely. He needed the producers to believe that this was his honest ending to the show and that he didn't mean to destroy their production company behind the study walls. He was a teen after all and teens wouldn't think of consequences such as that. The doorbell sounded two times in rapid succession. Drake's heart raced with a fury. The producers were watching and analyzing his every move. His actions and the plan needed to be believable, flawless. Drake hopped down the staircase and threw the door open, Dominick trailed immediately behind.

"Hey guys!" Jade squealed, pulling a rusty wagon packed with white plastic orange juice containers.

"Hey, Jade! You got the containers of water. Whoa, cool!" Drake shouted nervously, straining to stay calm. "Your early, uh, it's only seven!"

"Yea, sorry. I know you said eight o'clock but I had to get out of my house before my Aunt arrived. Then, I would have been stuck going out to dinner with the folks. Uh, I'm sorry, Drake. The wagon is so dirty, I didn't realize it until I got here," Jade wheeled the rusted wagon into the foyer, dirt trodden wheels clashing with the pristine marble floor. "I should have cleaned these tires, how embarrassing!"

"It's all right, Jade. I'll tell my mom that me and Dominick played football out back and got too close to the water and got all muddy," Drake said dryly, hoping his secret plan wasn't too transparent. "We'll hide the wagon in the garage for now."

"I had to kill some time so I went to see my priest at the church around the corner from my house and he blessed the water for us, without question. Couldn't believe he didn't even ask me why! Thought it would save time once the priest you called arrives if it were already blessed. Also, I figured it would be better if the water were blessed outside of this house, you know," Jade shrugged.

Drake hoped her story sounded plausible.

"Perfect. Great thinking, babe," Drake said, leaning over to give her a quick kiss on her lips.

Drake took the wagon handle and wheeled it into the kitchen. He and Dominick unloaded the jugs onto the kitchen counter and dragged the wagon into the garage. He was relieved that his plan seemed to be working.

Drake had to tell Jade that the plan had obtained a huge flaw by the name of Briar. He knew Jade would be quick to cover. At least he hoped. He couldn't think of the best way to let her know without it being obvious.

"Did you guys watch that movie? So, do you know what you're doing now? Or, I guess the priest you called will know what to do, right?" Jade said, unscrewing the tops on the white plastic jugs.

The gasoline started to permeate the air. Drake had to maintain an expressionless face not to let on there was a volatile, pungent smell invading his nostrils.

"Uh, yea, we even took notes. We are good to go! You're right, the priest will take charge when he gets here, but I think it's great that Dom and I know what we are doing too, you know."

Dominick took hold of the issue regarding the flawed plan. He lurched to the base of the stairs and yelled in a scratchy voice, "Briar!" He waited patiently with no response. "Briar!"

Jade gazed at Dominick intently, a flicker of comprehension on her face.

Drake caught on and added, "Let's check on her and see what she's doing. She might have her headphones on."

By the time the boys ascended the staircase, they saw Briar in the playroom, standing next to Ella's room in front of the attic door. She looked as though she had been caught doing something she wasn't supposed to do. Drake knew the producers were watching and Briar knew they were watching so he shrugged it off as to not draw any attention to it.

"Let's just tell her," Dominick added. "She'll be cool about it."

"Briar, uh, Jade brought over some, uh, holy water. You know how we think this house is evil and stuff, well, we watched a movie that explained to us how to do an exorcism and we've called a priest to the house. You wanna help us?" Drake inquired, eyes blazing holes into Briar's eyes.

"Sure," Briar said in an uneasy tone, looking back shortly to the attic door, concern riddled on her face as a mask.

The lights flickered in the house a few times during their descent of the stairs.

"Whoa, what was that, Drake?" Dominick rasped, eyes widening as he arched a jagged eyebrow.

"Just get ready for the house to fight back. It's not going to appreciate our plan, Dominick. It already knows what's coming and we better get ready for a fight."

The study door opened violently and slammed back shut. Jade let out a startling scream from the kitchen as Dominick and Drake, still descending the staircase, pretended to be startled and frightened. Drake paused to grip onto the staircase rail and Dominick squeezed Drake's shoulder, gazing at him wide-eyed, mouth agape. The boys played their roles brilliantly.

"Great. This outta be fun," Dominick rasped, pretending to look cautiously around the house.

By the time they arrived into the kitchen, Jade had finished opening the jugs and had proportioned them for each person. Omen crept sleepily into the kitchen, the door slam having awoken him from his nap on the bed in the master bedroom.

"Hey, Drake. We should probably spread the water around the house before the priest gets here to save time. It seems like this house isn't going to be very patient. It already knows what is coming."

Drake now believed Jade to be a mastermind. This would be perfect. She pretended to extend a jug to Drake but willingly let go of it. They all watched as it plummeted to the ground, the gasoline fumes quickly filling the air. Omen snapped out of his sleepy haze and bolted from the kitchen, retreating into the master bedroom, his lips curling up aggressively at the volatile fumes as he shook the odor molecules from his long nasal passageway. Briar froze, looking down at the jug of gasoline as it spilled onto the floor. Her eyes melted into a gaze of horror. Jade looked down at the gas and realized it was obviously not clear and the producers might realize it wasn't water. She quickly covered.

"Oh no. I might have left a little orange juice in some of the containers. I did it in such a hurry. Oops!" Jade blurted, cupping her hand on her forehead.

"No biggie, the holy water has a little O.J. in it. Oh well! Maybe evil hates orange juice and it will work better?" Drake added serenely, chuckling under his breath at his dumb comment.

Drake realized that it wouldn't take long for the gasoline fumes to hit the air conditioning vents, circulate through the house, and make their way into the study. He searched for something to do quickly but remembered how stuffy those rooms behind the study were, and figured they most likely didn't have direct vents connected from inside the house but rather to the outside. This would buy them more time than they originally had expected.

"All right, the first step is to spread the holy water around the house. Everybody get a jug and spread it everywhere. Get it soaked into the carpets along the perimeter of each room. The priest will be here shortly and can finish the job with his chants and stuff and get this house back to normal. Be careful because the house will certainly try to stop us but we have to stay strong," Drake instructed, shooting a hard glance at Briar.

Jade snatched a container and rushed toward the master bedroom. Dominick grasped his jug and took off toward the dining room with Briar, eyes expanded and eyebrows ruffled in angst as she followed closely. Drake grabbed a jug and sprinted up the stairs, soaking the carpet of the playroom, pouring an extra amount at the attic door. He rushed back downstairs, and noticed Omen panicking in the middle of the foyer.

"You need to go out, boy? Here ya go!"

Drake held open the door for Omen who was continuing to bare his teeth, shake his head and sneeze at the intense gasoline odor filling up the house. Omen would give their plan away if he didn't get him out of the house immediately. It was also a safer scenario not to have to save Omen from the fire once it started. Emily and Ivan were gone, Briar was with them, Omen was now outside and Drake could care less about the producers hidden in the rooms behind the study walls. It would be up to them to rescue themselves.

"I've soaked the master bedroom and the kitchen," Jade exclaimed, joining them in the backyard with a half-empty jug.

Random doors started to slam in the house as a black oozing, substance poured down the walls from the crown molding surrounding the foyer. The scene in the house was terrifying or at least it would have been if Drake hadn't known the criminals behind the walls of the study were orchestrating it.

"Sick, Drake. Check out that gross stuff coming down the walls. I hope that priest gets here fast!" Dominick shouted, still playing his role.

"Hurry, one more room and then we'll be ready for him."

Drake knew it was time for the study. On the way, he stopped off at the kitchen and opened the junk drawer. Emily always kept matches in the junk drawer. Eerie mantras sounded from the walls of the house, wailing and moaning echoed throughout. The producers were playing their role perfectly to make the house an absolute horrifying experience. Briar was wide eyed, pleading silently with Drake not to do it. She looked upward. Drake assumed she was trying to convey that there was somebody watching them. He knew this. Random wind gusts rushed through the house as doors continued to slam violently, vague figures of ominous faces appeared randomly in the windows. The producers obviously approved and accepted Drake's design to the conclusion of the show. He leaned over the drawer to conceal his grab of the matchbook and then quickly scooted into the foyer, toward the study.

"Come in here, Briar. Stick with me. I'm about to soak the study!"

As he lunged into the study, he started pouring the rest of the jug of gasoline along the wall while Dominick joined him. The doorbell rang. The priest had arrived. Drake looked at the time on his iPhone.

"Wow! He's early! It's only 7:20!" Drake said with resignation, gazing at Dominick to search for a plan in his eyes.

"No biggie. Let's get this done and then we're ready to go, right?"

"Yup! Good idea, he can wait out there for a few."

Jade added the remaining contents of her jug, splashing a copious amount onto the walls. The smell of gasoline was thick in the air, pungent, making it nearly impossible to breathe. Drake drew out the matchbook from his pocket and struck the match. He dropped it onto the floor, a thin film of flames spread along the black shag carpet.

"No! Drake!" Briar shouted, Dominick took her by the hands and pulled her out into the foyer.

The house grew silent at an instant.

"I hate this house! It's evil. This house is haunted and needs to die! I've just decided the exorcism won't be strong enough. I'm burning it down!" Drake screamed, implementing his plan to make it appear as if he had just thought of it on a whim and didn't mean to burn down the production company on purpose.

Rumblings could be heard from behind the walls of the study. The producers were scrambling, now aware of the fire. The flames saturated the study with a violent roar as the heat singed the hairs on Drake's arm. Drake and Jade sprinted out of the study and into the foyer with Dominick and Briar. The fire followed them, spreading out instantaneously into the foyer. Flame trails separated, radiating along the marbled floor towards the dining room, kitchen and master bedroom. It was blatantly obvious the blessed water was not water, but rather an accelerant. Drake hoped the producers wouldn't be able to detect the gasoline fumes by the time they evacuated the study. He counted on the fire combusting the volatile fumes instantaneously, the ensuing smoke acting as an additional odorant mask. However, he didn't think about the gasoline trails igniting so obviously prior to the rest of the rooms catching ablaze. He crossed his fingers that they would be too busy scampering behind the study walls in a feeble attempt to save their production equipment to watch the monitors. The bottom floor of the house was nearly immersed in flames in mere seconds. The doorbell continued to ring.

"Let's get out of here!" Drake shouted, lunging for the front door.

"No! Wait! Ella! She's upstairs!" Briar shouted in hysterics.

Briar rushed for the staircase as Gaven Phoenix stormed out of the study's secret door, bursting through a wall of flames in the study.

"What the hell are you trying to pull here, Drake?" Gaven shot a scowl at Briar who was at the base of the staircase, "You, stay right there!"

Drake took a few steps backward, trying to avoid contact with the massive build of Gaven Phoenix. He tensed every muscle waiting for the initial blow.

"It's the ending. It is the big conclusion you wanted, right?" Drake yelled through the roar of the flames surrounding them.

"For that, you'll never see your mom, dad or little brat sisters again. I hope it's worth it," Gaven snarled, grabbing Drake by the shirt and tossing him like a rag doll to the ground.

Dominick lunged at Gaven who countered the attack by shoving Dominick's lanky body against the wall directly into a trail of flames, catching his pant leg on fire. Jade quickly patted Dominick down to extinguish the flames. Briar, seeing that Gaven was occupied, started to climb the stairs.

"Briar no! I'll go get her, you go outside. Where is she?" Drake shouted before taking a stiff blow from Gaven's beastly fist on his temple.

Drake's body smacked the wall like a sack of potatoes before he crumpled and fell to the hard, marbled floor. Briar screamed and Jade rushed over to his aid.

For an unknown period, Drake's world went black. The familiar scent of smoke invaded his nasal cavity, bringing him abruptly to his senses as he coughed violently. Gaven stood over him, a glare so intense it was overwhelming, smoke filling in the spaces surrounding him.

"You, your family and friends are about to die. Get up," Gaven said, his husky voice low and intense.

"Why? We didn't do anything! We did what you wanted!"

"Leave him alone!" Jade shrieked as Gaven shoved her back a few feet.

Jade stumbled as she avoided the flames on the ground. As Drake staggered to his feet, he caught sight of a shadow in his peripheral field of vision. Gaven grabbed both of Drake's wrists with one iron hand, squeezing, causing intense pain to shoot up his arms. Sweat poured down Drake's face as the heat intensified in the foyer from the surrounding blaze.

"You did this on purpose, punk. That was gasoline, not holy water. We're not idiots; we saw the pattern it made when you threw the match down—

"But you wanted a big ending, a conclusion for the show!" Drake's words were a choked whisper.

Gaven's lips curled back from his teeth, his deep set eyes narrowed with hatred, his chest muscles twitching with the strength he was mustering to restrain Drake by the wrists. The pain in Drake's arms was immense, intolerable, and nearly incomprehensible. Drake felt as though he would lose consciousness first from the pain that seared every nerve, second to the smoke surrounding him like a blanket. His lungs tightened like a vice with every breath. The shadow became more visible behind Gaven. Gaven raised his free arm and with a clenched fist, every muscle in his arm flexed in preparation to deliver a deathblow to Drake's head.

"I just hope it was worth dying for—

With a loud clang, a metal object struck Gaven in the head. His neck pushed forward as he immediately released his grip on Drake's wrists and his massive stature plummeted to the floor. Blood streamed from Gaven's temple onto his neck and onto the marbled floor. The black ooze seeping down the walls met up with his unconscious body, contrasting with the white marbled flooring.

Dominick dropped the iron skillet by Gaven's head, cracking the tile next to his neck.

"Shut up!" Drake gasped, shaking the pain from his wrists. "Thanks, Dom. Hey, get the girls out of here, call the cops using Jade's phone," Drake scanned the room and saw Briar heading up the stairs, the doorbell continuing to ring.

"Where are you going?"

"To get Ella! She is in the attic! We don't have much time, Drake!" Briar's voice faded in horror as she whirled her arms around in panic.

Drake's face morphed into a grim mask of critical mass. As a Five Star General going into battle, he took control of his troops.

"Briar, go with Dominick and Jade outside. Tell me exactly where Ella is. Also, when you get outside, find Omen and keep him with you guys. Dominick, watch out for any more of the production crew as they come outside and stay clear of them and watch over the girls. They might have another exit from the side of the house. Tell the actor priest guy at the front door to get lost. Kick his ass if you have to but don't let him back in here."

Dominick nodded, lunging for the front door, waiting for the girls to follow.

"Ella is in the attic. You have to turn on the second light switch. Just feel along the left hand side of the wall. Hurry!" Briar screamed, choking from the smoke cloud surrounding her, reluctantly trailing Dominick and Jade out the front door.

"Be safe, Drake. I love you!" Jade sobbed, tears rolling down her cheeks as she followed Dominick onto the front porch.

"I love you too," Drake shouted, turning to ascend the stairs three at a time, dodging the flames as they randomly burst into the air.

Drake bounded into the playroom and dashed over to the attic door. It was unlocked. He felt along the wall, found the switch and popped the lights on. He followed the attic passageway into a quiet, open room. It was a nursery. Fully equipped with a crib, television, play area and anything Ella could desire. This is where she had been. She was never missing. She hadn't been kidnapped. The walls were covered with carpet, most likely for soundproofing. Ella was sleeping peacefully in her crib, television monitors watching over her as she slept. Drake reached down and picked her up, her tiny blue eyes opening to gaze at Drake, wrapping her arms lovingly around his neck.

"Dwake," she mumbled, nuzzling her head into his chest.

"Let's go Ella. Time to get out of here, baby girl."

Drake jetted out of the attic, facing the playroom that was now ablaze, random crashes from downstairs vibrating the floor. The fire was consuming the bottom floor of the home rapidly; the gasoline had performed its duty all too well. Drake knew his time was limited before the upstairs crumbled down into the blazes of the first floor. He knew that taking Ella downstairs through the vivacious flames would be too risky.

He darted back into the attic and grabbed a few of her blankets and a long sleeved jumper. He leapt into his room, shutting the door behind him, stuffing the blankets underneath the door to block the smoke. He silently thanked himself for forgetting to put the gasoline inside his room. Drake was surprised and relieved that Ella didn't offer much resistance as Drake put on her jumper.

"Wait right here, Ella girl," he gently placed Ella down on the bed, away from the window. "It's time your big brother got you out of here."

Drake snatched the baseball bat that was still propped against the wall from the possum fight. As he approached the window, his world swirled silent, still. His mind catapulted him back to 5150 Rosamond drive. Uncle Basil's house. He was now standing there, in the master bedroom and had just rescued Omen and searched for Basil to no avail. Instead of a moonlit lake, he now saw the fire trucks outside. Nobody noticed him standing in the window. He felt dizzy. Eyes stinging, he grew disoriented and thought he would lose consciousness at any moment. He struggled to breathe; smoke surrounded him, getting thicker by the second. His entire body throbbed with each breath. Omen raced frantically back and forth in the front yard between Drake and the firefighters. Dominick was standing by a firefighter, his lanky arm extending to the front door of the blazing house. Drake pleaded with Dominick in his mind to notice him as he stood there helpless in the window. He was being consumed by the smoke and invaded by the flames now entering the bedroom. The room was unbearable. The temperature in the room began to rise once again and beads of sweat raced down his flesh. His heart began an odd arrhythmia as it thrashed inside of his chest cavity, lungs tightening with the haze of smoke trickling into the room. He heard a tiny cough in the distance. It was Ella. At an instant, Drake fell back into reality, shaking the past from his mind, wiping the veneer of sweat from his forehead. He surveyed his room, pausing on Ella.

"Don't look Ella, put your hands on your face, all right?"

Ella nodded slowly, cupping her tiny hands over her face. With one foot propped on his windowsill, he drew the bat backward behind his head, gripping it tightly. Looking back at Ella a final time to ensure she wasn't moving toward him, he took the first swing, shattering the inner glass into a million pieces, immediately relieved it wasn't shatterproof glass as he had guessed. He dropped the bat immediately, lunging backward and shielding Ella from the shower of glass fractures and shards. Ella let out an ear-splitting wail followed by a surge of intolerable, breathless shrieks. She broke free from Drake and lunged for the door of the bedroom, trying to escape.

"Ella, baby girl, it's all right. Get back here! There's a fire in there and we have to go out this way! It's hot! Very hot!"

Ella's face reddened as she continued to scream, tightening every muscle in her body. She inhaled deeply after holding her breath and entered a violent coughing spell. Drake knew he had to hurry and get them out of there. After a few minutes to calm her and talk her into staying, Drake secured the towels underneath the door to stop a slender stream of smoke from entering the room before clearing the glass shards from the floor in front of the window with his foot. He grabbed the bat and placed a foot on the ledge as he did before. He curved the bat behind his head and, using all of the strength in his muscle fibers, took a swing. The bat rebounded from the glass with great force, nearly knocking him in the face.

"Crap. The outer window's shatterproof," Drake lamented, his face bewildered in a panic. "Hold on Ella, cover your face for me one more time, o.k.?"

Ella, still sobbing, complied with his request. He swung again, this time with as much strength as he could muster. The point of impact left a circle of bulging cracked glass but the entire window was still intact. Ella started screaming again, backing up against the chest of drawers. The pressure from the playroom fire caused the towels from underneath the door to shift and smoke billowed into the room.

"Ella it's all right. We are gonna have to go out this way and go on the roof. It will be fun, right? Don't you wanna climb on the roof?" Drake said cheerfully, trying to talk Ella into something absurd.

Ella slowly nodded her head, sobbing, smoke surrounding her as a blanket. She coughed violently, her face reddening with each cough.

"I have to hit it again but it won't come down like the other one. It will all go outside in one piece."

Ella slowly nodded her head, trying to stifle her weeping, coughing forcefully.

"Here we go, batter up!"

Drake choked the bat and with two successive hits, he created a larger dent in the center of the window with small sections of the window in various places having pulled away from the windowsill. Figuring he wouldn't have enough time to break out the window this way; he chipped away at the residual glass shards of the first window and inspected the windowsill. A brilliant idea popped into his head. He flew into his closet and grabbed the tool chest his father had bought him for Christmas the year before. He dragged it over to the window and pulling out a pair of needle-nosed pliers, he grabbed the thin strip of caulking from the bottom of the window and yanked, removing the strip with ease. Chucking the pliers aside, he snatched the screwdrivers one by one, sizing up the screw sizes next to the window until he found the right one. He rapidly removed the screws, looking back frequently to check on Ella who was fighting the smoke with every breath. The smoke was quickly filling up the room, the temperature rising to a boiling hot day in Phoenix. Ella blinked her eyes fiercely, stifling her sobs. Drake picked her up and set her against the wall next to the window with the least amount of smoke.

"Ella, it'll be one minute and we'll be out of here. We'll get to climb on the roof! Awesome, right? Hold on!"

She nodded slowly, cupping her hands over her tiny mouth, oppressing the next round of coughs. Drake's lungs were in a melee with the smoky air, his heart pounding in the familiar pattern as before. He fought visions of Rosamond drive as he became disoriented, dizzy from smoke inhalation.

"I'm not doing this now. Be strong, Drake," he counseled himself, grabbing the bat with sweaty palms.

He struck the window a few more times, the bulge became bigger, the bottom of the window started to move away from the track.

"Almost there, Ella!"

Ella, red as a beet, appeared to be fighting a loss of consciousness. For a moment, her eyes rolled to the back of their sockets as she steadied herself, gazing at Drake, helpless. After three more strong hits, Drake kicked the window furiously and it shoved off into the darkness in one mangled piece, hitting the ground with an epic crash.

Smoke rushed outside into the night air. The air was cool and felt blissful against Drake's skin.

"Let's go, baby girl. Grab my neck," Drake whisked Ella onto his side.

Ella clung onto Drake with her miniature arms as Drake dredged carefully out onto the roof, the smoke escorting into the night air, dissipating into the shadows. The flames surfaced at his bedroom door, jetting underneath the door and around the door jam, charring the door and the walls as it invaded the room. With Ella in tow, Drake climbed his way to the side of the house where a firefighter bellowed at him from below, Jade standing immediately beside him.

"Young man, stop right where you are," a stern voice sounded from a megaphone. "We're coming up with a ladder right now."

EPILOGUE – Deadwood City

Drake hopped down the stairs, the homely smell of bacon whirled in his nostrils, comforting him. Omen trailed closely behind. The eggs sizzled and popped in the frying pan as the toaster clicked loudly, toast rising from the slats. He rounded the corner to the kitchen as the phone sounded, rattling the cradle. Ella waved hello from her high chair with a spoon in her other hand, a bowl of cereal on her tray. Emily was standing at the stove, tousled golden hair, stirring the scrambled eggs as she hummed a soothing tune. She tossed the spatula on the counter and lunged for the phone, nearly tripping on her long pink fleece robe.

"Hello, this is Emily Henry!" she chirped in a happy voice, glancing over at Drake with a short-lived smile.

A period of silence ensued, Emily's smile hidden by a pensive mask as she listened intently. Drake sprinted to the stove, grabbed the spatula and took over tending to the eggs and bacon, periodically glancing over his shoulder each time Emily responded to the caller.

"Really? Wow, that's, well, that is great news!" Emily sparkled, her eyes twinkling in joy.

Another period of silence followed but this time, longer than the first. Briar arrived from upstairs and took a stance in front of Emily, bemusement riddling her expression. Ivan sprinted from the master bedroom, taking a stand immediately behind Briar, head cocked slightly as if to help his understanding of the half-heard conversation.

"Well, thank you for letting us know! Good bye!"

Drake finished cooking the eggs and bacon and had buttered and cut the toast into triangular slices before joining his father and sister in front of Emily. The family stared patiently as she dropped the phone into the cradle. She spun around, facing her captive audience before scooting around toward Ella in her high chair. Ella was calmly eating her cereal with her spoon. Drake was proud that Ella was showing signs of growing up, had stopped throwing her food, deciding to eat like a big kid. Emily pivoted around, grinning as she took turns glancing at each one of them.

"Well?" Ivan asked impatiently. "Who was that on the phone?"

Emily cleared her throat and responded, "It was the District Attorney in Austin. It seems as though they solved Basil's case."

"He did it, didn't he?" Briar spurted, tapping her foot erratically on the ground.

Drake shot a glance at Briar, mouth stretched into a humorless sneer.

Emily raised a stern hand toward Briar's direction, swishing her index finger from side to side as she retorted, "Not quite, Bee. He's off the hook. The murderer was one of your Aunt Kerstin's acquaintances back in Austin."

"What? Really?" Drake stated flatly, his tone brusque, his eyes cocked into an angle of puzzlement.

Ivan gasped, eyebrows raised into fierce arches.

"Well, they said she hung around a bunch of seedy crooks behind Basil's back and I suppose it caught up with her," Emily returned, pushing back her cat-eye rimmed glasses onto the bridge of her petite nose.

Briar let out a gasp, outwardly ashamed for believing her uncle had been guilty of such heinous crimes. Drake, wide eyed, gazed musingly at Emily, waiting for the details of the story. Ivan's weathered face was frozen.

"I'm surprised, actually. Are they *sure* of this? And so who started the fire in his house?" Ivan spouted, a hand pressed firmly against his hip.

"Same person was responsible for the fire. A female. They uncovered some strands of her hair, obviously pulled out in a fight during the murder. They collected it that night at the crime scene but for some reason didn't process it while they were investigating Basil as the suspect. They were so certain that Basil was the guilty party. However, when they recovered fingerprints on a gas can found by the creek immediately behind Winding Heights Estates, well, they analyzed it and it was a positive match to the same suspect. They said it was a financial motive, something about your Aunt Kerstin owing her a ton of cash and after the murder; she probably burned down the house to destroy evidence of some sort. Maybe she couldn't find what she was looking for and so she torched the place?"

"Whoa," Drake said absently.

"Wow. Never would have guessed it. Guess it makes sense, as a friend of Kerstin's would have known that dog. A stranger could not have broken into that house and shut that dog into a bedroom without being mauled. What a sick, twisted person to try to burn up an innocent dog," Ivan pointed out, shaking his head in disbelief.

"No doubt," Drake added sternly, shaking his head in unison with Ivan, reaching downward to stroke the fur on Omen's neck.

Drake stared at the table for a few moments, deciding upon getting some fresh air before breakfast. Briar tapped him lightly on the shoulder.

"Want to see if Jade's doing anything, Drake?" Briar asked eagerly.

Drake nodded fervently. Briar had read his mind.

"Sure, let's grab breakfast to go," Drake responded, grabbing a piece of toast and placing an egg and two strips of bacon on top, folding it over.

They took off on foot through the neighborhood, turning the corner to face a nicely sized stucco home, palm trees lining the front façade. They strolled up to the door, bacon and egg sandwiches in hand. Drake pressed the doorbell button and after a short minute, Jade surfaced at the front door, gazing at Drake with a loving grin spread across her face.

"Hey, neighbor! Want to go hang with us at the pool? Or maybe play some tennis?" Briar purred, taking a big bite of her breakfast sandwich.

"Uh, I'm not playing tennis with *Drake!* I think the champion might be a little much for my game," Jade giggled.

"Well, I'm only the state champion in 4A this year thanks to Coach Walter for arguing my case to the board, of course!" Drake laughed.

"No, it is because you are the best tennis player in the nation of your age, Drake. That's why! Your coach in Austin only did what was right!"

Drake and Jade gazed adoringly into each other's eyes for a long minute while Briar looked on in disgust.

"All right, you two. No more *love fests*," Briar scoffed, waving her hand in between Drake and Jade to break their gaze. "You told me that you'd be chill if I was around! I won't hang with you guys if you're gonna do this!"

"Got it, Bee!" Drake smiled, shooting a glance of acknowledgement at Briar.

"Let's go hang at the pool. I bet a bunch of people are up there since it's spring break. Hold on just a minute," Jade said brightly, retreating into her house while Drake and Briar turned to take a seat on the steps of her front walkway.

Drake smiled, thinking about how happy he was to live in Deadwood City. Ivan had taken a job as the Forensic Lab Director of Deadwood County. The family reasoned that there wouldn't be many high-toned cases with hardened criminals capable of threatening the family. With diligent research, Ivan found that the forensic lab was slow paced, with an occasional burglary or stolen car stereo case. In addition, the salary was more than he made in Austin. Since Deadwood City had nearly a third of the cost of living as Austin, the salary increase over Austin felt even more impactful, easing Ivan's constant financial worries. Ivan and Emily purchased the perfect home in Deadwood City. Drake was exceptionally excited that their new home happened to be around the corner from Jade Amity and it wasn't much smaller than the mansion in Shady Oaks. Dominick had continued his bimonthly visits to Deadwood City and the two had expanded their friendship with many students at Deadwood High School, many of them skateboarders that loved to travel around the city to find new and exciting places to skate.

Uncle Basil had found a job in Deadwood City as a manager of a chain restaurant but found a quaint place in the town of Shady Oaks to call his home. He liked the small town living and had made many friends there, many of which hung around the local pub. Drake was happy for Basil but even happier that he was independent and not living with their family. Basil did make an occasional visit to see the Henrys in Deadwood City but it wasn't too overbearing and Drake learned to get along with him, nearly finding him likeable at times.

"Let's go!" Jade said airily, returning to the front porch wearing a metallic gold bathing suit, holding a black plastic vinyl beach bag. "Ready, you two?"

Drake gasped, scrambling in his mind at the site. Frozen, he greatly admired the site of Jade in her bikini. Briar slapped him in the arm, forcing him to return to the plane of reality as they both ambled to their feet from the front steps.

"Sure 'nuff!" Briar shouted, skipping down the sidewalk, pulling Drake by the arm. "You know what? I don't have a swimsuit, duh! I'm going to run home and change very quick and meet you guys there. It won't take me but a couple of minutes!"

"Hey, is this a Dominick weekend, Bee?" Jade shouted, shooting a smirk at Drake.

Briar giggled sheepishly, "Yes, he'll be here this afternoon. He's staying the whole week!"

"Awesome!" Jade chirped, squeezing Drake's hand as they strolled down the sidewalk.

Briar took off jogging toward the Henry house as Drake and Jade continued toward the swimming pool.

"That's awesome that you finally allowed them to be together, Drake. I know it must be hard on you!" Jade whispered.

"Yeah, I guess Dominick has always had a big crush on her and I always knew she felt the same for him. I suppose if they still want to be together after all these years, why should I stand in their way. But I'll kill Dominick if he hurts her."

"I think he knows that, Drake, and I doubt he will. You can tell that he really loves her."

"Yeah, I agree," Drake smiled, gazing lovingly at Jade as they meandered down the sunny sidewalk. He brushed his fingertips along her cheek, trailing them to outline her jaw, beaming as he spoke, "Just as I love you, Jade."

An intense smile appeared on Jade's face as she leaned up to kiss him gently on the neck. As they walked up to the community pool's front check in, they each flashed their membership card to the guard who in turn, nodded for them to enter. The pool was a popular hangout for the kids in the neighborhood, most of which attended Deadwood High School.

"Hey, have you still not heard anything about that reality show? Do you think the producers salvaged enough film to put it on the air?" Jade inquired, pushing the turnstile handle with her beach bag.

"We still, after all this time, have no idea what happened to them, actually," Drake shrugged, waiting for Jade to get through, extending a hand to her. "It's all a mystery but no news is good news to us."

"Still, no news? Wow. I thought you'd hear something by now, you know," Jade said softly, bemusement sparkling within her expression.

Drake looked over his shoulder to see Briar jogging up the pathway, flashing her membership card to the guard at the check in.

"Well, every time the phone rings, we all freak out, thinking it will be news about that show. Dad's lawyers have contacted every television network. They notified them of the situation, warning them all about what a legal battle it will be if they pick up the show on their network. He's pretty sure that either those guys didn't save the film or they're being blackballed by the networks. Either way, the show should never hit the airwaves."

"I hate to say it but it just sucks that they all made it out of that fire," Jade whispered loudly.

"Well, they *barely* did, actually. Don't be sorry, they would have gotten what they deserved if they hadn't."

Drake chuckled softly, running his fingers through her silky auburn tresses. He winded a strong arm around her shoulders, she countered with a nuzzle, leaning her head upon his chest as they neared the entrance to the pool.

"Drake! I just got a text message from one of my friends back in Austin, Sadie Dawson! Guess what!" Briar was animated, holding her iPhone up toward Drake and Jade.

"What is it, Bee?"

"Sadie's is moving to Shady Oaks! Her family is moving! Her dad got a transfer with his job, a big promotion!"

"That's awesome, Bee! Sadie was one of your best friends."

"Yes! It's awesome news. But guess where she is moving!" Briar was anxious, waving a hand erratically in front of her face to fan herself. "You'll never believe it!"

"You said Shady Oaks, right? So, what's so crazy about that?" Drake asked, shrugging a shoulder.

Briar nodded, swallowing a lump in her throat. She paused and took two deep inhalations; gazing at Drake to be certain that she had his full attention.

"She's moving to 614 Scarlet Court."

Want to continue the story and find out what happens next at 614 Scarlet Court? Host a Murder Mystery Party! Go to www.MyMysteryParty.com and purchase the instant download version or have the staff prepare your Party Ready Pack!

Murder & Mayhem at 614 Scarlet Ct.

The Block Party to Die for!

DR. BON BLOSSMAN has written more than 100 murder mystery parties as well as other teen/ adult fiction novels such as *The Chronicles of Zombie Town* and *Take Heed to your Nightmares.* Dr. Blossman lives with her family in Dallas, Texas.

Visit Dr. Bon at www.bonblossman.com.

Made in the USA
Middletown, DE
09 December 2014